"Compelling . . . Couldn't p... on vacation and could have some uninterrupted reading time to just keep going."

—Julie Sisson

"My normal cup of tea is sci-fi/fantasy, so this is outside what I'd usually grab, but I'm so thankful the cover and first glimpse into these characters drew me in. A joy to read—something I'll recommend to my friends and the readers in my life, and perfect for bringing on the road when travelling, especially during the holidays."

—Cassandra Moffitt

"Engrossing story with the relatable, quirky characters to carry it. With each chapter I kept thinking, I WANT TO KNOW WHAT HAPPENS!"

—Terra Osterling

"I truly loved it! I found the story and the characters engaging and enjoyable. It kept me interested and often made me smile or laugh . . . I was thoroughly invested and had to keep reading to find out what happened. Started reading Friday night, rushed through my chores Saturday so I could keep reading, and finished that day. The characters, both believable and relatable, read as flesh-and-blood people. The humor of the book came through and gave them a human touch that I greatly enjoyed."

—Marcia Sisson

PRAISE FOR CLARISSA J. MARKIEWICZ

"Writing in a distinctive, effective voice, Clarissa Markiewicz makes many salient and often quite funny points about human interaction, empathy, and co-existence. In her big-hearted, literate, and frank approach, the author brings to mind a younger Tony Earley."

—Author Paul McComas

"This story is subtle and rich at once, creating dramatic tension between desire and reality. It is written with a poetic flare, and fully achieves in a brief space, both plot and psychological portrait."

—Poet Betsy Sholl

"She's quite ethereal, isn't she?"

—Unintentional compliment by
high school science teacher

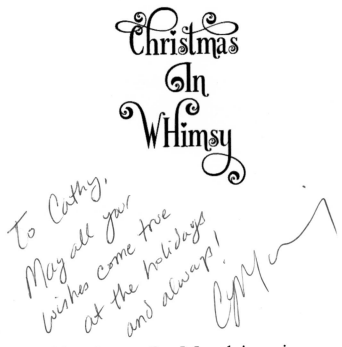

Christmas In Whimsy

To Cathy,
May all your
wishes come true
at the holidays
and always!

Clarissa J. Markiewicz

Unanticipated

✿

Dimension

Printed in the United States of America

First Printing, 2019

ISBN: 978-1-54399-068-3

www.ClarissaJeanne.com

For Mom and Dad and Papa and Mama:

my own personal Spirits of Whimsy

The windblown whisper of holiday snow
tells us magic is coming; look out below!
For love's twinkle appears when least you expect
and gray halls, in a flash, turn so festively decked.
A frothy hot cocoa, a Christmas Eve toast
shared with fam'ly, friends (and maybe a ghost!)
Bells in the morning chime joy and delight
or reverence in moonbeams of one silent night.
If ever you're down and hope seems to be lost
just wait for the kiss of the season's first frost.
For when climates turn chilly, warmer our hearts grow
to embrace all the whimsy of holiday snow.

—Inscription on town square plaque:

Whimsy, New York

From *Upstate Magazine,* Thanksgiving Edition (Vol. 16, No. 3):

CHRISTMAS BACK IN WHIMSY
by Lexie Moore

There is a town not far outside Manhattan's bustle, past the speed of the interstate, beyond the gray walls of winter. The snow always glistens here. It's a lovely town, with a lovely name: Whimsy. There's magic in that name, and at Christmastime, legend has it, there's magic throughout the town, from Orange-Clove Marketplace to the Gallantry Bridge. Some folks wish upon that Christmas magic of Whimsy, and this is the story of three women who did just that: a widow still longing for the past, a struggling actress with a hidden talent, and a magazine reporter.

This reporter.

It all started just about one year ago. . . .

Chapter One

Lexie Moore's interview with Santa had gone off the rails. If there was one reality she'd learned in her nine years since graduating J-school, it was that news stories were like kids: they could have a mind of their own. She sat across from the jolliest elf in front of Santa's Pavilion on the second floor of the Orange-Clove Marketplace, the unofficial "Official Mall of Whimsy, New York," as all the directories said. Amid the jeans and yoga pants dressing most people's Saturday morning, Lexie wore her own comfy weekend attire, of wide-legged trousers, a blouse and vest, and a blazer. The blazer, though, currently hung on the back of her chair, along with her coat and scarf. It had gotten pretty warm in here for Lexie. Sunshine gleamed through the mall's glass roof, and what she'd said to her boyfriend at breakfast had her sweating.

"Yes," she'd assured him for what was, by her count, the hundredth time, "I am looking forward to tonight." Since then, she'd tried to keep her mind on more pleasant, relaxing topics, like her job.

It seemed as though every child in Whimsy was out this morning. An interview with Santa? What kid in her right mind was going to miss that, especially with Christmas only three weeks out? Already, the kids had been springing up like popcorn from their spots on a huge vinyl mat in front of Santa and Lexie, but then Mrs. Claus had come around with warm chocolate chip cookies. The sugar boost sent the little ones into a frenzy, calling out their own questions. Lexie might have been annoyed by the hijacking of her interview if the hijackers weren't so darned cute.

So for a little while now, Lexie had sat back, listening and taking notes and trying to ignore the platter of those warm chocolate chip cookies. They were barely into December and Lexie's diet, admittedly not the healthiest anyway, had already given her the unwanted gift of extra pounds on her thighs and hips. In between taking notes, her fingers found their way to playing with the ends of her straight shoulder-length auburn hair. This was apt to happen whenever she was denied something she wanted. Then she jerked her hand down away from her hair, as was apt to happen whenever she caught herself doing it.

Finally, Lexie tried to take the interview reins once more. "Everyone," she said sweetly but firmly over the hullabaloo, "we don't want to keep Santa from his important duties, do we?"

"No," came the somewhat horrified response. Keeping Santa from his duties, dear God. That had to land you on the "Naughty" list, right up there with finger-painting with Mom's nail polish and sticking bubblegum in your sister's hair. No kid was going to mess with such things this close to Christmas.

Well, almost no kid.

A freckly redhead about seven years old jumped up. All the parents stood behind the mat, and this little boy's mom had come over to him three times already to calm him down. The mom sent Lexie an apologetic look, but it was Lexie who felt for the mother.

This little one had to be a handful, she guessed. At thirty-two, Lexie was no stranger to the biological pangs telling her it was time for motherhood, but one of her many worries about having children was having a child like him. She didn't know what scared her more: a pint-sized whirlwind, or that he'd stop spinning just long enough to look to her of all people for guidance.

She snuck a glimpse at her boyfriend, Theo, standing off to the side and chatting with his sister. Lexie's heart fluttered as it always did when she spotted his downy brown hair, glasses, and muscular build across a crowded room. In the three years they'd been together, she had never heard him express doubts about fatherhood or how their lives would change with a family. She'd never revealed her doubts to him either.

The little redheaded boy fairly wriggled with excitement, standing before the Big Man in Red. With a lisp that could've landed him a record deal singing, "All I Want for Christmas Is My Two Front Teeth," he spouted, "Thanta, could you tell uth the Legend of Whimthy?"

"Please," his mother urged at him in a whisper.

"Pleathe?" the boy asked.

The adults in the crowd laughed gently. Lexie was no exception. She went back to scribbling notes on her legal pad.

The Legend of Whimsy. She had to admit, this was turning out better than her interview could have. Her editor at *Upstate* magazine was going to love this as the crowning jewel in Lexie's cover story for the upcoming issue. She'd been working toward this for months between other assignments, culling research, talking to scads of townies, simply observing, and crafting the longest, most in-depth cover story in the magazine's recent history. This was what their readers craved. *Upstate*'s circulation was heaviest among busy and bustling Manhattanites, who thrived in the concrete jungle and yet dreamed of spa retreats, artisan boutiques, hiking trails, and cozy small-town getaways.

For the five years she'd been working at *Upstate,* Lexie had wanted to do a holiday profile in her hometown of Whimsy. It was perfect with its rolling, snow-covered hills an hour outside the city. The outdoor kids' rink, just past the golden pedestrian Gallantry Bridge, had skaters day and night. The Orange-Clove Marketplace—with the Holiday Hutch,

Brûlée Bakery & Café, and OC Fare where singing elves bagged the groceries—never ran out of cocoa and pumpkin pie samples. Whimsy was the North Pole on overload this time of year, and it even came with its own legend.

Santa gave an ebullient, "Ho, ho, ho," and tugged on his—luxurious and genuine, thank you very much—whiskers. "Well, children, the Legend of Whimsy . . ." he said, and then he stopped himself with a curious glance at Lexie. "Actually, I think Ms. Moore might want to field this one." He winked at her. "You do so love the tale."

Lexie froze. She muttered to Santa, "How did you know that?"

Santa's eyes just twinkled.

Odds were, he was either guessing or this was someone Lexie knew and just didn't recognize. She'd lived here her whole life, and "Santa" was probably an old high school teacher or neighbor. Whimsy was small—small enough that if you were out walking at four a.m. on the west side, you could smell the bread baking at Harvest Loaf on the east side.

But Christmas and the Legend of Whimsy weren't about logic and odds. They were too magical for that. And that's exactly what Lexie liked most about them both.

"Legend has it," Lexie said to the redhead, "that our little town of Whimsy has a magic all its own that comes with holiday snow."

"What'th holiday thnow?" the redhead interrupted.

"Oh, it's the best kind," said Lexie. "There are two types

of snow. There's the kind that comes in January or February, sometimes March or April, and it seems a little sad. It's cold and wet and sort of gray. But then there's holiday snow. Holiday snow is fluffy, and it's fun, and it sparkles like glitter."

Santa chimed in: "My reindeer and elves find it's the best variety of snow for making angels, and it has a sweet yet robust flavor for catching on your tongue."

The adults chuckled, and the kids cheered.

"But there's another special thing about holiday snow," said Lexie. "Holiday snow brings the Spirit of Whimsy, a daughter of Mother Nature. Some say she's an angel. Some say she's energy all around us, watching over us. But one thing everyone agrees on is she wears a magic watch that begins to run when the first flakes of holiday snow fly. The watch tells her when it's time for her to visit us again: from approximately a quarter to winter to half past New Year's."

The redheaded boy called, "How can Whimthy wear a wath?" He held his wrist in the air. "Energy can't wear a wath. You need a writht to wear a wath." The boy's mother groaned.

Lexie flicked her evergreen eyes to Santa, and sure enough, Santa stepped up.

He leaned forward toward the child. "It's magic, my boy," he said through a conspiratorial smile. "Whimsy is all magic. You know that feeling of goodwill that fills your heart at Christmastime? It makes older folks feel like children again, and fills us all with wonder? That's Whimsy. Sometimes, she even helps Santa make wishes come true."

The children oohed and gasped. Then Santa laid a finger aside of his nose and winked at the boy.

"Wishes like a QuikSilver Raptor Racer Car with remote control, Lucas."

They boy's jaw dropped. His eyes popped. In hushed astonishment, he uttered, "That'th me. I'm Lucath."

A warm feeling filled Lexie's chest.

Lucas scrambled to his feet. "Mom," he called, whipping around to face her, "we gotta go. I gotta clean my room." He ran to his mother and tugged on her hand.

"Well, I'm not going to argue with that," said his mom.

"Thankth, Thanta," yelled Lucas as he hauled his mom off. "Thankth, legend lady."

"Yes," the mom called over her shoulder. "Thank you both."

Lexie caught Theo's eye. Even amid such a crowd they shared an intimate moment and a smile, both charmed by the scene. The magic, the near-completion of Lexie's best article to date, the wings Theo's loving gaze set upon her heart, all of it began to put Lexie's mind at ease about tonight. After all, it was just a date. Yes, an extravagant one. Yes, an "important" one, as Theo had said. He'd reserved them a table at Rendezvous in the city, and called in about fifty favors to secure just the right horse-drawn carriage ride around Central Park with just the right coachman. They'd been out on swanky dates before, and he'd given her no real indication this one would be any different, thank goodness. Here she'd started to let her fears get the best of her and she'd read too much into his plans. They would go, have fun, be in love, and tomorrow everything would be exactly the same as it was right now, period.

Theo leaned over and murmured to his sister. He was still smiling. His sister's smile, however, faded with her response, and suddenly Lexie knew what they were saying. She knew as her heart came crashing back down, its wings clipped. She knew as the magic around her faded.

As she heaved a petrified sigh, she knew.

Theo was going to propose tonight.

What a ridiculous thing to be scared of, Lexie told herself. Wasn't this her dream? Wasn't it everyone's? To fall in love with your best friend and share an incredible fairy-tale night that ended with a glimmering ring and a joyful, "Yes, yes, a thousand times yes!"

Lexie kept a smile on as Santa continued to talk to the kids, and she tried to keep her hand moving and notes flowing across her legal pad, even as her stomach tightened and she kept sneaking glances at Theo and his sister, Anna. Maybe Anna could talk him down, she hoped. The two women got along famously. Often, one invited the other to go shopping or meet up for breakfast-for-dinner after work, sans Theo. All three of them commuted to Manhattan, but Lexie and Anna happened to work in offices uptown, near their favorite charming little dive, Bradshaw's Diner on 118th. Theo was way downtown, working in rare manuscripts at the New York

Public Library. It may have been possible, one evening over sunny-side-up eggs and rye toast, that Lexie could've let slip her doubts to Anna about taking that next, serious step with Theo.

She imagined the conversation going on now between the siblings:

"Tonight's the night," Theo said. "I'm going to ask Lex to marry me."

"I don't know," said Anna. "I don't think she's ready to settle down."

"Of course she is. She's a senior reporter at the magazine, with some real creative control. She doesn't have to go off chasing every story anymore. She already is settling down. Besides, my girl can juggle it all. She's my superwoman."

His superwoman. At least once a day he called her that. For the longest time she'd struck a pose at the somewhat un-conventional pet name, hands on hips, chin jutted proudly. Lex always thought she had too sharp of a chin, and this was the one scenario it seemed to work in.

Only she didn't think a real superwoman would lay awake nights, worrying in the dark of her bedroom and the dark of her mind about how to keep all the balls in the air at once. A superwoman wouldn't nervously play with her hair and then chastise herself for playing with her hair. She felt at times she was barely keeping it all together as it was. Just how was she supposed to do all this with a husband and a child or two? A child or two! The most serious responsibility she'd ever take on was bringing a person into this world. His entire survival would depend on her. Sometimes she barely felt she was taking care of herself. What would she do as a mom when a deadline kept her working through dinner? Order Chinese and let her kid gum a scallion pancake? What would his first words be, "Mother, for the love of God, please dust the bookshelves"? Lately, Lexie hadn't been striking her superwoman pose, only giving a wan smile when Theo made the reference.

"Ms. Moore?"

Lexie blinked back from her thoughts and saw Santa watching her, expectantly. "Oh. Yes? Sorry."

Santa held his belly as he laughed. "No apology necessary. I know I get that faraway look when I haven't had my cookies." He pointed at her. "But your, ah, cellular phone seems to be buzzing."

Sure enough, the thing vibrated in her belt clip like it was trying to escape. "Right. Excuse me, Santa, kids." She jumped out of her seat and took the call as she stepped away from the group. Behind her, Mrs. Claus asked the children who'd like to tell Santa what they'd like for Christmas. The entire room erupted in a volcano of "Me! Me!" and Lexie had to plug her free ear and scurry into the stairwell to hear her caller.

Theo slipped into the stairwell with her, just before the fire door clicked shut. The two were alone . . . except for Spark, Lexie's assistant, who was currently speaking so fast on the phone that Lexie could barely understand her.

"Whoa, Spark, hang on," said Lexie. Theo tried to nuzzle up to her, but Lexie gently brushed him away. She couldn't make out what Spark was talking about, but she knew her assistant. Something was seriously wrong. "Take a breath, try again. What's going on?"

"Sorry," said Spark. "Okay. The article's gone, Lex."

Lexie reached out to the railing to steady herself. "What article?" she asked, hoping it was not what she thought. She had to mean some other article, a blurb, a quick profile, anything else.

"*The* article," said Spark. "Little thing you've been working on? Cover story you've referred to several times as your baby that you're wrapping up today with Santa?"

"No, no, no," Lexie moaned. "What do you mean, it's gone?"

"I mean you got a virus on your computer and the thing is toast. Your whole hard drive."

Both women said to each other simultaneously, "Please tell me you backed this up."

Spark squealed, "Me? Last time I tried to touch your work I believe your exact words were, 'Spark, it's bad luck for anyone else to even look at my writing before it's done. If you go near it, I will be cursed and may never write another word. Do you want me to never write another word? Is that what you—'"

"But I told you this time to back up everything each night, Spark," Lexie yelled. Her voice echoed in the well, taking on a cold, metallic tone. Theo had backed off, arms crossed, lips pressed together in concern. "I was trusting you to do it this time. You didn't do it once?"

"When did you tell me to do that?" Spark asked, her pitch reaching an octave normally unattainable without helium.

"The day I started writing this. I . . ." Lexie thought back. She'd brought a flash drive to the office and stuck it in her top drawer with a sticky note attached that said CHRISTMAS ARTICLE, FOR SPARK. "Oh, no. Spark, are you at my desk?"

"Yep."

"Can you open my top drawer? I need you to look for something for me. You may need to dig around a little."

"Sure." The muffled noises of Spark shifting papers and general junk came through the phone. "I honestly don't . . . Hey! There's a little flash drive here with my name on it. Aw, you did a purple sticky. I love purple stickies."

Right around the time Spark said the words "flash drive," Lexie began quietly knocking her forehead against the wall. Now she remembered. She was *going* to tell Spark to back everything up when she gave her the flash drive. She just, apparently, hadn't *actually* done it, and in the interim the thing had gotten buried by desk detritus.

Theo grabbed the phone from her. "Yeah, Spark? It's Theo. Lex'll call you back in a few, okay? Yeah, I think it's safe to say you should stay at the office. She'll be there soon, I'm sure."

Theo hung up and put his arms around Lexie. She'd stopped the banging, but her head was still pressed to the wall. The concrete, cooled by December gales blowing around outside, felt good against her skin. Right now this was a perfect little spot. She could revel in both the refreshing season and the warmth of Santa's Pavilion, for although the fire door muted it all, she could still smell the chocolate chip cookies and hear holiday music and children's laugher.

Lexie mumbled in a miserable little voice, "The Santa interview was the final piece of the whole feature."

"I know," he said into her shoulder as he held her.

"I was going to write it up this afternoon, send it to Belinda for the final edit, and have an evening out with you."

"I know."

Proposal or not, the last thing Lexie wanted was to have her job hanging over her head during dinner and a carriage ride. The prospect of her job blowing up in her face was not an extra headache she needed on top of the inevitably horrible conversation that came when the answer to "Will you marry me?" was "Let's talk."

"And it's not like we can push the deadline," she said. "People think that because we're a monthly magazine and we go to press on Saturday, somehow that means we're not as strict about deadlines as a daily." She turned to face him, and he let go of her. "If I don't have a cover article for Belinda by seven tonight, you know what's going to happen? A week from Monday, six big, blank pages'll hit newsstands. Right about the time a big pink slip is hitting my desk."

"You really think Belinda would fire you over this?" Theo asked. "She's never struck me as the type who would throw you or any of her reporters under the bus."

"I don't think she'd have a choice." The more Lexie stood there envisioning the worst, the sicker she felt. "I'm so sorry, hon, but I have to fix this," she said. She kissed him quickly on the lips and flew around him toward the fire door.

"I know you will," he said. "Our reservation is at six, so don't forget to bring a change of clothes with you to the office."

She froze.

"No, Theo, I won't be—"

"I'll meet you at the office at, say, five thirty. That should give us enough—"

"I won't be able to—"

"You're absolutely right," said Theo. "I won't come up to the office. I'll keep the cab. That'll give you a little extra time, so if you're in the lobby no later than five thirty-five—"

"Theo, hang on," said Lexie in her investigative journalist's bark. Granted, she didn't have a lot of opportunity to use the bark doing light pieces for *Upstate,* but she'd honed it as a junior reporter years ago in anticipation of the day she'd interview some evil dictator, or at least a scandalous politician or two.

Theo blinked at her. "Okay," he said. "Hanging."

Lexie closed her eyes so she wouldn't have to see his disappointment. "I'm going to be late tonight. Deadline's seven o'clock. I'll be writing right up until then."

She gave him a second to digest that. Then she slowly peeled her eyelids open.

His brow was furrowed and his nostrils a bit flared, the way he looked when a book he was reading had a lousy ending. He jabbed his glasses up on his nose.

Lexie tried closing her eyes again.

"You know what I had to go through to pull this night together," said Theo.

The fire door, her escape, seemed far away. "Hon, I wish I could be in two places at once, but . . . You know, seven is a more normal time for a Saturday night swanky dinner anyway."

"I couldn't get seven," he said. "I could get six."

"Well, who eats dinner at six o'clock on a Saturday?"

"People who managed to get six o'clock despite a two-week waiting list," said Theo, getting louder. "I had to call in more than one favor to get it, too, same as the carriage ride."

"We can't reschedule this for a couple weeks out? The favors won't keep?"

"I get charged a fee for cancelling this late, on dinner and on the carriage."

"Fine," said Lexie as she threw her hands out in exasperation. "You get the table and order an appetizer and take an hour or so to eat it."

"That'll throw off the carriage ride. We have to be there at eight."

"Then maybe I can just meet you at the park."

"I don't want to get crammed into your to-do list."

"And I don't want what's supposed to be a nice, relaxing evening scheduled to within an inch of its life."

Theo let his hands fall against his jeans, and he paced around the tiny square landing. "You can juggle anything. How come it's all or nothing, tonight of all nights?"

Lexie rolled her eyes. "What's this all about, really? A couple fees on your card? A missed dinner? Are these now things that throw you into a spiral? They never used to be."

"Don't do that," he said.

"What?"

"I'm not some guy you're interviewing. Don't spin this and throw it back on me."

Lexie's phone, still in Theo's hand, buzzed again. He glanced at the screen and then handed it back to her. "I'd like to finish discussing this," he said pointedly.

She held the phone, buzzing, buzzing, with Spark's name beckoning her from the caller ID. Theo's eyes had turned from frustrated to a sadder, more desperate color.

"I'm sorry," said Lexie as she thumbed the screen to pick up. "Spark, hang on a sec?"

Theo turned away from her, his hands dug deep into his pockets. She came up behind him, yearning to run her fingers through his hair to get him to look at her, embrace her. The way he held her meant the world to her, his arms enveloping her like the safest, homiest cocoon. She loved to nuzzle into his chest. That's the only way she could smell his cologne, he wore such a faint trace of it. He wore it just for her, only to be inhaled by her, that mix of a little lavender and a little spice. Would he turn around and hold her now, if she reached out to him? She didn't know the answer to that, and for the first time in her life, she didn't want to ask the question for fear of what she'd learn.

She said to him, "Keep the reservation. Maybe you can take Anna to dinner. I'll meet you guys at Rendezvous and wait at the bar, okay?"

"Sure, I'll have a romantic dinner with my sister while my girlfriend drinks martinis alone. That's not weird."

"Theo, it's the best I've got. Text me if you have a better idea, but I have to go."

"Fine." He started down the steps without a second glance at her.

His footfalls on the metallic steps sent a cold rush over her just as she felt an unwelcome lifting in her chest. It was relief, just a hint of it, that she wouldn't have to face a proposal tonight. Even if they kept the reservations and were able to salvage the tail end of the evening, the idea of a fluffy proposal and fireworks of kisses if she said yes seemed laughable now. She hated herself for feeling relieved. Guilt took its place almost instantly.

"Theo," she said, and he turned around to face her, pausing in his steps. They always said it upon parting: "I love you," she said with her full heart.

He shook his head as though she'd tacked on an irrelevant sidebar to the main article. She felt she might as well have said, "I love chamomile tea."

It seemed like hours he gazed at her. Spark was on the phone, asking if Lexie was still there. Lexie held Theo's gaze. Spark would have to wait.

"I love you too, Lex," he said finally. He turned and was out of sight. Lexie watched after him a second more. Then she banged back through the fire door to do what needed to get done.

After giving Spark a few more instructions, Lexie hung up with her. She thanked Santa—she'd gotten enough material, thanks to the extempore chat with "Lucath"—and then she grabbed her blazer, coat, and scarf, pausing only long enough to toss them on. She hustled through the marketplace crowds, down the central winding staircase, and out the front double doors. On her way, she shoved her phone and legal pad into her oversized purse.

She got socked in the face by the wind and Whimsy's omnipresent perfume this time of year: chimney smoke. Normally she loved the smell, but just then it left a bitter coating down her throat. The gales decided to play tug-of-war with her scarf, whipping one tail off her shoulders. Lexie managed to grab it just before it got away.

"Ten minutes ago," she muttered to herself, "this was going to be a great Christmas. Now I can't even keep my scarf on." The Spirit of Whimsy legend popped back up in her mind. "Whimsy, if you're out there, I could use a little of that holiday magic you've got twirling around. Ugh!"

The scarf had dislodged itself again and this time succeeded in flying away. Lexie whipped around to go after it, shoving strands of hair out of her eyes. Standing behind her, holding her scarf, was a motherly woman. Lexie put her in her fifties. Her skin was the deep color of chestnuts, and she had raven black hair that fell in soft curls over her shoulders.

"Here you go, miss," she said with a smile that sparkled, holding the scarf out to Lexie.

"Oh, thank you so much," said Lexie. She dropped her purse between her feet and crunched it tightly between them, lest any of her other belongings fly. Then she crunched her feet in even tighter with a burst of frustration. The perfect image she'd pulled together had devolved into a runaway scarf, messy hair, and a purse on the ground still damp from melting snow. Superwomen were not disheveled, and if they ever were, they didn't show how much it bothered them because nobody wanted to see that.

With a pop-up smile and a bubbly tone, Lexie stopped just short of saying, "Fiddle-dee-dee," and instead went with, "This weather is crazy, huh?" She tucked her head down, watching herself knot the scarf under her chin. "I say we change the name of this town to Windsy. What d'ya think?"

When she got no response, Lexie looked up. The woman was gone. Lexie glanced over the shoppers milling about, surrounded by their bright din of chitchat and the odd ice patch crackling underfoot and paper bags swishing against each other, but she couldn't see the woman anywhere. All that was left where she'd been standing a breath ago was a little whirlwind of snow, sparkling in the sun.

Chapter
Two

Navigating Santa's Pavilion this close to Christmas could be quite the feat for the uninitiated, but luckily, even in her rejected state, Robin Russell knew the ins and outs of the quirky central space, its cubbies and corners. It was helpful that she also knew exactly who she was looking for: her roommate, Anna Walker. Robin had a little time before her shift started at the Holiday Hutch, and she needed her friend. A few moments ago, Robin spotted Anna across the pavilion talking with Theo. Then Theo's girlfriend, Lexie— whom Robin had met once or twice and liked very much— marched over to the stairwell and disappeared behind the fire door, with Theo following.

Robin sidled up to Anna, and said glumly, "You don't happen to have any pistachio ice cream in your pocket, do you?"

"Oh, no," Anna said, throwing her arms around Robin. "You didn't get the part?"

Robin's arms remained listless at her sides. She didn't even have the will to clear Anna's frizzy blond bob from her face. "I didn't get past the first round. What else do I have to do? This part was made for me: African American woman, aged twenty-one to twenty-six, athletic, tall enough to have presence but not taller than the guy who plays her love interest. I wouldn't have even had to wear a wig: a little wavy, bangs. I have the bangs! No one else there had bangs."

"I know, I know," Anna said in a comforting tone. She patted Robin's back and then parted from her. "Did they give you a reason?"

"Apparently I'm great at taking direction," Robin said, "but this is a short rehearsal period and they need creative people who can bring their own vision to the show. Do you believe the director actually said to me, 'You ain't got it, kid'?"

Anna grimaced. "Did he also have a cigar hanging between his teeth and look like he stepped right out of a black-and-white screwball comedy?"

This at least elicited the blink of a smile from Robin. "You haven't heard the worst part. He finishes off with, 'But keep your head up. Just because you're not right for us doesn't mean—'"

Anna groaned, and finished with her: "'You're not right for someone else.'"

"Like that's helpful," said Robin. She held her arms out wide. "I mean, has that ever helped anyone in the history of anything? Tell me exactly what you need, I'll do it. I can do it. How do they know I'm not creative? Take a day and work with me, and then tell me if I can't handle the gig. They're killing me, Anna. They are slowly and painfully ripping my resolve out one strand at a time until I, like Samson, have lost all my strength."

"Well," said Anna, applauding, "I'd hire you based on that little performance alone."

Robin bowed deeply at the waist. *"Grazie. Grazie."*

She giggled with Anna, only because she didn't want to show just how disheartened she was and bring her friend down too. Robin had been at this professional acting thing now for years, and except for a few parts here or there, mostly at the Whimsy Playhouse, she'd had little luck. When she was in middle school and high school, she'd nabbed nearly every leading role. Even in her fairly competitive theatre courses at Brixby College, a small campus a little farther upstate, she was among the core group cast in everything. Apparently, school was one thing; asking people to pay you for your creative work, she was learning, was an entirely different bowl of oat bran. She was beginning to wonder if she didn't have what it took to land the types of roles she'd been going after, or if she simply didn't have what it took, period. The feeling was dreadful. Acting was all Robin had ever wanted to do. She liked working at the Holiday Hutch, but she didn't want to do that the rest of her life. She ached to fulfill her dream.

Through it all, Anna had been a terrific friend. They celebrated their successes, like when Anna had gotten her catering business off the ground, and they commiserated in woe, like the time both of their boyfriends happened to break up with them just before Valentine's Day. Robin's parents were down in Texas, along with her younger brother and sister, who were both in various stages of their graduate degrees. It wasn't that Robin was estranged from her family or they still harbored their initial misgivings over Robin's choice to go into acting, though there had been lots of discussion over that at one point. They just led very separate lives, with not much in common. There was plenty of love there, but most of their phone conversations were long, blank stretches between bursts of small talk. Anna had become the family Robin missed.

Robin returned her hug. "Thanks for the shot in the arm," she said.

"Of course," said Anna. "And I hope you remember that I'll do anything I can to make you feel better, and I'm your friend, and I will get you all the pistachio ice cream you want because I have another log of bad news to throw on the fire?" As Anna spoke, she drew out her words longer and longer until they landed in more of a reluctant question than anything. Questioning what, Robin didn't know. Her ability to take more disappointment today without flopping over? Probably.

Robin groaned. "Do I have a choice?"

Anna shook her head. She wore little jingle bells on her ears that gave a cheery ring contrary to her wary expression. "The landlord—"

"No," Robin moaned.

"He's raising the—"

Robin put her hands on her ears. "I don't want to hear it."

"He's raising the rent again," Anna rushed out.

"How much?" Robin asked, hands still on her ears.

"Ten percent."

Robin sank to the floor. Santa's Pavilion was so crowded that even the "adults" area was getting overrun by kids, and Robin found herself sitting in the midst of an impromptu parade. Boys and girls marched around her, tooting on noisemakers and ringing bells that someone apparently thought was a good idea to give them. One little girl gently placed a tissue-paper crown on Robin's head and then patted it with sympathy, it seemed.

Anna sat down too. Robin said to her, "Ten percent? Does he know how much that is to someone living paycheck to paycheck?" She shrugged, resigned. "I guess I can give up my train pass and walk to the city for auditions. That'll only take, oh, seventeen hours one way."

"I can float you for a little while," Anna offered.

"Oh, thanks, but it's not like you're rolling in it either," said Robin. "Besides, I need to come up with a sustainable solution. Let's face it, acting might just be a pipe dream. Tons of people want to be actors. Only a few can make a living at it. Maybe I'm just not one of the few." She said this matter-of-factly, without self-pity, and yet as she heard herself her stomach turned.

Anna seemed keyed into her true feelings. "You don't really believe that, do you?" she asked.

"No," Robin fairly burst out. "My mother taught me that if you work hard enough for a dream, somehow, someway, you'll achieve it. There are always obstacles, but that just separates out those who really want it. It's going to take a little ingenuity, a little elbow grease, and a little grit, but I'm not ready to throw in the towel."

"Now that sounds like a prelude to a rousing, uplifting Broadway song," said Anna and threw her arms open wide. "Belt it, sister."

Robin stuck her tongue out. "No." She pushed Anna over before jumping to her feet and helping her friend up.

Anna brushed herself off. "Seriously," she said, "you're a great actress. And you know what a tough critic I am. You heard what I thought of the Playhouse production of *Annie.*"

"That cast was, like, ninety percent kids."

"Yeah, really awful kids." She glanced down at one of the boys marching around, who'd overheard her and sent her a frown. "What?" she said to the boy. "Were you in it? If you were, you were the one really great kid." She ruffled his hair and sent him away while shaking her head furtively at Robin.

"I've got a few minutes before I start my shift," said Robin, "so I'll try to track down Charlotte. Maybe she can give me some more hours. I don't know when I'll make time for auditions anymore . . ." She shrugged.

"But . . ." Anna prompted with a grin.

"I don't know," said Robin. "Eventually I'll figure something out, I guess."

"No, no, no," said Anna. "Rousing song, rousing song. Annie sings 'Tomorrow,' not 'Eventually I'll Figure Something Out, I Guess.' Nobody's going to see that show."

"We'll see what Charlotte says. If I get good news, I'll sing the whole musical in our living room tonight, rousing renditions and all," Robin promised.

Meekly, Anna said, "Can you do *Little Shop of Horrors* instead? I never really liked *Annie,* even with a good cast."

Robin rolled her eyes. "Whatever you want."

Charlotte Lejeune would most likely be in one of two places this time of day: either in the back office with her husband, René, with whom she owned Orange-Clove Marketplace, or at the Holiday Hutch, which she managed. Robin's first stop was the right one. The office was tucked back in a nice little administrative cove, where the bookkeepers and security were also stashed. Robin waved at the security guard manning the front desk, and then she paused just outside the owners' door, waiting for the right moment to break into their conversation.

They were talking about Charlotte's cousin, whose husband had been killed in a car accident six years ago. Charlotte seemed to think it was time to give her a little push to get back into life, maybe even start dating again. "I'm just saying, Margot and Kyle barely even decorate for Christmas," said Charlotte. "A couple days before, they throw up the tree. She's got to get her heart back into something, don't you agree?"

Apparently, René did not. In his thick French accent, he said, "Kyle is only *quatorze ans, oui?* Ehm, fourteen this year. Perhaps she thinks he is not so ready for his mother dating. Perhaps she must focus on Kyle's dating, she thinks. This will be coming on soon enough."

"I feel like if she could just get going," said Charlotte, "maybe the Christmas spirit would grab her. Maybe the Spirit of Whimsy would grab her."

"Do not push, *mon trésor,*" René said.

From her listening post, Robin smiled. She loved René's pet name for his wife: my treasure.

"I'm not pushing," said Charlotte. "If I were, I'd set her up with Gavin. Talk about a match made in heaven."

René said, "Ah, but if it is to be a match made by destiny, we must allow destiny to make the match."

Out on the promenade, the grand cuckoo clock rang out, signaling that Robin was officially late for her shift. She tapped on her bosses' door and poked her head in.

"Sorry to interrupt," she said, and then thumbed out toward the clock. "Guess I'm going to be a couple minutes late at the Hutch."

"That's fine, honey, come on in," said Charlotte. She was short to René's towering figure, with "a little extra pudding," not padding, as she was fond of saying. The sleeve of her sunny orange and yellow crocheted sweater, a Charlotte original, sagged as she reached her arm out to Robin for a quick hug. Charlotte loved to crochet. She wasn't especially good at it, but if you got a Charlotte original for Christmas, you knew you were loved. Robin had four.

"How was the audition, *mon petit oiseau?*" René asked his "little bird."

Robin gave them a similar rundown to what she'd told Anna, and then explained why she was there. "I wouldn't need a lot of extra hours," she said, "and I don't think my schedule could handle a whole lot more anyway. But even four or five hours a week would help immensely."

"Aw, sweetie," said Charlotte, "I want to help, but we're maxed out on holiday hires. We can see how the profit bump plays out in the New Year, but right now I don't see how we can make it happen. We're just not projecting enough."

Robin tried to sound casual. "Okay. I understand."

"Let me make a few calls around. We both will," Charlotte said, and René nodded in agreement. "There're lots of businesses I'm sure would love to have such a capable employee. We'll give you references like you wouldn't believe."

Robin thanked them both. A job was a job, she knew that, and she was grateful for their help in finding extra work. But it felt like finding more retail work was going in the wrong direction. Extra hours at the Holiday Hutch was one thing. She loved that place. She loved her coworkers. She loved that grand cuckoo clock ringing out every hour, and that the Hutch smelled perpetually of Mo's Popcorn Palace next door. She even loved the cutesy alliteration surrounding her. It was as warming to her as the working fireplace displays they had this time of year at the Toasty Tent on level one.

Was she at the point, though, where she had to start thinking of a retail career? Should she start putting all her energy into sending out résumés and setting goals that had more to do with bottom lines than chorus lines? Might she even have to give up the one thing she actually liked about working retail, the Holiday Hutch itself, in order to make ends meet? In a matter of seconds, the questions flitted and chirped around Robin's head like her very own *"petits oiseaux."*

She envisioned a black-and-white, silver screen version of herself in this predicament. All she'd need then, she thought wistfully, would be a fainting couch, some smelling salts, and a handkerchief to dramatically draw across her poor, overextended brow, and the answers would magically appear within an hour forty-five runtime. Of course, her heroines had come far since the romantic swoon. These days, they went after their goals tirelessly, delivering perfect roundhouse kicks to anything that stood in their way, in perfect four-inch heels and perfect hair, no less. Yes, these were movies, make-believe, but that heroine was everywhere; to Robin's thinking, there must be real-life versions that inspired the character. Maybe they weren't as airbrushed, but there must be lots of real women who made their own luck, and made it look easy.

As she took her leave of the Lejeunes, she turned back. "By the way," she said, "I couldn't help overhearing about your cousin. Why don't you send her over to me at the Hutch? Maybe she just needs a good idea or two for decorating to get her in the spirit of things."

"Ah-ha," Charlotte exclaimed. She clutched Robin's face in both hands. "I could kiss you. You see?" she said to René. "I told you, Margot just needs a little help. One brilliant idea from our Christmas angel here and she'll be on her way to finally healing." Charlotte snapped her fingers and turned back to Robin. "I'm going to make you my grandmother's *arroz con pollo.*"

Thankfully, Charlotte's cooking ran circles around her crocheting.

"And I'm going to make those calls. *We're* going to make them," Charlotte said pointedly to René.

"*Oui, mon petit oiseau,* we will," René echoed.

"Please tell them, too," said Robin, "that I'm a fast learner. I mean, if you find someone who's hiring. I might not be perfect right off the bat. Maybe I'm doing something wrong, but I just . . . I just need someone to point me in the right direction."

"Fast learner and a brilliant thinker," said Charlotte. "Just brilliant."

Robin left them then, desperately hoping for her own brilliant idea to help her out of the hole she felt she was slowly slipping into.

Chapter
Three

When the elevator opened on *Upstate*'s offices, Lexie bolted out and nearly ran smack into Spark holding a mountain of files.

"Whoa, whoa, whoa, boss," Spark yelped. She got the files back under her control, balanced them in one arm, and then patted her purple swoosh of hair. Apparently satisfied that no strands were harmed in the making of this potential slapstick, she fell into step behind Lexie, rushing to her desk.

"Talk to me, Spark," Lexie called over her shoulder. She'd stopped home quickly and traded her purse for her laptop bag, which was currently banging against her thigh as she marched. Lexie was sure it was leaving a black-and-blue mark roughly the size of the Gutenberg press. "What d'we got?" She stopped and turned to grab some of the files off Spark's pile, which Spark dumped neatly over to her. Neither woman missed a beat. On some level, despite the crisis in front of her and the relative calm of the weekend's mostly empty offices,

Lexie still felt that reporter's rush and romance: racing the clock to meet her deadline against the backdrop of the city.

Spark said, "We got research in the top three folders, original notes and legal pads under that, and . . ."

"Drafts?" said Lexie. "We have part of a draft that—"

"Belinda has redlined already," Spark finished, sidestepping over to her own desk, three down from Lexie's. "I've got it here." She ripped stapled pages from one of the teetering paper mountains on her desk. "IT is on their way but no one's here—"

"Because it's Saturday," Lexie said, nodding. "Yeah, I didn't think we were going to get anyone. But you—"

"Talked to 'em on the phone, did everything they said." Spark gestured to Lexie's computer with all the hope of the Coast Guard who's just come upon a beached whale. "The thing's dead, Lex."

Lexie stood behind her swivel chair, her fingers digging into the faux leather. Behind her loomed the open floor plan and desks of the "newsroom," as the staff called it with affectionate smirks. Most reporters here had grown up with Woodward and Bernstein as their heroes. They imagined their own workplace as the chattering *Washington Post* circa 1973, despite that the most sensational story these walls had seen was when the Sorkum sisters up in Canajoharie got into a heated legal battle over rightful ownership of a rogue pair of Teddy Roosevelt's shoes.

Rothco, Inc. owned *Upstate,* just as it owned a half dozen other niche magazines and housed them all in this high rise. *Upstate* was lucky in one sense; the newsroom offices were on the eighteenth floor, and boy, if writers needed inspiration, all they had to do was look out the window. Beyond the newsroom were the glass walls of the conference room, and to either side of it, the glass walls of the editorial offices. Chances were at least several offices and the conference room were open at points throughout any given day, and reporters were known to scuttle in their chairs across the newsroom and just stare at the city vista. In the daytime, the urban landscape was an ocean, with sunlight sparkling on the skyline's glass waves. At night, stars gleamed both from the heavens and in the towers of lit windows. All seemed close enough to touch.

The downside to being up this high, as far as Lexie was concerned, was twofold. First, layout and the presses were located on the ground floor, so getting there in a hurry was a dash few enjoyed running. And second, when the power went out and you had high heels on your feet, eighteen flights of stairs was cause for a legitimate grown-up hissy fit.

Lexie spun her chair around and flopped down into it so she was facing the conference room, which was full with the regular Saturday editorial meeting. A few other reporters in the bull pen were typing away at their desks and chatting on phones, but even though this was a workday for some, it was only mandatory for editors, layout, and as needed by reporters up against a deadline.

"Do you think I can do it?" she asked Spark.

"What, rewrite the article?" Spark shrugged. "Sure, boss. No problem. Like a walk in the park. Ooh, or a carriage ride! That's tonight, right? Theo's taking . . . you . . . umm . . ." Spark's words melted into mush under the heat rays Lexie was shooting at her.

"Please," she said. "I don't want to talk about it. No, what I was asking is, do you think I can convince Belinda and Stu I can do this?"

"Well," Spark said, jutting her chin at the conference room, "they're all finishing up. Guess we'll find out pretty soon. But what's their other option? They've gotta let you try."

"I'm guessing from the rather calm way they're sitting in there that they have no idea I'm about to drop a huge bomb on them?"

"Lex, I'm assistant to four other reporters besides you," said Spark. "You're my favorite, don't get me wrong, but I don't get paid near enough to be the bomb warning system around here."

"Say no more," said Lexie. The editors had begun packing up notes and standing. Lexie took a breath and strode toward the conference room.

She held open the glass door as a few editors said hello and walked past. The room smelled perpetually of paint and new carpet, even though the place had last been remodeled before Lexie had started working here. Lexie nodded to

Belinda and Stu. "Can I have you two for a minute?" she asked.

They sat back down, Belinda in her standard three-piece skirt suit—pinstriped, always—and Stu casual with his wild, curly hair, untucked button-down shirt, and cords. It amazed Lexie years ago the first time she heard Stu mention his husband; she couldn't imagine him letting Stu go out of the house looking like a twenty-two-year-old college bachelor. She really couldn't imagine it the first time they met at a magazine function, given that his husband wore a gorgeous suit, tie, and pocket square that came right from Milan's Fashion Week that year. That was the first time Lexie really understood the phrase "opposites attract."

Lexie stood at the other head of the conference table, across from Stu, and she planted her hands out in front of her. "Stu, *Upstate* has a major problem, but I can fix it for you," she said.

There was a time she never would have addressed her editor-in-chief with such command, especially without first consulting her own senior editor, but she was no longer the nervous cub who started here five years ago. In fact, as Lexie's senior editor, Belinda had mentored her and coaxed her to break out of her shell. Her best advice to Lexie had come early on: make every word count, in your articles, in your life. It was advice Lexie had taken to heart, especially since practically everyone she interviewed embodied that very wisdom. They were successful business owners, driven artists, adventurers who spent their holidays spelunking the Herkimer caverns and hiking Mount Marcy and then went back to their everyday lives of parenting and the office. Those people inspired her to never squander a second, never leave any path unexplored. She didn't want to wake up when she was sixty and regret the road not taken. She was determined to take all the roads open to her, and such ambition left no room for timidity.

Stu sat forward, folding then unfolding his hands in front of him. "First things first, Lexie. What's the problem?"

"You know how you send out those occasional reminders to back up our work regularly because computers notoriously pick the worst times to fail us?"

"Yes," said Stu guardedly.

"Turns out my backup system failed right along with my hard drive." In point of fact, Lexie's backup system had failed. She'd failed to give Spark the flash drive, so Spark had failed to back it up.

Belinda sat back with her legs crossed and flicked a hair back from her face. The motion, like any other she ever made, did nothing to muss her other shiny, straight tresses. Her Iroquois heritage had provided her tan skin, which made her look sun-kissed throughout the year, high cheekbones, and dark hair. It had also provided her an unflagging meditative calm. "Please tell me we're not talking about your cover that's due to layout in"—she daintily lifted her wrist and glanced at her watch—"five hours, twenty-seven minutes?"

"I am," said Lexie.

"Oh, God," said Stu, right before dropping his forehead to the table.

"Stu, Stu," Lexie rushed on, "I'm telling you, all I need is this room and a few undisturbed hours, and I can turn this right around."

"You can?" he asked.

"Absolutely," she said. "What if I told you this might be a blessing in disguise?"

"I'd fire you," he said with a queasy look.

"Ah, see, that would be a mistake, Stu," Lexie said.

"Because you can fix this," he said.

"By seven tonight, layout will have an even better article than before because now I'm pumped," said Lexie. "The fire's within me, Stu."

"You didn't just say, 'Fire me, Stu,' did you?" he asked.

"Mark my words," said Lexie. "We're going to be in here in a couple weeks celebrating how I saved the day, and saved you right along with it." She marched over to him and stuck out her hand.

Stu gave her a skeptical shake. "What are you doing?" he asked.

"Thanking you," she said. "Thanking you for making the right choice, not firing me, and not running some other article in its place."

"I haven't made those decisions yet," he said.

She winked at him. "Thank you, Stu."

He turned to Belinda. "You got anyone you can call in to help her?"

Lexie said, "I don't need help."

"What are you talking about?" he yelped, springing up out of his seat. "Who's copyediting? Who's proofing? Who's fact-checking? Even if you can rewrite the thing—"

"If you force me to work with anyone else, it'll slow me up," Lexie said. "Stu, I know this material backward and forward. The research has been fact-checked right along, by me and Spark, and no one can touch my grammar."

"Really?" he said. "This from the woman who just said, 'me and Spark'?"

"Okay, no one can touch my grammar on the page. The time it would take me to explain what I need to someone else isn't worth it."

With a loud sound somewhere between a growl of pain and a groan of defeat, Stu ran his hands through his hair. He asked Belinda, "Can she do this?"

"If she says she can," Belinda said without hesitation, and without taking her eyes off of Lexie. "When she's done, I'll read through it and get it to layout. She has my complete confidence."

Stu shook his head and marched toward the door. Lexie called out after him. "What's the verdict?" she asked.

He whipped open the glass door. "You don't already know? You thanked me already, didn't you? I'm going to eat a bottle of Tums." With that, he was gone.

Belinda got up, moving like silk. As she walked around the table, she gave Lexie a little smile. "Relax. You can do this. I'll be here if you need me before seven. And, ah, try to give me at least thirty seconds before the layout deadline to glance over the thing."

Lexie nodded. "Thank you, Belinda, you know, for telling him you have complete confidence in me."

"Just don't make me a liar," she tossed out as she left the room.

Moving just as coolly as her mentor, Lexie followed her out. She relaxed a little, relieved that she hadn't lost her job—not yet, anyway—and that her bosses were trusting her to pull off the impossible.

Now, of course, she had to actually do it.

When she saw Belinda was back in her office, Lexie dropped her calm façade and ran over to Spark. "Files, please," she barked, fingers curling up madly in a grabbing motion.

Spark dumped all the folders into Lexie's arms, papers sticking out of them, pages flipped over the tops of legal pads starting to scrunch and wrinkle as they were jostled. A curse or two slipped from Lexie's lips when one paper's edge sliced into her finger. With her arms cradling the messy pile, Lexie shuffled back over to the conference room and tried maneuvering her fingers around the door handle.

"Need a little help there, boss?" Spark suggested, her eyebrows lifted in a knowing and somewhat amused look.

"No," said Lexie, still struggling. "I can do it myself. I'm a master, Spark. Not everyone can do it all by themselves, but I can."

As if punctuating her sentence, the files slipped from her grasp, plunking down at their feet. Loose pages sailed out from their folders.

Spark frowned. "Pretty sure anyone can do *that* all by themselves."

Lexie slumped a little and curled her lip at the mess. "The master could use a hand."

Together they gathered up the papers, and then organized them in neat piles across the conference room table, according to subject and interview. Spark set up Lexie's laptop, went back out to her own desk, and came in again with her own laptop tucked under her arm.

Lexie looked up from the last pile of papers she was organizing. "What's that?"

"I'm here to help."

"I appreciate it, but I need to be alone to get this done."

"But I can—"

"Catch up on your own work at your desk, and I'll call you if I need you," Lexie finished for her. "Please, Spark."

Spark threw up her free hand in an exaggerated shrug. "Okay, you're the boss." She turned to walk out and had just gotten to the door when Lexie called her back.

"Wait, Spark, I do need you."

Spark spun around with a grin on. She wagged her finger at Lexie. "See? You almost had me there. I thought for a second you were seriously going to try to do all this alone."

"I need you to find the biggest peppermint-cocoa latte in a two-block radius and buy me four," said Lexie. "Thanks."

"I quit," said Spark as she started for the door again. It was her standard response whenever Lexie felt the pressure of a deadline and relegated Spark to coffee delivery girl.

"Okay," said Lexie, "but not before I get my—"

"Yeah, yeah," Spark called out without turning. She waved her hand. "You'll get your caffeine."

The glass door huffed closed behind her, and Lexie relished the silence. She breathed in the paint and new carpet smells. They smelled even fresher when no one else was in here. She kept her back to the window, not allowing herself to be distracted by the view. She could bask in that later, after her success. Now was the time for taking off her blazer and rolling up the sleeves of her blouse. She dipped into her pocket and pulled out an elastic band for her hair, whipping it into a messy ponytail to keep herself from playing with it and losing valuable seconds.

Just as she sat down, finally, in front of her laptop, her cell phone buzzed on the table. Lexie hadn't brought it in, and she hadn't seen Spark bring it in, but there it was, like a stray puppy that had somehow nosed its way into the house. She snapped it up, but her annoyance evaporated when she saw Theo's name lit up on the screen. Her stomach dropped a little.

It was funny, the different stomach drops of Theo. It could drop in excitement when he kissed her, and in nausea if she couldn't get a hold of him late at night. Then it would always drop in relief when she eventually did get a hold of him and it turned out he'd fallen asleep or had been out with the boys and the time had gotten away.

Just now it had dropped in panic. She hadn't liked the way he'd said, "I love you too, Lex." She hadn't liked how long it took him to say it. And she hated that they hadn't resolved the argument.

But her job was on the line.

Lexie got up, grabbed the phone, and turned it off. For the last time until the article was finished, she left the conference room and went to her desk. She paused, and then stuck the phone in her top drawer.

"One crisis at a time," she whispered to herself as she walked away.

Chapter
Four

margot Kobeleski stood just outside the Holiday Hutch. All around the Orange-Clove Marketplace, children were laughing and neighbors were oohing and aahing over Christmas gifts with hot cider in their gloved hands. The scene gave Margot one thought: *I don't belong here.*

She tucked her hair behind her ears and kept her head down. When she walked around this way, she felt nice and invisible. Every six months she cut the split ends off her long curls, and she hadn't colored out the gray in years, so it had become sort of a tabby ash brown. She was in jeans, but she wore the faux fur coat her husband had bought her seven Christmases ago, and the cashmere scarf and crystal brooch he had bought her eight Christmases ago. She wore them almost exclusively every winter since he'd died.

Margot hardly knew why she was here. A few hours ago, her cousin Charlotte had called up, telling her to drop by the

Holiday Hutch and find a clerk named Robin. Robin could help her decorate this year. Robin was a jewel, a genius who could take an ornament or two and bring a tree to life. "You know the sad little tree in *A Charlie Brown Christmas* that just needs a little love to turn from a dying twig into full-on bloom?" Charlotte had said. "That's what Robin can do."

At first, Margot had said no. Thank you, but no. Charlotte, however, was not just Margot's cousin. She was her best friend. She was concerned. And, possibly, she was a pertinacious little elf who would never stop calling until Margot gave in.

"Margot," Charlotte had said, "think of Kyle."

She'd said it gently enough, but pointedly. Kyle was fourteen. He'd simultaneously mourned and taken on the "man of the house" role for the past six years since Darren's death, despite Margot's continued attempts to keep that responsibility away from him. She hated that no matter what she'd tried to do to keep his childhood intact despite the tragedy, it still seemed to slip through their fingers like sand.

"You're right, Char," Margot had said, curled on her couch and keeping her voice down so her son couldn't hear her from his room. "He deserves a proper Christmas. Maybe I don't know how to give him that anymore, but you're right. I can try."

"Don't you think you deserve it too?" Charlotte had said. Margot had changed the subject, and now, two hours later, she was working up the nerve to walk into the Hutch.

That was proving to be harder than she'd thought. There was no reason she had to do this today, she told herself. Christmas was three weeks away. She and Kyle didn't put up the tree until a couple days before anyway. Yes, she decided as she pulled her woolly blanket of a coat tighter around her. She'd go home and work up to this.

"Are you Margot?" a woman's voice called from behind her.

Margot looked back toward the store and saw a lovely young woman smiling at her. She wore a Holiday Hutch apron over her sweater and trouser jeans. Margot tugged on her coat again. "You're Robin?"

"I am." Robin came over to her, holding out her hand, which Margot shook. "I knew you from your brooch. Charlotte told me about it once."

By reflex, Margot's fingers went to the rough yet comforting ridges of the red crystal brooch, which had been fashioned in the shape of a music note perched on a treble clef staff. "It was a gift," she said, barely audible and glancing away.

"Are you a musician?" Robin asked. There was a soothing tone to her voice, Margot felt. Normally, Margot wasn't one for sharing personal information, especially with strangers. She wasn't big on social media sites and posting about events in her life. Kyle did it all the time, of course, as did Charlotte and René and their two little ones. Margot had tried it once, sitting at the computer to post her feelings one day when she was especially missing Darren. She'd pulled up a picture of him that was already saved to the hard drive, she typed up the post from her account—she did, still, have an account, which sat dormant unless she saw a funny or inspirational thought of someone else's to share—the post was all ready to go, but then she couldn't bring herself to hit the share button. Mostly it was because she couldn't imagine that any of the few friends she had online would be interested in hearing her brood. But beyond that, she just didn't like opening any door that would get into "her story."

Questions about her brooch, she was sure, would do just that. And yet when Robin asked, with compassionate, insightful eyes, Margot opened the door herself. "No," she said, "I'm not a musician, but my husband owned a music store, For the Record. I took it over after he died." To slide them both past any "I'm sorry's" or "That's terrible's," Margot rushed on: "We specialize in buying and selling old records. There's actually a bigger market than you'd think for that, especially in a place like Whimsy."

"Sure," said Robin. "Small town, quaint. That's one of our big draws: traditions and the past. I know For the Record, been in there a few times. I love the vibe."

"Well, thank you."

"And vinyl's been making a comeback for a while, even with digital."

"That's what we've found," said Margot. "People value the old right alongside the new."

"I have scores of digital music," Robin said, and then laughed. "No pun intended."

Margot's lips turned up into a shy smile, and she let a dollop of a chuckle escape.

Robin continued, "But there are old records you just can't find online. I even have one of those record players that converts the tracks to digital."

"We've sold a few of those," Margot said. Kyle told her from time to time that she was stuck in the past. Usually he admonished her when she refused to post things online. Then she would remind him he had homework to do or the dishwasher to load, or she always had her old standby of, "I was in labor for seventeen hours with you." She could pretty much win any argument with that.

"You know," Robin said, "you might really like our antique and novelty ornaments. I don't get a lot of buyers for them."

"Just the out-of-touch folks like me, huh?" Margot asked good-naturedly.

"Actually, I was thinking it takes someone special to appreciate how beautiful they are. Come on, let me show you."

Margot started feeling uncomfortable again. The Holiday Hutch was alive with carols over the PA system, a brisk flow of customers in and out, and all manner of lights dancing overhead and on tree displays. Scents of peppermint candy canes and pine wafted out through the open glass doors. "Maybe another time," said Margot, moving away.

"Please," Robin said, jumping to stop her. "You'll be doing me a favor if you come in, just to look around for a second."

"Oh?"

"Charlotte's worried about you."

"Charlotte's always worried," said Margot. "Really, I'm fine."

"But I told her I'd help you look for decorations," Robin continued, "and I really need to make sure she stays happy with me. I need this job more than ever right now. I can't afford to let her down."

This didn't sound quite right to Margot. Charlotte had spoken highly of Robin when she'd mentioned her. Besides, neither Charlotte nor René was the type to come down on an employee for something as silly as not persuading their cousin to buy an ornament or two. But Robin's hands were clasped in front of her like a plea. *Or a prayer,* Margot thought. Either this clerk truly feared for her job, or she was certainly putting on a good performance. No matter what, Margot figured, this must be important to her.

With a shaky nod, Margot let Robin steer her into the store. She regretted it almost instantly. What had begun making Margot uncomfortable outside now gave her full-on claustrophobic panic. She'd read about this and experienced it herself before, the effect that fluorescent lights could have on anxiety sufferers. That was why stores were one of the most common places to trigger a panic attack, she knew. The lights, and the decisions to be made. So many choices, so much activity with shoppers buzzing up and down aisles, could cause even the strongest constitution to falter from time to time.

And Margot's constitution had not been strong for, oh, about six years now.

She'd learned, though, how to contain the frightened feelings. She'd had to; she had a growing son who needed whatever strength she could muster. How many times had she nearly gone dizzy keeping it all inside? How many times had she wanted to run away from the grocery store or not take Kyle shopping for new clothes at the start of the school year? She did it, though, trying to keep life as normal as possible for him, especially when life had been so unfair taking his father away. Kyle came first, and whatever Margot had to deal with, she would not lay that on him. As far as she was concerned, that was just called being a mom.

Navigating the Holiday Hutch was no different, then. Margot took deep breaths and reminded herself that fluorescent lights, loud music, and the pandemonium lite of a December Saturday at the marketplace couldn't hurt her. She wouldn't even faint from sensory overload. The good thing about panic was that it raised blood pressure, not lowered it, and so fainting in this scenario was virtually impossible. All she had to do was ride out the discomfort.

A wonderfully strange thing happened, though, when she and Robin turned down an aisle near the back of the store. The cloud lifted. A moment ago, it felt as though the entire store would come crashing down on her in a plume of glitter and sugar plums. Now the world spun just a touch slower. Maybe it was because the lighting wasn't quite as harsh back here. Maybe it was because there weren't as many customers flooding this aisle. Or maybe it was the aisle itself.

"Oh!" said Margot, a sough of genuine enchantment coming through her shy smile.

"I thought you'd like this," Robin said.

The shelves were stocked with all sorts of ornaments, music boxes, picture frames, centerpieces, tree toppers, and stocking holders. Some looked practically ancient and so delicate Margot didn't want to touch them. These were, wisely, displayed on the top shelves, far from the curious hands of little ones. Some were intriguing knickknacks with unique features. One set of stocking holders smelled like gingerbread, and another smelled like a freshly built fire crackling away.

Margot had reached for salt and pepper shakers that played "Jingle Bell Rock," when she pulled her hand away at another sound. Down at the far end of the aisle, a man about her age, in a woolen overcoat, was laughing with delight at a plastic ornament in the shape of a saxophone. He'd lifted the cover on the sax's bell, and it played a few tinny bars of a recording.

He glanced at Margot and Robin when he seemed to sense he had an audience. He took off his fedora and revealed a head of sandy blond hair streaked with gray. "Isn't this just the most marvelous thing?" he asked with a light in his eyes.

Margot pointed at the ornament. "That's 'I Sing You Starlight,'" she said. "It's an old big-band ballad from the forties, but I don't know that I've ever heard the lyrics." She nodded at the sax. "Does it say who the crooner is?"

The man turned the ornament over. "Al Francis," he reported. "Of course."

Margot's hand went to her heart. "Oh, I love him."

"Who doesn't?" he said. "Man's voice could melt an iceberg."

Robin chimed in, "That's a one-of-a-kind buy. I mean, I promise I'm not working on commission or anything. But I'll tell you that's truly a find. Can I put it aside for you?"

"I'd love that," he said, handing the sax over.

"Just need a name," said Robin.

"Gavin," he said. "Gavin Aberline."

"Margot, would you excuse me for a minute while I put this up front?" Robin asked.

"Sure," Margot chirped. She gave Gavin a tiny wave and meant to round the aisle to see what other treasures awaited her, but he stopped her.

"You're not Margot Kobeleski by chance, are you?" he asked.

"Uh, yeah," she admitted.

"I'm a friend of René's," he said. "Well, and Charlotte's, but René and I have known each other for years."

Now that Margot knew the context, she recognized Gavin's name from various times Charlotte had mentioned him. "Oh, of course. I thought you lived in . . . is it Ohio?"

"Indiana," he said. "And I did until about six weeks ago. I needed a change of scenery and wanted to get back to New York. Used to live up near Syracuse, but René talked up Whimsy pretty good." He held his hands out. "One whirlwind move later, here I am."

"It's so strange, I don't know why Charlotte wouldn't have mentioned . . ." Then, suddenly, Margot knew exactly why Charlotte hadn't mentioned one of their good friends moving to town. It was because this particular good friend had gotten divorced a couple years back, now she remembered. Margot's eyes moved slyly to his hands, and she confirmed that he wore no ring.

"Gavin," she asked delicately, "Charlotte and René didn't happen to send you over here today, did they? To the Hutch, I mean."

"No," he said, giving her a curious smile. "Actually I haven't spoken to either in a couple days. Why do you ask?"

She shook her head. "I was just wondering how you came to find this little trove."

"I guess I just let destiny guide me," he said. "Or what is it you have here? The Spirit of Whimsy, that's it."

That discomfort was starting to sneak in again. "Well, Gavin, it was nice meeting you. I'm sure we'll see each other around," she said, starting to back away, almost tiptoeing as though walking too stridently would break this nice noncommittal ice.

"Say," he called out to her.

Crack, went the ice.

"Yes?" said Margot. She'd stopped walking away, but she didn't move back toward him.

"I'm going to be taking Veronica and Andy to the skating rink next Saturday," he said. "Figured my Christmas gift to Charlotte and René this year could be watching their kids sometimes. And with my own out of the nest now, I guess I could use the company. Would you maybe like to come along?"

Margot heard her voice croak a bit as she tried to say no. She cleared her throat to try again when she heard behind her, "Oh, the rink is great. The kids'll love it."

Robin had returned, mercifully, but the last thing Margot needed was for this man to be spurred on. Out of the corner of her mouth, she tried whispering a hint to Robin: "No," or "Not," or "Please for the love of Al Francis don't encourage him." But Robin apparently took Margot's muttering the wrong way.

"Wait," said Robin, "you're talking about the kids' rink by Gallantry Bridge? Or the indoor rink that also has the huge outdoor rink this time of year?"

"The latter," he said.

"You're gonna love it," Robin said. "Hey, don't you have a son?" she asked Margot. "Charlotte mentioned him. So, are they cousins too? Your son and the kids of your cousins? Or are they, like, second cousins twice removed or something like that? Are you still their cousin?"

"I think the kids are just second cousins, technically, and I'm a cousin, but they call me Aunt Margot," she said rather stiffly, wondering if this was perhaps the most painful discussion about family since the days of Richard III. "Thank you for the invitation," she said to Gavin, "but I'm not sure if we're available."

"Aw," he said. "That's too bad. I bet the kids would love to see each other."

Margot remembered what Charlotte had said about thinking of Kyle. She knew for a fact they had no plans next weekend. The last thing she wanted was to stunt him any more than he had been. He loved to skate. He was a winger on his hockey team, after all. Besides, all he had to do was hear from Veronica and Andy that his mom hadn't let him come to the rink, and she'd have a bitter teenager on her hands. She could practically hear the stomping up to his room and the door slamming.

"You know what?" Margot said. "On second thought, I think we are free. We probably won't stay very long, but you know, for a little while."

"Great," said Gavin. "That's great." He gave her a visiting card with his phone number and address—a touch Margot had to admit she appreciated, for rarely did anyone carry visiting cards anymore—and they made plans to meet at the rink next Saturday afternoon.

As soon as he was gone, all of the discomfort Margot had been holding at bay rushed in full force. "Thank you, Robin, but I have to go." She hurried toward the door, happy the registers were in the other direction. If Gavin was buying his trinket, she could slip out without having to talk to him anymore.

"Oh, no. Wait," said Robin as she chased her. "We didn't find you anything. Come on, we can do a grand Christmas tree, a *Nutcracker* theme, how about that?"

"I like my tree fine, thank you," Margot said without pausing.

"No problem," said Robin. "Same tree. But we have lights in the shape of jukeboxes. How cute is that?"

"No, I don't think so," said Margot. At the store's threshold, she turned back to Robin. "But you're very good at this. You are. I mean, don't base your success rate on me, I'm a mess. But you've got a knack for knowing people, what fits them. You're a . . . a Christmas helper. A little elf who can give people perfect gift ideas and creative ways to decorate. I've heard of those, Christmas helper people. Do you have a business card? I'll be happy to give it out to some friends."

"Oh, no, I'm not . . ." Then Robin's eyes lit up. "Your own personal Christmas elf. Yes! That's perfect. That's how I can . . . Thank you," she said to Margot.

Margot gave a tiny laugh. "I have no idea what I did, but you're welcome."

Robin seemed to fly back into her own thoughts. "A card! I need to get cards printed. Cal Simmons owes me, and a rush order on some cards is how Mr. Stationary Store is going to pay me back." She whipped her Holiday Hutch apron over her head, stuffed it in Margot's arms, and took off.

Margot waited.

Robin scuttled back, grabbing her apron again as she passed Margot. "He's going to pay me back when I go on break. But if you come back in a few days, I'll have those cards for you."

For a heartbeat, Margot actually felt lighter on her feet, caught up in whatever had Robin floating so high. Then Gavin came out of the Hutch, a little plastic bag in his hand. His fedora was back on his head. He and Margot locked eyes. He touched the brim of his hat, giving her a nod and a smile. She almost smiled back, and that's when the song over the marketplace PA system changed, stopping Margot's heart.

"Sometime, at Christmastime, you'll walk through the door," sang the recording of Joan Goff, a folkie-pop singer from the seventies. Margot and Darren had connected over her, over this song, in fact. Instantly Margot was transported to the day she met him, at For the Record, when they'd talked for nearly an hour about their shared love of sixties and seventies pop. "A Christmas Sometime," as the tune was called, had become Margot and Darren's song that year.

Yes, it was a holiday song, and yes, this was the time of year for it, but it was obscure, forgotten by most on a B-side somewhere. Certainly this was the first time Margot had heard it publicly in a long, long time, since ages before Darren's death.

"'Only this time of year, dear. Make our future a happy one,'" Margot found herself singing along, hardly above a whisper. Gavin had become a fuzzy blot in the corner of her eye. Her focus was on Darren, for there was his face, in the crowd on the promenade.

She was used to seeing his ghost. He came often to her, at night or during opening or closing of the store when no one else was around. But that was just it—usually, no one else was around. Longing and despair clutched her heart as she stood there, not wanting to move or blink or breathe, for fear she'd lose him again, lose his blond mop of hair, his loving and impish brown eyes, her one true love. That's what many people didn't understand. She had never shared such a connection with anyone else, ever, and to have that connection severed so coldly, by such a cruel twist of fate, when they should have had most of their lives left to live together, that was what had left her in pieces.

Someone walked in front of him. Margot took in a gasp of breath, craning her neck to find him again. But he was gone.

Gavin started to come her way, but Margot turned, tears blurring her vision, and she hurried off.

Chapter
ᏏFive

Spark hopped around nervous as a rabbit on the first day of hunting season. At least, that's what Lexie likened it to whenever she glanced up from her laptop and saw her on the other side of the conference room door. Throughout the afternoon, Lexie had stuck her head out three times and asked her to please cool it, and Spark would for a little while. Then she'd find her way back, working herself up from a saunter pacing back and forth to this hippety-hopping thing. As the sun set, turning the skies from white-blue to purplish red, and finally star-studded black above the city's constant dome of light, Spark got more jittery. Now that they were coming up on seven o'clock, Spark was talking, too.

"We're not gonna make it," she said, shifting from one foot to the other, staring at her watch. "You said you could do it, and I really believed you could do it, but I don't know." She bit her lip. "Six fifty-one," she said, still biting her lip and doing her dance. "I knew you were gonna need help. How many times did I offer help? 'Need some help, Lex?' But, no, you didn't need help. Because you're the master. The master of what? I don't know. Getting fired? Because that's what's about to happen. Don't say I didn't warn you. I'm talking to a door."

"No," Lexie yelled from inside the room, "I can hear you."

"Are you done yet?" Spark all but screamed.

"You've asked me that twenty-seven times in the last hour alone," Lexie yelled back.

"Six fifty-two!"

Lexie jumped up from her seat and shot a toothy grin to Spark. "Done."

For the first time in hours, Spark stood perfectly still. "Seriously?"

Lexie waved at her to come in, and Spark crashed through the door. "I'm emailing it off to Belinda," Lexie said. After a few moments of mad typing, her keystrokes fell silent. "Oh, no. No!"

"What?" said Spark.

"Cannot connect?" Lexie yelped. "What do you mean, cannot connect? You stupid computer. You are stupid, stupid, stupid and I hate you. I hate all the computers!" She snatched up the flash drive she'd been using all day, saving manically every twenty minutes or so. No way was a crashed hard drive going to foil her again, and now, no way was a lost internet connection going to do it.

She flew out of the conference room and down to Belinda's office. Spark stayed on her heels, chanting, "Ohmigosh, ohmigosh, ohmigosh," over and over and fanning her hands, looking like she was one newt's eye short of casting a spell. Belinda's office was dark. Lexie spun around, nearly smacking into Spark.

"Where's Belinda?" they yelled out together to the few reporters still working at their desks.

"Layout," came someone's response.

Lexie and Spark raced to the elevator. Lexie jabbed the call button as her other hand started to sweat clutching the flash drive so tightly. She kept jabbing, her head swiveling as her gaze flitted from the wall clock to the numbers on the elevator panel. The second hand was moving much too fast; the little indicator light encircling each floor's number not fast enough. Spark still hopped and flapped, but had switched from chanting to hyperventilating as Lexie just kept jabbing, head swiveling.

Finally the elevator binged, the doors opened, and Lexie and Spark flung themselves inside, where another chorus of jabbing and hyperventilating commenced, this time with Lexie chanting, "No, no, no," to magically stop anyone on any other floor from pushing another call button. When they stopped on six, Spark joined her, and both screamed, "No!" at a startled young man from *SoHo Beat Digest*. Lexie went back to jabbing until the doors had closed and they were back on their way down.

After a geological epoch or two, the elevator doors finally opened on the ground floor and the women spilled out, running to their left toward a sign announcing LAYOUT: ROTHCO, INC. PUBLICATIONS. A man pushing a library cart full of magazines and DVDs nearly T-boned them as he came through a swing door off to their right. Entirely by reflex, Lexie grabbed Spark's sleeve and tugged her out of the way just before the cart could catch her ankle. That move, however, threw both women into a spin and off-balance. Lexie careened, bouncing off one of the huge, framed photos on the wall of famous moments in journalistic history, and it was Spark's turn to catch Lexie before she went down. "V-J Day in Times Square" shimmied a little, but everyone came out of the collision relatively unscathed.

They burst through the doors of the layout department, and called to Belinda, who was on the other side of the room. "We have it," yelled Lexie. "We're here," yelled Spark. They waved their arms like castaways at a low-flying plane, and then ran through the aisles of long tables full of scanners and giant monitors and printers and humming CPUs and buzzing fans. The place had a smell that always reminded Lexie of the last century, like the magnetic tape of audio or VHS cassettes, and she chalked that up to the sheer amount of all kinds of hardware running long hours in here, seven days a week for the past thirty or so years.

Belinda was half a table away when Lexie's heel—low enough, thankfully, or she never would have been able to run so fast in the first place—slipped on the concrete floor. Her foot went right out from under her. She landed on her side, dropping the flash drive in the process, and took Spark down with her.

A shot of pain hit Lexie's elbow and radiated down half her side, and she panicked. Not because of the fall, but the first thought that blared in her head was, *where's the flash drive?* She rolled onto her stomach, searching madly, until she spotted it and felt a wave of relief. It had skidded just out of reach, half under a CPU. Lexie reached out, snagged it, and got to her feet.

After helping Spark up, Lexie limped to Belinda, who had run over to them. "Good Lord, are you all right?" said Belinda. For a woman who Lexie had always known to be unflappable, just now she was, well, quite flapped.

Lexie held up the drive. Her hair, still pulled back from her face, was a mess of flyaway chunks sticking out from the elastic band, her clothes were dirty from the floor, and her skin was already working on a collage of black-and-blue marks to match the one on her thigh from her laptop bag.

She hadn't felt this good in a long time.

"Six fifty-eight," she said to Belinda, and handed her the drive.

Belinda's posture eased back into its normal impassive and fashionable slouch. She said, "You know, I was joking earlier when I asked you for thirty seconds to look over the thing."

"I know," said Lexie. "I gave you two whole minutes." She patted her own back. "Employee of the year, right?"

"This better be the cleanest copy I've ever seen," said Belinda as she walked it over to one of the layout designers.

"Oh, it's clean," Lexie said, limping after her. "It's so clean you can eat off it. It's white-glove inspection clean. It's the after photo in a dishwasher detergent commercial clean."

"Okay, I get it," said Belinda. She handed the drive to the designer, and told him to bring it up on his monitor and another for him to place the text as she finished proofing it. Lexie and Spark ambled out, banging through the door with cocky smirks on their faces, and then each fell back against either wall in the hallway, grinning at each other.

"You did it, boss," said Spark.

"I did, didn't I?" said Lexie. "Couldn't have done it without your moral support, Spark. And the lattes. Let's not forget those."

"Well, that's true. Really, I am the hero of the hour here."

They both giggled. Lexie felt such a surge of happiness at having saved her job, and maybe even writing a better article than the first version had been anyway, that her giggles snowballed into a hearty laugh. She felt a little lightheaded, but in the best possible way, like after celebrating a win with a glass of smooth champagne.

And celebrating was exactly what she felt like doing. "Hey," she said to Spark, "you wanna grab a drink or something? Or a bite to . . ." Her stomach plunged, and she leaned her head back against the wall. "Theo."

Lexie led the way back to the elevator, filling Spark in on what had happened earlier with Theo—not on all the details, but that they'd argued and she was supposed to be meeting him right about now. "Or maybe I'm not," she said as they got off, back on the eighteenth floor. "I can't for the life of me remember what we decided."

"You okay?" said Spark. "Need to talk more about the argument or—"

Lexie waved her off. "Thanks, but it was nothing. A spat. Not even. A mini-spat. A spatlette."

Spark threw on her coat and turned off her desk lamp. "Well, call me if you feel like chatting. Otherwise, I'll see you Monday."

"Will do." Lexie thanked her again, and after a hug, they said good night.

Probably dawdling more than she should have, Lexie finally opened her desk drawer. There was her phone, powered off, its screen blank, like its spirit had been broken. She turned it back on to find nine missed calls, three messages, and four texts, all from Theo. They all amounted to him sounding calmer about the reservations, especially after he invited their friend Steve to take Lexie's place. Anna, it seemed, couldn't make it, and Theo seemed relieved that he wouldn't have to dine at a romantic restaurant with his sister. Lexie had no idea why the idea of dining with Steve—a big, burly teddy bear of a man—bothered him less, but she wasn't going to start asking questions. Her article was safe, her job was safe, and her man seemed mollified. A day of fires popping up left and right had ended with all of them being put out. For the time being, Lexie was happy.

In Theo's last text message, sent around four, he said he was heading into the library for a little while to catch up on some work, and he'd be meeting Steve at Rendezvous. He'd wait for Lexie there until seven thirty, if she could make it, and if she couldn't, he asked her to call and let him know whether she could meet him at the park at eight. It was about ten after seven. With a little luck, she could catch a cab, jet over to Rendezvous, and meet him just in time.

For once today, what she wanted came easy. The first cab she flagged outside the Rothco building swooped in and picked her up. On the way she did her best to pull herself together, brushing off the grunge from the layout room floor, buttoning up her suit blazer, touching up her makeup. She shook her hair out after pulling it free from the elastic band, and she brushed it until it was at least silky, if not flat and smooth.

As they headed down Frederick Douglass Boulevard to Central Park West, Lexie found her thoughts returning to the carriage ride. To her surprise, she was no longer dreading it. In fact, it was a picture-perfect night for a ride. A light snow fell, but it wasn't that cold. It actually felt a little warmer than it had earlier in the day, probably, Lexie figured, because there was no wind to conjure that biting chill. Nor was there much snow accumulating. Just enough fell to add a magical stroke to the city's nighttime painting.

They passed the Hayden Planetarium and The Dakota, and then cut down West Seventy-first. "I can walk from here, thanks," said Lexie. She handed the cabbie some cash and hopped out of the car. Then her body reminded her she'd just fallen on concrete a half hour ago, and she made a mental note not to hop anywhere for a while.

Walking, though, felt nice. She only had a third of a block to go, and she spent it daydreaming and inhaling the Manhattan winter's eve: the invigorating, fresh air mixed with roasted nuts and hot dogs from the street vendors. There was plenty of air in Manhattan that was about as fresh as a landfill, but for now, all she could smell was sweetness. As she came upon the soft light spilling from Rendezvous' marquee sign, she got swept up in an exciting thought that quickened her heartbeat. This was the perfect romantic setting for a proposal, an engagement ring slipped onto her finger, and an enchanting kiss with the man she loved. The cotton-candy clouds of her fantasy grew and grew in her mind, until there was no room left for her misgivings.

As she approached the front door, she looked in the restaurant's huge picture window, and her excitement vanished. She stopped in her tracks. She felt like she'd been hit, like the fall she'd taken earlier was a love tap in comparison.

Inside, at a table, was Theo, but he was not with Steve.

Unless Steve had suddenly become a beautiful, leggy blonde.

Lexie had never seen this woman before. Yet they certainly looked familiar with each other, laughing and talking with big, animated gestures, especially the woman. *Who has to fling their arms out like that while talking?* Lexie thought with contempt. *What, is she batting away flies? That wouldn't be surprising. She probably has hygiene issues.* But the petty thought did nothing to comfort her, and in fact made her feel worse for sinking to that level, even in her head.

When Lexie was eleven and the boy she dreamed of was thirteen, she'd seen him through the window of an ice cream shop kissing a much prettier, much more mature girl. She felt now like she did then: foolish, and young. But the boy at the ice cream shop hadn't belonged to her. Eleven-year-old Lexie had run home, tears in her eyes. Thirty-two-year-old Lexie's eyes were clear and glaring.

This gesturing is bordering on obscene. How pathetic, when a person had to make a scene to bring attention to herself. Of course, Lexie herself felt like making quite the scene right then and there.

She wouldn't, though. At least, not unless Theo or his fly-infested buddy started it.

With a confident strut and her head high, Lexie walked through the restaurant's front doors.

Chapter
Six

"**m**adam," said Rendezvous' mustached host, returning Lexie's wide smile as she approached
him, "may I help you?"

Maître d's in the city, Lexie had found, were like your
friendly neighborhood beat cop: considerate with helpful hand
outstretched, until you stepped out of line in their bailiwick.
Give maître d's blue uniforms and the legal authority to use
handcuffs, and you'd be hard-pressed to tell the difference.
Once or twice since her days on the college newspaper, Lexie
had learned the wrong way to trying sneaking past a maître d'.
Asking politely to be let in, slipping him a bribe, pretending
to be his long-lost niece, none of those things worked these
days. Now, however, she knew the right way.

"Hello, yes," she said to him. "I'm meeting . . ." She
glanced over toward the gold and marble-top bar beyond the
host's station, and her face lit up. "Ah, there he is," she said,

waving at one of the unaccompanied men at the bar. None of them happened to be looking her way, but the maître d' didn't know that. She whispered to him, "I think tonight's the night," and wagged her ring finger.

The host seemed just as excited. "Oh, good luck. And if it's not premature, congratulations."

"Thank you." She winked and strode past him. Only when she glanced back and saw he was busy with the next customer did she veer off. The winsome twinkle in her eye disintegrated as she neared Theo and the Laughing Girl.

Theo's back was to Lexie. When she landed behind him, she laid a hand on his shoulder. Obviously, they were waiting for the table to be cleared. The sight and smell of picked-apart steak, potatoes, and some kind of peppercorn sauce on both plates like remains of a vultures' feast were enough to make Lexie retch. But she did nothing of the sort. She kept a pleasant look on her face and kept her voice in the low tones of civility. To anyone looking on, this would be a casual encounter, a friend coming over to say hello.

Theo and the woman looked up. Lexie said to her, "My, Steve, how you've changed. Just in case they gave you a lobotomy while you were under the knife, let me remind you who I am. Lexie Moore. Theo's longtime, serious, devoted, serious girlfriend. Did I mention we're serious?"

"Lex—" Theo tried.

"Quite serious, actually." Lexie squeezed Theo's shoulder, and not in a loving way. Occasionally, she glanced around the dining room, sharing a sociable nod with anyone who might give them a glimpse. "Steve . . . Are you still going by Steve, or is it Stephanie? You know what? I don't care. I just stopped by to tell you both how incredibly inappropriate this is. Actually, that's not true. I stopped by to try catching up with a romantic evening my boyfriend planned for us, one that, I was told, was a very special night and I was starting to feel pretty bad about missing. And I guess I'm not telling you *both* how inappropriate this is, or how I'm so hurt I could scream and throw that little swan carved out of butter you've got by the rolls there." She turned fully to Theo. "I'm telling you. You're the one who was wrong."

"Are you done?" he asked.

"For now," she said, and turned back to the woman. "Enjoy the rest of your evening. The carriage ride should be especially nice."

Lexie gave them both a wave and walked out. As she emerged into the cold outside—it was colder than before, she was sure—and she flipped up the collar on her coat, two thoughts occurred to her. She wondered if the maître d' had seen her as she blew past the host's station. She had kept moving and there were quite a few people waiting to be seated, so it was entirely possible he hadn't noticed her. But what if he had? Would he wonder what happened with her beau, such a short encounter when it was supposed to be a romantic night? Belinda had once called this type of musing the "journalist's curse." Everyone had different stories and a journalist wanted to know them all, even the silly ones, even the inconsequential ones.

And that was what led to Lexie's second thought. *"As a reporter, you ask questions. You don't answer them yourself or jump to conclusions."* She heard Belinda's voice in her head, though Belinda hadn't been the first one to tell her that. That was pretty much a Journalism 101 decree. Before a few minutes ago, Lexie didn't know the last time she'd charged head down with steam and judgment, as opposed to eyes up in cool curiosity.

Slowly, she walked to the nearest subway station, occasionally checking over her shoulder to see if Theo would come racing after her. She'd made it halfway down the block, well out of Rendezvous' warm light and into shadows of apartment buildings, and he still hadn't come. She slowed her pace down more. Why was it men never came racing after women the way they did in the movies? Didn't Theo know that "I'm done for now" was code for "it's time to fight for me and show me why I'm wrong for assuming the worst here"?

Finally, Lexie turned back in Rendezvous' direction and stopped in place, waiting. That didn't last long. The snow-flakes were obnoxious, the roasted nuts smelled burned, and she'd noticed a rivulet of dirty, gooey water running curbside into the sewers. She was starting to feel like a world-class jerk for coming down on Theo, and that poor woman. Maybe the day had exhausted and frustrated her more than she thought. Maybe her fear of the proposal had magically turned her into a high-school girl who saw her date for the prom dancing with another girl and overreacted. Whatever the case, it was time to go home.

She dug her phone out of her laptop bag and called Spark as she walked. Spark sounded alarmed when she answered. "Hey, boss, you okay? Did Belinda call you back in or anything?"

"No, no," said Lexie. "I'm calling just to, you know, talk."

"To me?"

"Spark, we've been . . . Yes, to you. We've been friends for five years."

"Well," Spark said with a little laugh, "we've been froworkers for five years."

"We've been what?"

"Fro-workers. Friends who are coworkers. Actually, more like coworkers who are friendly, but I don't know what you'd call that. Cofrerkers? Coworkends?"

"You said to call you if I felt like chatting."

"Yeah, but I didn't think you actually would. You almost never do. Hey, I thought you were meeting Theo."

"Me too." Lexie filled her in, this time including that she'd thought this night would end in a ring, not disaster. "Now I just have this gnawing feeling in my gut."

"Maybe that's just the four peppermint-cocoa lattes and no food on your stomach."

"Somehow I don't think that's it."

"You still in the city?" Spark asked.

"Yeah, but I'm about to head downtown, catch a train back to Whimsy."

"Why don't you just crash here tonight? Sofa's a foldout. Of my sixty roommates I'm sure no more than twenty will have a problem with you."

"Yeah, well, I already have one person mad at me, possibly two depending on how Blondie feels. Twenty's probably more than my luck can handle tonight. They might collude to stick my hand in a bowl of warm water while I'm sleeping. Freeze my bra or something."

"Seriously, I'm only a few stops up from where you are. You're welcome to—"

"I really just want to be alone," said Lexie. "But thanks for keeping me company on the walk."

"Anytime, Lex."

She hung up with Spark and tucked her phone away again. Santa rang his bell a few storefronts away, and all the bare trees on this block had twinkling amber lights strung on their boughs. People of all kinds moved around Lexie, creating a kinetic light all their own. The city was getting its second wind, which would last until sunrise.

Lexie started down the subway steps. There was no one else on them, and they were sterile and perfunctory in comparison to life above ground. Lexie felt about as empty as the stairwell. She considered resurfacing, ducking into a coffee shop for a decaf and pastry, and telling her diet to take a hike.

But she had a bad taste in her mouth anyway, so she just kept descending.

Number 14 Milliner Street, just a couple blocks away from Whimsy Square, was the only home Lexie had ever known. It was a blue cottage-style beauty, two floors, red front door smack in the middle of windows framed with white shutters. She bought the place from her parents when they wanted to downsize, and now they lived on the other side of town. Well, they had a posh little townhome there. Most of the time they were traveling, enjoying a much-deserved retirement. They were older when they'd had Lexie, a surprise baby for a couple who'd been told for years they wouldn't get pregnant. Lexie was their first and only.

When Lexie finally got home that night, she slipped the laptop bag off her shoulder, dropped her coat on the floor, kicked off her shoes as she trudged into the living room, and flopped onto the couch. She'd barely had enough energy to turn the hall and living room lights on, and were it not for her growling stomach—loud enough to garner her some looks on the subway, which was saying something—she would have fallen asleep in front of the TV. As it was, she stayed put on the sofa for a good forty minutes or so before succumbing to the call of popcorn and leftover moo shu.

It was during the fourth episode of her classic sitcoms binge-fest that the doorbell rang. She'd been dozing, and the sound so startled her that her foot flew up and knocked over the last of the popcorn and dud kernels. "Perfect," she said. The rug would smell of artificial butter for days. She threw a blanket around her shoulders, went to the door, and peeked out the curtained sidelight window.

"Hi," she said, opening the door for Theo.

He leaned on the doorjamb, one eyebrow arched over his glasses and his hair tossed playfully by the wind. Even still upset with him, she melted a little.

He said, "Can we talk about this, or do you want to keep assuming you know everything and never hear my side of the story?"

"Come on in," she said, and after he did, she stood peering out to the street.

"What are you doing?" he asked.

"Oh, you didn't bring Blondie here too?" Lexie shrugged and closed the door. "I figured you invited her to my dinner and carriage ride, so why not invite her to my house?"

"You're being ridiculous," said Theo. "You're the one who all but cancelled on me."

"Last I heard, I was going to try to meet you, and Steve was taking my place at dinner."

"Well, you know what, plans change," he said, raising his voice. Where they stood, still in the front hall, the acoustics amplified the sound even more. "Steve couldn't make it."

"You left me seven thousand messages but you couldn't leave me one more explaining that?" she said, her own voice getting louder.

"I was done having one-sided conversations with your voicemail. It gets a little tiring."

"Why didn't you call the office? Spark would've put you through."

Theo backed up, putting more space between them. "It is not my responsibility to check in with you every time my plans change. And by the way, you never called either."

"I never called?" Lexie pointed at herself, her pitch jumping up. The throw blanket over her shoulders dislodged itself a little, and she tucked it under her arms to keep it in place. "When was I supposed to call?"

"Whenever, Lex," he exploded. "'Theo, I'm on my way.' 'Theo, Belinda pushed the deadline after all.' 'Theo, just wanted to call because—surprise, surprise—I spared you one lousy thought while I was off saving the magazine.'"

Lexie shook her head and threw her hands up, turning her back on him. "You're just . . ."

"What? I'm just what, Lex? What am I?"

"You're just . . ." She spun back around and folded her arms. "Did she enjoy the carriage ride?"

He rolled his eyes and sat on the bottom step of the staircase leading to the second floor. "Oh, my God."

"No, really. Did she have a good time? She didn't, like, get trampled viciously by the horse and trapped under the carriage wheels or anything, did she?"

Theo stood up again. He took her by the arms, stared her straight in the eye, and said, "She and I are colleagues. We work together. When I went into the library for a few hours this afternoon, she was there. She was available, Steve wasn't, and I didn't have any options left. There is nothing, nothing going on between the two of us."

Lexie put a hand to her head, which felt like some mossy swamp heap after the day she'd had. She felt like running and never stopping, and at the same time crawling upstairs to her bed and hiding under the covers for the foreseeable future. She was done. She was done arguing, done with the animosity. What she really wanted was to tug Theo over to the couch and cuddle up with him and forget the fight, the ruined evening, even the proposal, the stupid proposal that she felt was partially to blame for all of this.

"I know there's nothing going on between you," she said quietly. "Don't you think I know that? You're not a cheater. You're also not stupid. If you were going to cheat on me, I hardly think you'd bring her to a spot you were pretty sure I was going to showing up to eventually."

Theo squinted at her. "Then why—"

"This was our night, Theo," she said, trying to make him understand her, even though she didn't fully understand her. "Whatever it was going to be about, whatever crazy form it was going to take, especially after my hard drive died, it was ours. Our special night. And you shared it with some other woman."

He gave an exhausted shrug. "And you shared it with Spark and Belinda, a computer, and what, a couple lattes, I'm guessing?" He gestured to the leftovers in the living room, and the paused television. "Then you topped it off all by your lonesome. Lex, you can juggle anything. How come I got dropped tonight?"

For whatever reason, those words just now, "You can juggle anything," made her feel like she couldn't breathe. Suddenly the smell of the overturned popcorn and the mess in the living room, the mess of her "lonesome" end to the disastrous evening, weighed on her. She went back to the living room, tossed the throw blanket off her shoulders, and got down on her knees to start picking popcorn bits captured by the nubbins of her frieze area rug.

Theo said dryly, "Let me help you with that."

"Just let me do it," Lexie said.

He did, for a minute. Then he got down next to her. He hardly had a chance to grab one kernel when she said, "Theo, I mean it. I made the mess. Let me clean it up."

"This is silly, Lex. What do you want me to do, watch you clean?"

"I need a little time," said Lexie.

He slapped his thighs as he stood up again. "Fine. Be stubborn. I'm going to get some water. You want anything, or are you not deserving of refreshment during your popcorn penance?"

She looked up at him and sat back on her haunches. She wasn't even sure where her words came from in the first place. They just sort of dribbled out, maybe from fatigue, maybe from distress still roiling around in her belly and her heart. But maybe they weren't created by mistake out of her confused state. Maybe they were exactly what she wanted to say, and she had no filter left to second-guess them.

She said, "I mean, I need a little time. Time to assess what's got me so upset, so on edge. Maybe we shouldn't . . ." She couldn't finish the sentence. It felt too specific to say, "Maybe we shouldn't see each other for a while." Cryptic was the only way to go. It was easier to cope with. "Just give me a little time, okay?"

"You want to cool things off because of one lousy night?" Theo asked.

He looked crestfallen, and she felt terrible. "Yeah," she said softly.

"That's not what you do in a strong relationship, Lex. You don't walk away when things get tough. You work them out."

"That's what's telling me I need some time," she said. "You're absolutely right. One lousy night shouldn't make me question our relationship."

"But that's what you're doing."

"I guess so."

He nodded, but slowly, like he was underwater. "How much time?"

She only had enough energy to lift one shoulder in a tired shrug. "Couple weeks?"

"Weeks?" he blurted out. "At Christmas?"

She spoke to the floor. "Maybe." When she lifted her eyes to his again, she thought she saw tears forming behind his glasses, though maybe it was just a reflection of the light.

With a scratchy voice, he said, "Merry Christmas, Lex," and he walked out of the house, closing the door behind him.

She stopped cleaning and leaned back against the couch. "Bah humbug," she said.

Chapter
Seven

From *Upstate Magazine,* Thanksgiving Edition
(Vol. 16, No. 3):

WHIMSY (CONTINUED)
Each year, as the calendar days fly away and
Whimsy gets closer to Santa's big day, the
town's whipped into frenzy by gifts and
décor and shoppers who want just a little bit
more. . . .

It had been a week since the light bulb had gone off
over Robin's head, and she'd officially begun taking clients as "Your Own Personal Elf." She even
had a hashtag that had gotten a decent amount of traffic:
#WhimsyYOPE. So far, she'd given lots of gift advice and

answered decorating questions, minor stuff that didn't take very long, only an hour or two per client. But it had been enough to bring in a nice little addition to her Holiday Hutch direct deposit. It was true, she didn't have her own office or storefront, but between the Hutch and Brûlée Bakery & Café, she was doing just fine on where to meet clients. Charlotte and René didn't even mind that she was using the Hutch, considering many of her ideas came from their shelves. "It's synergy," Charlotte had told Robin a few days ago, when Robin had asked whether she minded bringing her YOPE clients in. "Hutch sales are ahead of where they were this time last year. I'm thinking of making your YOPE a permanent fixture."

It was a nice thought, transitioning from a clerk to managing her own niche business, but Robin was having enough trouble keeping up with the additional work even on this temporary basis. She'd had to miss one audition already, because Mrs. Meiers was willing to pay Robin extra for coming over the day of her Christmas party and setting up the decorations she'd picked out. And of course the Hutch was still Robin's primary source of income, complete with benefits, tax withholding, FSA, and retirement planning. Over a slice of the bakery's limited-edition eggnog tiramisu, she'd punched a few numbers into her phone's calculator. If YOPE was going to be a full-time gig, she'd have to be earning a whole lot more money, which meant finding a whole bunch more clients, especially since this was pretty much a once-a-year market.

Robin didn't imagine there was nearly as much call for "Your Own Personal Easter Bunny" or "Your Own Personal Halloween Witch." Maybe at some point she could branch out to help with gifts and planning for any holiday, and in fact the idea did light a little fire in her belly. But that fire wasn't nearly the all-out blaze she still felt about acting. As difficult as it was breaking into show business, she wasn't ready to stop trying.

Robin had been rushing around the Holiday Hutch all day this Saturday two weeks out until Christmas. She rebuilt a pyramid of boxed outdoor lights after a couple kids decided the display table was a good spot to play tag. She brought customers over to their desired section and explained the difference between this tinsel and that garland. She fixed the model train in the front window when the acrid scent of burned-out motor had caught her attention. And every time the clerks on registers rang their jingle bells, Robin flew to the back to help with the long lines. The piped-in holiday music had already cycled through one round of its songs and was on its second pass. Robin was fairly sure she'd hear those songs in her sleep tonight.

She'd just finished gathering several stockings to put aside for Mr. Demopoulos to pick up later on—stockings, she was pleased to say, that she'd recommended as YOPE—when a girl, about nine years old, came running up to her with a sheet of paper.

"Excuse me," she said. When she peered up at Robin, her two long braids reached halfway down her back. "Can you help me?"

"Sure," said Robin. "Is that a list? Did your mom or dad give it to you? If you're looking for something in the store, that's fine, but if your parents are looking for me, you know, Your Own Personal Elf, I'd rather talk directly to them. You know, rates, delivery, et cetera and so on. So which is it? Holiday Hutch list or YOPE list? Wow, I need a break."

"Uh," said the girl, "it's not a list." She handed Robin the paper. "Can you put this up on your board over there?" She pointed at the "Community Herald" corkboard near the front of the store, chock-full of fliers and bulletins for all sorts of Whimsy announcements.

"Oh," said Robin, looking it over. "Sure. *A Holiday Spectacular,* huh?" she said as she read. Players from an off-Broadway production were coming to town on Christmas Eve, it seemed, to perform in the children's wing of Whimsy's Mercy Hospital. "What a great thing to do," she said. She added to the girl, "And it's very nice of you to help out by spreading the word."

The girl turned bashful, blushing a little, before she thanked Robin and walked out. Robin went to the corkboard and started rearranging other fliers to make room. Her mind wandered. What if one of the actresses couldn't make it that night? Oh, she didn't wish harm to anyone, certainly not. What if, though, the actress were offered the chance of a lifetime out in Hollywood, and she had to leave that very night? Robin could see it: the director knocking on her door. "Are you *the* Robin Russell? I've asked all around town and everyone tells me you're the best actress here," he'd say. "Would you mind filling in for our prima donna?" And then he and the whole company would be blown away by her talent, her ability to learn a part so quickly and so profoundly. "Brava!" they'd call. All the kids in the hospital wing would cheer for her, because of course she'd give them her best performance. Anyone stuck in the hospital deserved her best, especially kids and especially at the holidays. And the director would offer her a place in the troupe, where she'd happily perform until Broadway came calling.

The flier slipped out of her hand and she dropped a thumbtack on the floor. "Oh, cripes," Robin muttered. She dropped down to find the clear tack, running her hand over the vinyl tiles and inwardly cursing their busy pattern.

As she searched, she felt a tap on her shoulder. "Hang on, kid," she said without turning. "I promise I'm working on getting the flier up."

"Well, no one's called me 'kid' in quite some time," came a rich tenor voice.

Robin glanced up and saw a man crouched beside her. A man in a gorgeous camel coat. A man with deep brown eyes and full mahogany lips and a dimple in his left cheek, shown off by his smile. "Sorry," said Robin, "I thought you were . . . Never mind." An alarm was going off in her head, alerting her that she was awfully close to this man and she'd had garlic in her pasta at lunch. She tried turning her head and getting to her feet at the same time, which only succeeded in throwing her completely off-balance and landing her on smack on her tailbone.

"Ow," said the man, wincing with her. "That's gotta smart." He stood up and reached his hands out to help her up.

"Oh, you know," she said, taking his hands, standing up, and resisting the urge to further humiliate herself by rubbing her backside in public, "nothing a little ibuprofen won't cure. Taken with a bottle or two of wine."

The man held out the tack to her. "Is this what you were looking for?"

Robin raised her hands to the heavens in gratitude before collecting it from him. "Yes. Thank you. I am never using another tack again if I can help it. Hear that, tack? You are my arch-nemesis." She held up the flier, which was a bit wrinkled from her fall, but not unsalvageable, and she shoved the tack through it onto the corkboard. "Ha. I win."

"If you're done denouncing thumbtacks everywhere," said the man, "can I ask, are you Robin Russell?"

Robin's daydream about the director fresh in her head, she bridled with surprise. Her heart leapt into her throat. She leaned in a little, but only a little, for fear the garlic breath would do her talking for her. "Are you a director?" she asked.

"No," he said with a chuckle. "Ah, a guy in reindeer antlers downstairs at OC Fare told me you're the one to see about gift-giving advice? Actually, he sang it to the tune of 'Roxanne,' which was a little weird. 'Robin,'" he sang in a falsetto, "'she'll help you with gifts for your family.'" He cleared his throat as Robin laughed. "I don't think Sting or the reindeer bagging groceries has to worry about competition from me."

"Hey, you sound great," said Robin. "That's probably Jamie you met. He's a struggling singer. Half the folks who work here are struggling artists of one form or another, but Jamie's the biggest fan I know of eighties' Brit pop. And, yes, I'm Robin."

"Nice to meet you," he said. "Scott Donovan."

"And you need 'gifts for your family'?" she asked, matching the song's cadence.

"To start," he said. "Usually we all go to my parents' for Christmas, but my sister somehow corralled me into hosting this year at my apartment, and I'm not big on decorating." He frowned. "Well, that's an understatement. I've never decorated for Christmas."

"Really?" said Robin. "Not even one of those little tabletop ceramic trees with the multicolored bulbs all over it, and all you have to do is plug it in and it all lights up?"

"Yeah, I have no idea what you're talking about."

"Wow. Okay. And you said you need gift ideas, too?"

"The whole shebang. My mom, my sister, and my dad are all coming over Christmas Eve morning and spending the whole holiday." He nodded to himself. "And I should probably tell you that my dad and I aren't . . . close."

"Okay," she said, prompting him for more.

"Well, since I'm hosting this year, I just . . . I need to impress him. I can't get him another tie sorter or travel shaving kit or some other gewgaw you grab from a department store just before they close on Christmas Eve."

"Another?" said Robin. "You've already gotten him those things?"

He gave a curt laugh. "Several."

"Jeez," she said, nudging him comically with her elbow, "you ever wonder if that's why you're not close?"

His smile withered.

Acutely aware she'd just crossed an uncomfortable line, Robin regrouped and said soberly, "I'm sure we'll be able to find the perfect gift."

"Great," Scott said. He reached into the breast pocket of his coat and pulled out a checkbook. "What's your retainer fee?"

"Oh," she said, "that's not necessary," but he had propped the book up against the corkboard and was already filling out a check.

"Two L's or one in Russell?" he asked.

"Uh, two, but you don't—"

"Let's say . . ." He scribbled down a figure and started writing out the amount.

"Really, Mr. Donovan—"

"Scott," he said, still scribbling.

"Scott," said Robin. "I don't need any kind of—"

He tore out the check and handed it to her. The retainer, as he'd called it, was enough to pay the extra 10 percent rent until spring. She felt lighter than she had in ages. Even the business she'd been doing hadn't made her this happy. She nearly threw her arms around him, but then she came crashing back to earth.

She held up the check. "You don't even know me," she said. "What if I'm terrible?"

"Are you?" he asked.

"No," she said with a confidence that took her aback. She repeated it, even stronger this time: "No. But you don't know that."

"I listen to my gut," he said simply. "And my gut tells me I need to hire you and make sure you can spend the time you need on my project."

Robin's own gut was talking. Sure, she'd been able to handle small requests for clients so far, but what if, fleeting confidence notwithstanding, she couldn't do this? Was she really up to finding the perfect gift for a man whose son had been getting him generic presents his whole life? Decorating an apartment that had never seen a twig of holiday cheer? All within two weeks? She had enough doubt about acting kicking around her gut like a stomach virus; what if she couldn't do this either?

"Just so you know," she said, "I don't do this full time. Technically, I do *this* full time." She gestured into the Holiday Hutch. "And I'm an actress. Sort of."

She thought his eyes glazed over for a second when she mentioned acting, but before she could ask him about it, he came back to her. "I can work around your schedule," he said.

Again, she glanced at the check. There was a lot going on in that little paper rectangle: faith in her supposed skills, validation that she could do what she set her mind to, trust that she would keep her promise. She held it back out to him and said, "How about you just pay me if you like what I do?"

He put his hands in his coat pockets, and seemed to mull something over as he glanced around the busy promenade and inside the store. Then he said, "My dad doesn't like that I'm a mechanical engineer."

"Okay," said Robin, waiting to hear where that came from, but then she realized what he'd just said. "Wait. What? I mean, I could see his beef if you were an, oh, I don't know, out-of-work actor"—they chuckled together—"but 'Son, I'm disappointed you're an engineer who's successful enough to have your own apartment and hire strange ladies to decorate your place' was never a trope on any family TV shows I watched growing up."

"I didn't go into the family business," he said.

"Oh, well," she said, "that sounds a little more familiar."

"Yeah. I love trains," he said. "That's how my career started. I wanted to build trains. I loved the whistles. That's the sound of adventure, of history, of new horizons. I think to Dad it was the sound of his only son leaving him behind."

A quip ran up to the front of Robin's mind about how she could've used his help fixing the train in the front window of the Hutch, but in a rare instance of self-editing, she kept her mouth shut.

"My point," said Scott, "is that I had no idea what I was doing when I started college, and I had my father's doubts to contend with on top of it. At some point, you have to believe in yourself, but it helps when a friend believes in you too." He nodded at the check. "I believe in you."

"So we're friends?" said Robin, happy at the suggestion. "When in the three seconds I've known you did that happen?"

He bobbled his head side to side like he was thinking it over. "I'd say right about the time you told the thumbtack off. I've had one or two encounters with rogue thumbtacks. And don't get me started on staplers."

Finally, Robin folded the check in half and stuck it in her jeans pocket. "Okay. Okay. Thank you for believing in me."

"Great," he said, and there was that dimple again. "When do we start?"

"Well, I can brainstorm a few ideas, but I'll need to meet up with you, talk about your space. You live here in Whimsy?"

"No, actually," he said. "I'm in the city."

"Really? What brings you here?"

"The gift for Dad," said Scott. "I've heard of this town and the marketplace and how Christmas sort of takes over here. I figured it'd be a good place to start, and with a little luck I'd find what I was looking for." He gestured to her. "I was right."

They agreed to meet early the next week at Brûlée, at Scott's suggestion. He loved the storybook town. He also loved that he had to take a train to get there from the city. Scott would bring photos of his apartment, and Robin would come armed with ideas to fit just about any space. He'd tell her more about his family, particularly his dad. Robin gave him one of her cards, and after writing his cell phone number on the back of one of his, he did the same. His parting words to her were, "This'll be the first year in ages I won't disappoint my father. Yeah, I think it's very lucky I met you this Christmas. Take care, Robin. Watch out for those thumbtacks."

After he left, Robin sauntered to a quieter spot in the store to digest what had just happened. She was totally oblivious to kids bumping her as they ran through aisles, the unflagging holiday music, and the taste of garlic pasta lingering unpleas-antly on her tongue desperately in need of a Tic Tac. She felt a bit lightheaded, a bit overwhelmed with excitement about setting out on this project, along with trepidation. The check in her pocket and all its expectation weighed her down.

The quieter spot in the store she'd ended up in was next to a locked glass display case of angel figurines. Front and center was a ceramic motherly figure with wise lines around her eyes and smile. Her skin was the deep color of chestnuts, and her hair spilled over her shoulders in black tendrils. An engraved nameplate at her feet read SPIRIT OF WHIMSY. Robin winked at the figurine, hoping the spirit would bring her the same luck it had apparently brought Scott.

"Because," she muttered to herself, "an out-of-work actress and part-time personal elf is about to play therapist to a warring father and son. What could possibly go wrong?"

Chapter
Eight

The Whimsy Ice Rink, as anyone in town would attest, was really the better place to go for serious skaters, as opposed to the kids' rink down by Gallantry Bridge. The kids' rink was more picturesque, it was true, particularly at Christmas with the Art Nouveau scrollwork of the bridge all lit up by strings of multicolored bulbs, steam rising from cups of cocoa, and red cheeks and noses nipped by the cold. But the Whimsy Rink had a huge outdoor area for figure skating, and an indoor arena as well. It was where Margot's son had practiced and played hockey since he was a little tyke. Margot had always liked the rink, mostly because it had a concession stand that put all others she'd ever seen to shame. She would have looked forward to watching Kyle fly up and down the ice anywhere, but the Whimsy Rink's loaded nachos, which rivaled any restaurant's offering, were her one guilty pleasure, food-wise.

As she and Kyle parked in the lot, Margot tried to keep her mind on those nachos. She'd buy an extra-large plate of them for everyone, she decided. She hadn't seen Charlotte and René's kids since about a month ago, and catching up with them was always a treat. Andy had just turned nine, Veronica was twelve, and Kyle played the protective older cousin to them both, almost like a brother. Whimsy Rink nachos shared with the best kids on the planet, in her opinion, was a fine way to spend a Saturday.

What was not fine, Margot thought, was Gavin.

He was pushy, she'd decided when she had some time to think about it. He was overly confident. And she didn't like his hat. Well, that wasn't true. She loved when men wore fedoras. She'd been born a little too late, Charlotte had told her on more than one occasion. She should have been around in the forties when suits and hats and dresses with full skirts were the norm. So, all right, she liked the hat.

But she didn't like how Gavin wore it.

The day was quite mild for December, no wind or deep freeze, with sunbeams peeking through a light snowfall. As Margot and Kyle walked past the outdoor rink, their skates draped over their shoulders, they looked for Gavin and the kids. The rink was dotted with all types of skaters, from those with arms stretched to either side trying to hold a quivering balance, to near-professionals executing upright spins. But Gavin and the kids were nowhere to be found.

Kyle flipped his overgrown brown bangs from his eyes and offered, "I can run inside and see if they're in there." His voice teetered on the cracks of puberty.

"Thanks, hon," said Margot, though she had no idea why they'd go indoors when, really, it was a beautiful day. As Kyle took off, Margot lifted her left arm and wiggled the plush sleeve of her faux fur coat until it moved out of the way of her watch. Maybe they were just running late, she figured.

A minute later, though, Kyle pushed back out through the rink's double doors. He waved at her and called out, "They're here." He had a big smile on his face, and he rushed back inside right away. His obvious excitement pushed away any clouds Margot's mood had churned up. She tucked her hair behind her ears and started for the doors. Maybe they were inside on a break, she thought. Maybe Gavin liked the nachos too. If he did, maybe she was going to have to reassess him . . . or the nachos.

Inside the small arena, Margot's question was answered. They were there because they weren't actually skating. They weren't on the main ice at all. Gavin, Andy, Veronica, and now Kyle, were on the smaller rink, which Margot knew wasn't even called a rink. It was a curling sheet.

"Curling?" Margot asked. Veronica was helping Andy sweep a broom back and forth in front of one of the stones. Kyle had already headed over to the desk in the front vestibule, where they provided curling shoes.

"Sure," Gavin said, half-sliding and half-stepping over to her. "Skating's so cliché. Actually, I love skating, but I thought the kids might like something different."

He'd taken his hat off, and Margot felt a little disappointed by that. Though he certainly didn't need a hat, she found herself thinking. He had nice, thick hair.

She said, "If we weren't going to be skating, why did you tell me we were?" It sounded more like an accusation than anything.

"I didn't," he said. "I just said we'd be at the rink. Actually, I didn't know what the kids would feel like doing. But when I mentioned curling, they seemed interested."

He wore khakis and a wool sweater, but it didn't look like the itchy kind of wool, Margot thought. It looked soft and cozy. It was a deep purple. Margot wondered if Charlotte had told him purple was her favorite color. There'd been no sign from Charlotte or René that they had, in fact, orchestrated the meeting or the rink outing. But Margot knew her cousin.

This wasn't the first time Charlotte had tried fixing Margot up with a man. The last time was a little over a year ago. Margot got as far as telling the poor guy about her music note brooch when "dinner and a movie" turned into "half-eaten appetizer and the check." A panic attack had hit her, and the man, nice as he was, hadn't called her after that. The panic attack was probably just the straw that broke the camel's back, she guessed, and the rest of the straws were all pretty heavy to begin with: "middle-aged widow," "teenaged son," and "isn't interested in anything more than friendship anyway."

The nachos were smelling even tastier than usual right about now. Margot said, "Well, you guys have fun. I'll be at the concession stand."

Andy shuffled over, his mom's cherubic cheeks glowing. "C'mon, Aunt Margot. This is pretty fun."

"Yeah," Veronica, her father's beanpole double, called out. "I mean, Andy can't even hold the broom right but—"

"Can too!" he yelled at her, whipping back around to face her.

"You cannot."

"Guys," Margot intervened, holding up her hands. "I don't have the right shoes. Mr. Aberline here didn't tell me we might be curling."

"And if I had," he said with a sly smile, "you would've brought your curling shoes?"

"No, I . . ." Margot clasped her hands together. "I would've thanked you kindly for your offer and then declined, since neither my son nor I has ever curled. Or practiced curling. Or played curling. Or whatever you call it."

Kyle came back then carrying two pair of shoes. "Here, Mom," he said. "I think these'll fit you. Cool, huh?" He handed her pair off to her without stopping on his way to the nearest bench. He kicked off his boots and was on the sheet with his cousins in a matter of seconds.

To Margot, Gavin said, "Why don't we get you a broom and you can try it out? If you hate it, I'll treat you to whatever you want at concessions and we'll wait for the kids there."

The suggestion of spending time alone with Gavin was enough to make her blurt out, "Let's grab a broom."

Apparently, the rink manager had unlocked the curling equipment cage and Gavin signed for its use. Margot had no idea there even was such a thing as the curling equipment cage, but it made sense if they had a curling sheet. What were folks expected to do otherwise, tote their own stones and brooms in the biggest, heaviest duffle bag known to man?

She changed her shoes, took off her coat, and shuffled out onto the sheet, where Gavin held out the broom for her to take. As she did, she looked it over skeptically. "They really call this a broom?" she asked.

"Yeah," he said. "A curling broom."

"There's not a more technical name for it?"

He laughed. "Like what? A curling wand?"

"Pretty sure that's what I used on my hair this morning," said Margot.

Gavin laughed again, this time from his belly. In the mostly empty arena, the sound echoed along with the omnipresent piped-in Christmas music and the cheerful shouts of a few younger kids on the main ice, whose parents were leading them around. "Well," he said to Margot, "whatever you used on it, it looks great."

She swallowed hard and tucked her side strands behind her ears. "How 'bout we get started?" she said.

For the next hour or so, Gavin gave them all a crash course in stones and sweeping, and they played on teams: Andy and Kyle against Gavin and Veronica, then Margot subbed in for Kyle, and the teams switched up. They didn't keep score. That, Gavin said, would come later. When they had the basics, he moved on to strategizing, which, he said, was imperative to winning the game.

"You sound like an Olympic coach or something," Kyle said.

"Not quite," said Gavin. "But I have been a coach, and I've advised for the Paralympics. If you think this is tough, try playing from a wheelchair. I think the players taught me more than I taught them, in that case."

"How long did you coach?" Veronica asked as she crouched next to a stone and tried sliding it straight ahead to where Kyle was already sweeping.

"I was with the Bonspiel Curling Club of Central New York for almost ten years," he said. "But that was a long time ago. Then I moved out to Indiana."

"Didn't they have a curling club?" asked Kyle, his eyes on the stone.

"They did, actually," he said. He glanced furtively at Margot, though she didn't miss the look. "I just, ah, had other priorities at that point. Family, job, normal stuff."

Andy was still trying to move his broom smoothly back and forth, but it kept catching on the ice. "Mom said you got a divorce after your kids were all grown up and now you're all alone." He said it matter-of-factly and ended on a note of compassion.

"Shut up, Andy," Veronica hissed.

"You shut up!"

"Guys," Kyle called over them both. "Let's practice some more before we start scoring, okay?"

As the kids went back to playing, Margot went over to Gavin, who looked a little startled by Andy's statement. "Kids," he said to Margot with a shrug, like it was all he could think of to say. His cheeks had gotten a bit flushed.

Suddenly, Margot felt sorry for him. She cleared her throat and said, "So, strategy, huh?"

"Sorry," he said, shaking his head as if to focus. "What?"

"In curling, I mean," she said. "It isn't just about sweeping the ice and trying to get the stone in the bull's-eye?"

"The button," he reminded her. The easygoing glint in his eye was flickering back to life. "The button in the house."

"Right, right," she said. "You told us that. The button and house."

"There's so much more to it," he said. "It's about timing, and teamwork. And a little bit of guile, I suppose."

"Sounds a bit like life."

"Ah," said Gavin, "we have a philosopher in our midst."

Margot glanced down. She guessed that was something else Charlotte had told him about her. "Well, a bachelor of philosophy, anyway."

"You're kidding," Gavin said.

"Oh," she said, surprised. "You didn't know?"

"How would I? What area of philosophy?"

"Of the arts," she said. "Focusing on painters, mostly."

Once upon a time, after college, Margot had taken her degree and gone on to work as a procurement analyst for the Wilson University Museum and Gallery not far from Tarrytown, and from time to time she consulted for them from home until she took over running For the Record. This was the first she'd even mentioned philosophy in a long time, and she felt a gust of nostalgia nearly take her breath away. Discussing classical and contemporary works of art in the receiving room at the gallery had been her favorite thing to do, for the receiving room had been permeated by decades' worth of linen and oil paint, an earthy perfume that brought solace to Margot. The walls were a stark white, almost like a canvas, as though the room knew it was there only to serve the brilliant masterpieces that came in. When she was consulting from home, she yearned to be back in that room from time to time, despite how much she loved her life with Darren and Kyle.

"Hey," Kyle yelled from across the ice. His eyes went back and forth from Gavin to Margot in a silent inquisition that wasn't lost on his mother. "You guys playing or what?"

"Mr. Aberline and I," Margot said pointedly, "will be over in a minute."

Kyle rolled his eyes and shuffled back to his cousins. For the first time, Margot wondered if this bothered him, her talking with a nice, single man. But then, she asked herself, it wasn't just talking, was it? She'd accepted an invitation from this man to spend time together as a family would. Did he think his father was being replaced? The whole reason she'd come here today was because she thought Kyle might like it. Her own discomfort she could live with, but the last thing she wanted to do was make Kyle uncomfortable. Yet there he was, sort of dragging his broom behind him, his lips turned down like he had just tasted week-old bread and found that no, in fact, those white splotches on the crust were not just specks of flour.

She excused herself from Gavin's side and slid over to Kyle. Quietly, she asked, "Honey, do you want to leave?"

"I wanna play," he said.

"Because if you're ready to go, that's okay," said Margot. "I'm about ready myself."

He rolled his eyes again. "Can we just do this? God, Mom, you're being obnoxious. Why'd you drag me out here if you were just gonna stand around all day?"

It was the mouthiest he'd gotten with her in a long time, and it hurt. He started to shuffle away, but Margot called him back. "Hey, mister," she said. She spoke softly enough to keep the discussion between the two of them and away from everyone else, but there was nothing soft about how she laid down the law. "Cool it. Don't talk to me that way. I'm your mother. Did you forget that? Do I need to wear one of those 'Hi My Name Is' tags to remind you?"

"No," Kyle muttered, his eyes cast down.

"All right then. I'd like an apology."

"Sorry." His mouth barely moved.

"I couldn't hear that, probably because you were apologizing to your shoes. Wanna try apologizing to me now please?"

He looked up sullenly. "I'm sorry, Mom."

"Okay," she said, suddenly feeling a little tired. The few times she ever had to do battle with Kyle, even minor skirmishes, left her feeling like she'd just dashed up and down the block a few times.

And then, because the universe apparently hated her, she heard over the PA system, "Sometime, at Christmastime, you'll walk through the door . . ."

Margot closed her eyes. She shut the tune out as best she could, and when she opened her eyes again, she stopped herself from looking around the rink to see if Darren's face appeared as it had at the marketplace.

"All right," said Gavin, "are we ready to play for keeps?"

"For what?" asked Margot.

"Keeps," he said. "Are we ready to try keeping score?"

"Uh, yeah," Margot said. She pasted a smile on her face. "I think so."

She lasted another hour as they played teams again, subbing out here and there. The song ended, of course, and Margot was relieved it didn't somehow get stuck on repeat to turn the rink into the most melodious torture chamber ever. Kyle's mood seemed to lift, especially when he and Margot were closing in on a snowman in one end. They'd delivered seven of their eight stones closer to the button than Gavin and Andy had, not that their stones had been "close." It was hard to deliver a stone. They were unwieldy, and no one save Gavin knew the intricacies of how exactly to curl it. And boy, were they heavy! Margot had a decent amount of upper body strength—you didn't get through raising a boy and being a single parent for six years without building those biceps—but the kids had to push hard, Andy with all his might. Margot was fairly sure Gavin had held back. Otherwise, he would have won every end, easily.

Veronica was due to take Margot's place for the next end anyway, and Andy had already tasted victory with a steal in the last end, so Margot asked Veronica if she wanted to sub in early.

"Oh," Andy groaned, dropping his broom and throwing his head back to look at the heavens. "That's not fair. Veronica's gonna beat me and she's gonna rub my nose in it forever."

"Will not, baby," Veronica said.

"Will too, doofus face!"

"Hey," said Margot. "Enough."

"Yes, Aunt Margot," they mumbled together.

Andy shuffled over to the bench and plopped down. "I don't feel like playing anymore."

Gavin held his hands out. "You're gonna leave me high and dry?"

Andy looked sorry. He screwed up his face like he was thinking it over. Then he said, "Yeah."

Gavin looked up. "What d'ya say, Aunt Margot? I need a teammate."

Margot glanced at Kyle, who looked impatient. "You know what?" she said. "I think we need to get going anyway."

"Oh," said Gavin. "After this end?"

Not wanting to spoil the snowman for Kyle and Veronica, Margot agreed to finish out the end. She did it halfheartedly, and when Gavin tried giving her a high five after their delivery, she pretended to be preoccupied with a loose thread on her pants. As soon as the kids won, Margot all but ran off the ice. She kicked off her shoes, thanking Gavin in a rush and grabbing up her coat. Kyle's feet barely touched the floor she towed him out of there so quickly. She didn't even stop to get nachos to take home.

They were almost out the door when Gavin called out, "I'll be seeing you soon."

Alarmed, she turned back suddenly enough to cause the ice skates dangling from her shoulder to wrap halfway around her. "Why? I mean, what do you mean?"

"René and Charlotte's party," he said, jogging up to her. "Christmas Eve. Maybe we'll have a chance to talk more about . . . well, I don't know, anything. Records, curling."

Margot could practically feel the synapses firing to come up with an excuse why she couldn't be at the party, but she was too focused on getting out of there to land on one. She muttered some incoherent gray area between "okay" and "not on your life," and turned away.

"Philosophy," Gavin blurted. Margot turned back around. "What you said before about philosophy in the arts. I had no idea you studied that. It's fascinating. I mean, what constitutes art? That's gotta be a debate that's been brewing for centuries. When my kids were, well, kids and they brought home paintings of red and blue splotches, I remember thinking maybe I could sell it as a Jackson Pollock and no one would know the difference. I'd love to hear from a professional why one's a masterpiece and one brought home a B for effort."

How she managed to interest him in a second so-called date, when she'd been trying so hard to make this a one-shot deal, was beyond her. "I don't know if we'll be able to make it to the party," she said.

"Oh," he said. "I'd be sorry not to see you there. Well, maybe someone else will want to talk philosophy."

"Maybe. Okay, so, bye."

Kyle slammed through the outer door, not bothering to hold it for her. She scurried out after him. Because of the cloud coverage, which must have taken over the ceiling completely while they were inside, the sunset was little more than a gray, fading light. The snow had stopped, but the air was raw.

In the car, Margot turned to Kyle, who had turned grumpy again. "What has gotten into you?" she asked.

"I really don't want to talk about it," he said, looking her in the eye. "Can we please drop it?"

"Not if you're going to be walking around with a lousy attitude we can't."

"Mom, please. I just want to go home, okay?"

She turned the ignition, pushing the key harder than needed, she was sure, and pulled out. *Great,* she thought, *I've got a boy who doesn't want to talk to me at all, and a man who doesn't want to stop. Whimsy, I beg of you, please just get me through this holiday with my sanity intact.*

Chapter
Nine

Nearly every night since Scott hired Robin, they had talked on the phone about gift ideas, wrapping ideas, ideas for what type of tree he should buy, if he bought a fake tree whether he should use a subtle diffuser stick to scent the air with a touch of pine, down to the menu for Christmas dinner at his apartment. They'd met this past Monday night at Brûlée, as planned, for dessert and coffee. Scott had brought the photos of his apartment; however, "apartment" wasn't the word Robin would have used to describe the place. She and Anna had an apartment. Their apartment was on the second floor of a duplex, with two modest bedrooms at the back, a galley kitchen, a standard full bathroom, and a living room/dining room combo at the front. Robin didn't know from square footage, but you could easily stay in your bedroom and, as long as the door was open, eavesdrop on whatever was going on in the living room. That, Robin figured, was an apartment.

Scott had a palace.

All right, maybe not technically a palace, Robin supposed, since it was in an "apartment" building on a Manhattan street with other "apartment" buildings. But it was certainly palatial. The vaulted ceilings reached to the moon, the balcony—there was a balcony!—could seat a twenty-piece orchestra, and Robin and Anna's entire actual apartment would fit into Scott's living room about a million times over. At least, this was how Robin described the place to Anna. Anna, used to Robin's exaggerations, told her that even after whittling it down in her imagination, she was still impressed.

Yesterday—a week since they had met—Robin spent her coveted and rare Saturday off shopping in Whimsy with Scott. Usually, on coveted and rare Saturdays off, she'd sleep in until daytime streamed through her window. Then she'd roll over, snuggle under her warm comforter, and sleep some more until the alarm clock of her growling stomach went off. Yesterday morning, however, she'd popped up as soon as the sky was light, and kicked off the covers. She was dressed, her ebony hair in a high, wavy ponytail, and she was making pancakes by the time Anna wandered out of her room in bunny slippers and the frizzy poof her curls turned into each night. Robin made pancakes to kill time until meeting Scott at nine thirty outside Orange-Clove's main entrance.

Anna, over her stack of pancakes, had mentioned with a wry smile that she was sure Robin's enthusiasm had nothing to do with how cute Scott was. Robin had taken a selfie of the two of them at Brûlée, and the first words out of Anna's mouth had been . . . well, not so much words as an approving "mm-*hmm.*" Of course, his looks weren't lost on Robin, nor was the comment he'd dropped about not currently seeing anyone. His classic style wasn't lost on her, his laugh wasn't lost on her, whatever that woodsy aroma was—soap, cologne, moisturizer, she didn't know or, really, care—wasn't lost on her. But Robin's mind was on one thing only. She wanted to make her client happy. She told Anna this, and Anna wasn't so sleepy that she didn't think of the obvious cheeky joke, "I'll just bet you want to make him happy."

More than anything, though, Robin was having fun. Scott was easygoing. Their ideas seemed to click constantly. She was having so much fun creating a perfect holiday fantasyland for his place, in fact, that the doubts she'd had at first about whether she could deliver as Your Own Personal Elf had evaporated. Their ideas were pretty well fleshed out, and yesterday was the day they finally got to buy, buy, buy.

They'd spent the entire day together. Scott loved things off the beaten path. He had big-picture ideas about what he wanted, and Robin was able to translate them into a shopping list. They bought bolts of gold and silver mesh instead of garland or tinsel to enrobe the tree. They went with blue string lights instead of white or multicolored. They did, indeed, get an oil diffuser with peppermint, frankincense, and spruce scents, and his twelve-foot faux Fraser fir would be delivered by Tuesday. She brought him to stores she never imagined for her other clients. They ended up at Whimsy's hobby shop, Small Pursuits, weaving through the aisles of dollhouses and model planes before coming upon the train sets. Robin's idea was to turn miniature train cars into ornaments for his tree, and that was where the day's fun really began.

By seven that night, they were back at Robin's apartment and had spent the last couple hours hot-gluing loops of string to the backs of the cars. Anna had come home at some point and set up a hot cocoa station and s'mores on the dining room table. A few friends happened to drop by, and someone paired their phone to the Bluetooth ornament on their tree. Holiday music filled the whole place. As the afternoon shift was going off duty at the Holiday Hutch, Robin called over there and invited a few more people over. By the end of the night, they had an impromptu ornament-making, cocoa-drinking, s'mores-melting dance party on their hands, and none of them could remember the last time they had such a good time.

Scott ended up calling for a car to drive him back to the city, given that all the shopping bags he was loaded down with would've needed their own train ticket. After he and the chauffeur had piled them into the trunk, Scott had kissed Robin on the cheek and thanked her.

She couldn't stop thinking about that kiss, his soft lips on her cheek, the kind dark eyes that lingered on her longer than they had up to that point.

This morning, Sunday morning, she'd had an early audition in the city that had actually gone well. It was for a small part in a small theatre, but it was a speaking and singing role, and the director seemed to like her. Between the crisp, sunny day, the promising audition, and last night's kiss, Robin hardly gave herself a chance to think twice before she stopped walking to the subway station, and pulled out her cell phone to call Scott.

"Just wondering if you have time to grab brunch," she asked him.

"I'd really love to," he said, sounding disappointed. "I have plans already. For brunch, actually, at my place."

"Oh," she said, hoping her own disappointment didn't come through too much, "no problem. It was just off the top, you know. Maybe another time."

"You know what?" he said. "Why don't you come over here and join us?"

"Um," she said, "who's 'us'?" The last thing she wanted to do was be a third wheel, or a fifth, or any odd number. Just because Scott had said he wasn't seeing anyone didn't mean he hadn't suddenly met someone, and if that's what brunch was about, a date or a double date, Robin wasn't interested.

"My family," Scott said.

Well, that was worse than crashing a date. "Oh, no," she said. "That would be a huge imposition."

"It wouldn't," he said with a flat laugh. "You would be doing me a tremendous favor. Besides, we still have to find my father's gift." It was true. His mother and sister had been the easy ones. "Maybe this'll give you a chance to get to know him a little, see what he's like for yourself. Maybe you'll see something I don't."

"Oh, Scott, I don't—"

"Please? I had so much fun last night. You'd make my entire weekend if you came over."

Her breath caught and she felt her cheeks flush. Whether or not he was hinting at more than friendship, it sure felt nice to hear she was wanted.

He said, "Look, if they're abominable and you're having a lousy time, I won't blame you one bit for leaving. But I have this really nice spread set up with bacon and scrambled eggs, bagels and lox, mimosas, and a bunch of other things—"

"Stop," Robin said. "You had me at bacon."

Twenty minutes later she was standing in the middle of Scott's living room. He had already, sometime between getting home late last night and this morning, put up the decorations he could without having the tree in place yet. Robin tried not to gawk at the modern, open space, but she did have to keep reminding herself to close her mouth. There was a huge wreath on the bay window, strings of blue lights hanging over the balcony doors, and tufted garland draped over the mantle. He'd even set up the diffuser with the spruce oil. But the flavor of the air had been overtaken by the spread, magnificent as promised, on the dining room sideboard.

Robin's taste buds had to wait, though, because already seated at the table were Scott's family. They all had the same rich mahogany skin as Scott, the tone of proscenium arches at some of the sleeker theatres Robin had auditioned in. His mom and sister stood up immediately when Scott brought her in.

"Everyone," he said, "this is the famous Robin."

"I'm famous?" she asked, but she wasn't sure if he heard her because his sister squealed and rushed over to her with open arms.

"Thank you," she said, hugging Robin and swinging her a bit from side to side before breaking the embrace. She had Scott's deep eyes and dimple in the left cheek. Her long hair was done in Senegalese twists, she was tall and svelte, and she smelled like berries. "Thank you for injecting a little holiday cheer into this big old, cold apartment."

"Cold?" said Scott, his brow furrowed and his lips pulled to the side. "Pshh. My place is not cold."

Robin chimed in, "It's lovely."

"It's huge," said his sister. "Too big for one person. Westminster Abbey is huge and lovely too. No one's calling it homey."

Robin had to admit, she did sort of agree with his sister. There simply wasn't a lot going on in the living room, almost nothing of the sparkling personality she'd been getting to know in Scott. The living room of a home, Robin had found, was truly what set the mood of the whole place. The kitchen may be the heart, the bedrooms may be the sanctuary, but the room where a person entertained, relaxed, and did all manner of, well, living, Robin felt that room was the soul. Except for the Christmas decorations, that room looked like staging for a house on the market. Beautiful, yes, with high-end tables and chairs, and a beige suede couch big and cushy enough to lose yourself in, but not at all personalized . . . except for one thing.

In the corner of the room, with sprawling picture windows to either side, was an angled drafting table and stool. Robin had only gotten a glimpse of it, but it looked like it held schematic drawings of railway cars, along with various drafting tools: a T-square, compass, protractor, a handful of mechanical pencils, basically tools Robin always thought looked interesting but hadn't any use for since the days she'd bought them off a school supplies list. She wished she had the opportunity to make the room over with a décor based entirely on train design. At the very least, some of those schematics should have been framed and on the wall, she thought.

Scott's sister, done lamenting his home for now anyway, stuck out her hand, which Robin shook. "I'm Frankie. Nice to meet you."

"Francesca," said the man who was obviously Scott's father. "We didn't have a second boy. Your name is Francesca." He stayed put at the head of the table, his ample belly pushed up against it. As he worked on a teetering stack of syrupy pancakes, his jowls quivered. Robin didn't think she'd ever seen anyone frown while eating pancakes, but there he was.

Scott's mother, who wore glasses and had a stout but athletic physique, waved off Scott's father as she came around the table. "Don't you mind him," she said, and went in for her own handshake.

"It's nice to meet you, Mrs. Donovan," said Robin.

"Hush with that," she said. "I'm Tara. Let's get you some food, shall we?" She ushered Robin over to the sideboard and handed her a plate.

Even as she stood with her back to Mr. Donovan, Robin could feel his eyes boring into her. She didn't quite know how to approach him. Here Tara was talking about their holiday plans, and how nice it was to take a break from hosting this year, all the while scooping food onto Robin's plate. Robin couldn't exactly get a word in edgewise with Tara's bubbly personality, and Mr. Donovan seemed like he couldn't care less about her, yet she felt awkward about essentially ignoring him.

"Here," said Frankie, moving her plate and silverware down the linen tablecloth, leaving a spot open between herself and Scott. As they dug into the eggs and bacon, Frankie and Tara asked Robin about what exactly YOPE was and how long she'd been doing it. As they sipped mimosas and coffee, they asked her about Whimsy. As they spread cream cheese onto their bagels with lox, they asked about the Holiday

Hutch. Not that Robin actually talked all that much. Tara had enough stories for the lot of them. But they were amusing anecdotes, and Tara told them with aplomb. Robin could have listened to her all day.

Scott hadn't said much either, save a little sibling banter with Frankie and filling in when Robin missed a detail or two about their past week together. He did, however, spend the meal laughing and engaged, which was much more than Robin could say for his father.

The entire time, Mr. Donovan sat scowling at his plate, scowling at Scott or Robin, scowling at some random point across the room. Finally, when everyone was stuffed and plates were clear but for a few crumbs, he lifted his eyes, narrowed them suspiciously at Robin, and grunted, "What else do you do?"

His voice was startling. It left a resounding, harsh tone hanging in the large room. Robin jumped a little. "I don't . . . Uh, what do you mean?"

"This YOPE thing," he said disparagingly. Coming from him, it didn't sound like the cute little name Robin always said. It didn't sound like it should have a hashtag in front of it or be a marketing gem: fun to say, easy to remember. Coming from him it sounded stupid, and Robin felt a little embarrassed about it just then.

He said, "Sounds like you work a month out of each year."

"Well," she said, a little defensively, she couldn't help that, "I work at the Holiday Hutch." *Which I've already mentioned if you'd bothered paying attention,* she added in her head. "And I'm an actress."

This last part was new information, at least as far as Robin knew. Unless Scott had mentioned it to the family at some point, they had no way of knowing that. She wasn't sure how they'd take it, especially this wolf of a man who apparently already decided that he didn't like her. Some people, especially successful people, as she guessed Mr. Donovan was in his own right given his and his wife's clothes, haircuts, and manicures, had a hard time with struggling artists. They saw it as flakey, as pie-in-the-sky, even as lazy, when in actuality some of the hardest-working people Robin knew were struggling artists.

"An actress?" Frankie said. From the way she said it, Robin knew she had at least one ally besides Scott at the table. "That's so cool. I'm sure Scott told you Dad was an actor."

Robin's eyebrows shot up, and she turned to Scott, who was looking rather uneasy. "He didn't mention it, actually," she said.

"I was," Mr. Donovan declared, "at one time." Robin should have known, with a sonorous voice like that. He was projecting into the next time zone, for crying out loud. "Now I am tenured at Preston University, teaching the graduate-level acting workshop among other things. But, yes, I still remember my great soliloquys. My Hamlet was revered. My Amadeus was masterful. Even my Ebenezer Scrooge was inspired."

Big surprise there, thought Robin. What she said, though, was, "Preston's a formidable school."

"Between my innate talent for the stage and my head for investment management, I have been able to write my own ticket and that of my family," he went on, ignoring her compliment. He kept his eyes narrowed at Robin, and his chin was tucked in under his glower. The heavy breathing through his nose was almost as loud as his voice. "Are you on Broadway?" he asked her.

She held her tongue, almost skidding into a joke. It was like a nervous tick that hit her at times, throwing out a joke, usually a terrible one, when she felt backed into a corner. Thank goodness she caught herself. "No," she said. "Not yet anyway."

"Then you're off?" he asked.

"Oh, I'm off all right. At least that's what my parents thought when I told them I wanted to be an actor," said Robin with a snorting chortle. Immediately, she clapped a hand over her mouth as she felt the blood rush to her cheeks. "Oh, God."

Yep. The terrible joke popped out anyway.

Scott and Frankie laughed, just to be polite, Robin was positive of that. Tara gave her own gracious titter. Mr. Donovan was not impressed.

To try to save face, Robin chuckled shyly. Then she glanced at the windows behind her and contemplated a swan dive.

"I'm sorry," said Robin. "I'm . . . weird. Uh, were you asking if I'm off-Broadway or if I'm off of work, like, between shows?"

Mr. Donovan stared at her, then enunciated, "Off-Broadway."

"Oh," said Robin. "No, I'm not."

"Then you're between runs?" he asked.

"Technically," said Robin. "The last show I was in was a revival of *Starlight Express* at the Whimsy Playhouse. You think you've seen everything in community theatre but then you put it all on roller skates and, I'll tell ya, those images haunt you the rest of your life."

"The Whimsy Playhouse?" Donovan said with a sneer, like she'd said it was the Rats, Ebola, and Black Mold Playhouse. "Whimsy Playhouse. Why am I suddenly reminded of down-home folks solving all their problems by staging a show in the old barn?"

"Dad," Frankie admonished.

"Reed, really. That's unnecessary," Tara scolded him.

"More mimosa, anyone?" Scott said pleasantly, if a touch nervously. He jumped up, grabbed the pitcher, and started refilling glasses.

"When was this show?" Donovan thundered over them all.

Robin raised her chin and refused to look away from him. "About a year ago."

"You haven't worked in a year?" he said. "Oh, excuse me, what was I thinking? One can hardly call community theatre 'working.'"

"Hey," said Robin, "I got paid." She paused. "A little." She paused again, then haughtily admitted, "In chickpeas, in cans of chickpeas. The director worked for a distributor who sells . . ."

"Chickpeas," Donovan said.

"And chickpea products," said Robin. "Like hummus. And . . . well, I guess that's pretty much it. Chickpeas and chickpea product, singular." As Scott refilled her glass, she pointed at the windows and said to him, "Do these open?"

"So you're a checkout girl with a hobby," said Donovan.

Robin turned back to him and said seriously, "No. I'm a clerk at the Holiday Hutch. I do an honest day's work for an honest day's pay, and I wouldn't call Your Own Personal Elf a hobby because I get paid for that, too."

Donovan shook his all-jowls head. "I meant the acting. It's a hobby. You haven't done any shows in a year and the last one paid you in legumes. That's not a career. That's a hobby."

"You know," said Robin, "one thing theatre's taught me is how to take criticism. It's a tough world. So competitive. I just came from an audition in the city where I was up against Zombie Girl Number Three from that horror flick last summer. And that mom from the soup commercial, she was there."

"Ooh," said Frankie, "that commercial with the grandpa and the little boy?"

Robin nodded. "They do the whole collage of the family photos for the sick grandma and then they all—"

"Eat the soup," the three women said in sentimental unison.

"Oh, I love that commercial," said Tara. "Makes me cry every time."

"Acting was never so competitive for me," Donovan plowed over them all. "I'll tell you what I tell my students on day one . . . Of course, one day of my workshop would cost about a hundred seventy-five cans of chickpeas, but I won't even charge you for this. You can fill yourself with as many excuses as you like about the cutthroat world of theatre, but what it comes down to is you're either good enough to secure the role, or you're not. I doubt that Sir Laurence Olivier ever cried into his Pimms over stiff competition."

In that moment, Robin made a decision.

She sat quietly, tuning out Frankie and Tara coming down on Donovan for his rudeness. She tuned out the touch of confused dismay she felt over Scott, who apparently had no problem with the way his father talked to his new friend. Delving deep within herself, she sank into her doubts about whether she could make it in acting. All of it crashed and swirled around her, a whirlpool of rejections, the days that went by without a callback, the agents who told her she needed an impressive résumé, the directors who denied her that résumé because she didn't have an agent.

Heartache stirred in her chest until tears came to her eyes, which she tried to keep at bay. Frankie and Tara noticed and came over to her. Scott halfheartedly moved toward her too.

"No," said Robin, sniffing and dismissing the women's coos of encouragement. "He's right. I'm no good. I've heard it my whole life when it comes to acting. I've tried so many classes"—she almost lost the hold she had on her tears, and just barely regained it—"but the teachers just tell me to stop wasting my time and theirs. Other actors ridicule me, understudies ridicule me. One really nice director I had once convinced me not to go on after all because he didn't want me to humiliate myself. He thought he could work with me when he cast me, but he said I was hopeless. My own parents sobbed at one of my performances."

Scott finally spoke up. "That's a good thing," he said. "You moved them to tears."

Robin shook her head. "It was a comedy."

"Oh," he said.

She used her linen napkin to blot her eyes, and then held the back of her shaking hand to her lips, her eyes downcast. "I told myself I was going to quit altogether after this year. This morning's audition was it. If I didn't get it, I was just going to hang it all up, walk away from my dream. But I think . . . Yeah. I think I'm just going to withdraw my name from consideration."

Frankie rubbed Robin's back. "Honey, don't walk away from your dream. It takes a long time to succeed."

Tara glared at Donovan. "You apologize to this girl right now."

Robin managed to glance at Donovan, whose holier-than-thou expression had been replaced by one touched with shame. His mouth was open, like it was standing at the ready for his brain to form the right words. Scott's hands were hidden deep in his pockets, his head lowered in dismay.

Letting her gaze fall again, Robin said tearfully, "You don't have to apologize." Then she lifted her head with a smirk. "But I'll take a round of applause."

For a few seconds, everyone's mouth was open, just like Donovan's. Then Scott and Frankie burst out laughing, clapping, and whooping. Tara gave her an appreciative whistle and called, "Brava! Brava!"

Robin bowed her head. "*Grazie.*" When she came up again, her eyes landed back on Donovan, who'd clamped his mouth once more. She resisted the urge to stick her tongue out at the pompous toad.

Not long after that, Robin took her leave, in part because she was worried that if Mr. Donovan continued to stew, he'd boil over and leave quite the mess behind. Mostly, though, she knew if she didn't remove herself from the scene, she'd end up flicking Scott in the forehead repeatedly to see if she could hear an empty, echoing sound. She'd known he wanted to win his father's affection, which had already seemed strange to her. Why did he care so much about a person who apparently didn't care for him? But since he'd all but joined in his father's castigation of her, she felt betrayed. She thought they were becoming friends, but she couldn't imagine ever just standing by if any of her friends were treated with such disrespect, even by her own parents. Apparently, she'd been wrong about the nature of their relationship.

Scott walked her out to the elevator in the hall. When his front door was closed and they were alone, he said awkwardly, "I'm, um, I'm sorry for my dad's behavior."

She nodded. "Well, thank you for the apology." He was still her client. She still had a job to do. And so all the other things she thought of to add to that, including a few innovative ideas about what he could do with his rather feeble apology, went unsaid.

"Friday," he said. "Friday night, actually. I want to take you somewhere special."

She squinted, dubious. "Why?"

"My dad's gift," he said. "It's the only thing we haven't gotten."

"Right," she said, trying to keep her utter lack of enthusiasm to herself. "Fine, um, my shift ends at four at the Hutch, so as long as the train's on time I can meet you . . . where?"

"No," he said, "don't take the train. Just be at your apartment and ready to go by six, okay?"

"Don't take the train? What am I gonna do, sprout wings?"

"Just be there," he said. "Please."

She held her hands out to her sides in a sort of surrender. "Okay. See you Friday."

As she walked into the elevator and returned his wave, she was the picture of decorum. But as soon as the doors closed, she let go of her amiable expression and glared at the floor. By her shoes was a balled-up gum wrapper, which she amused herself with by toeing it until the doors opened again. She stalked off. Here she'd been starting to consider this man a friend. She'd even entertained one or two flights about their friendship someday blossoming into a romance. Now she felt about as special as that balled-up gum wrapper. Whatever the stupid gift idea was, she hoped it would work out so she could wash her hands of spineless Scott and his precious father for good.

Chapter
Ten

Two days before the winter solstice, Spark met Lexie at the elevator on *Upstate*'s eighteenth floor. Spark was wearing a silver headband over her purple coiffure, her "solstice" headband with tiny reliefs of geese, figs, and clovers. The headband was how Lexie recognized her, given that Spark held in front of her face the latest issue of *Upstate,* which featured the now-infamous cover article.

"Are you *the* Lexie Moore," she teased warmly, walking backward as Lexie marched to her desk. "Can I have your autograph?"

"Stop being so silly," said Lexie. "It's just an article. I've written dozens of them for this magazine alone."

"Just an article?" said Spark. "No. I don't think so. Do you know how many issues I saw on the bus this morning? And it just hit stands. You struck a chord, my friend. People are loving the Christmas getaway this year, and if our sales are any indication of where they're looking to go, Whimsy's tourism board isn't going to know what hit 'em."

Lexie dropped into her chair with a purely professional demeanor draped over her. But she couldn't contain herself. A grin leapt onto her face as she stretched back and kicked off the floor to spin the chair around. "I did good, didn't I?"

"You so did, boss."

"We did," said Lexie. "I couldn't have done it without your help."

"Oh, please," said Spark. "What did I do, get you coffee and run perhaps the longest marathon ever? At least, it felt like the longest getting the thing to layout."

The entire last week had been fairly light around the office, since Lexie had come in the Monday following Saturday night's debacle, and Belinda had praised her on the story. In fact, the office felt so good to Lexie that she stayed late every night, helping other reporters out, chatting with Spark or Belinda, or culling her own research for stories she was thinking of tackling in the New Year. She even brought takeout to share with Stu in his office, listening to him freak out about one supposed catastrophe or another. Taquitos from Señor Jalapeño's food truck tasted extra-special spicy when they were garnished with a sprig of Stu's hysteria.

Her house was depressing in comparison. It was the same old house, of course, and it wasn't like Theo lived there. His presence was not so ensconced that it would be obvious to anyone else he was missing. Lexie had thought about it late one night after finally coming home, legs folded under her on the couch, two ice cream sandwich wrappers discarded on the end table, TV turned off. She looked around the living room, into the front hall and past the staircase to her little home office she'd converted the dining room into. From where she was, she could see a framed photo on her desk of her and Theo. He was giving her a piggy-back ride after the heel had broken off one of her shoes, and the friends they were out with had insisted on taking the picture. The house didn't feel empty, really, or cold or dark. It was a comfortable seventy degrees, all the lights worked, and the décor was cozy with throw pillows and area rugs that coordinated with her blue and green walls. She had artwork around her and all her own furniture that she loved. But it didn't feel right, and it took Lexie some time to put her finger on it.

Then it hit her. It felt worn. Everything, when she was alone and not distracted by anyone else, felt worn out and old, like a Christmas tree still up in March. But when she thought maybe she should redecorate or change out rugs or pillows, the idea left her cold, like that wouldn't help anything after all. Her house would still be her house. And that made her wonder if it was really the house at all that bothered her.

Regardless, she'd spent yesterday, Sunday, a week and a day since her blowup with Theo, doing some Christmas shopping, hanging out at Orange-Clove, and then visiting with her parents, who were back in town for the holidays. They finally told her around eleven thirty that she could stay over or go home, but they were turning in and no one needed more coffee at this hour. She grudgingly went home and was awake before her alarm went off at six this morning.

But today was Monday, and in a reverse from practically everyone else on the planet, Lexie was looking forward to a whole nice long week before having to face the weekend again. That was, until she saw Belinda approaching her, and the grim look on her face.

"Uh-oh," Lexie said under her breath. "What now?"

"Lex," said Belinda, "Stu and I would like a word with you. Conference room, please."

Spark lifted a wary eyebrow at Lexie and patted her on the shoulder. "Well, I hope you enjoyed your success. All twenty seconds of it."

Lexie followed Belinda, stepping quickly to keep up with her long, sleek strides. The fluid way the woman could move in a pencil skirt had always left Lexie and Spark befuddled and awestruck. "Hey," Lexie said as they approached the conference room door, "is this all a ruse and you actually have a surprise party waiting for me in there to congratulate me on a job well done?"

Belinda halted so abruptly that Lexie nearly ran into her. Even in pants, Lexie wasn't as smooth as Belinda in her skirt. "Lex, do you see a party waiting for you?"

All she saw through the glass walls was Stu, his hand in his shock of hair, pacing madly. "No," she mumbled.

"We have a problem. I'll let Stu fill you in."

They went through the door, and Belinda closed it behind them as Stu gestured for Lexie to take a seat. "Belinda says . . ." Lexie started, but her throat had suddenly turned into a gravel pit. She cleared it and tried again. "Belinda says we have a problem?"

"We do." Stu sat finally in his normal place at the table's head. Belinda slinked into a chair next to him.

"Okay," said Lexie, taking a deep breath. "Well, give it to me."

Stu opened his mouth, but Lexie cut him off. "Let me just remind you, before you say anything, that I was in here a week ago Saturday, working my little fingers to the bone to make sure that a failed hard drive—which was not at all my fault, by the way—a failed hard drive didn't ruin an issue of your magazine. Our magazine."

Stu said, "Right. We know. Lex—"

"I say 'our magazine,'" she jumped in again, "because I truly feel like *Upstate* is a family. We all support each other, we're here for each other, my successes are your successes, and vice versa. Families help one another. For instance, when one has a problem, the others help her. Nothing bad happens."

Stu waited, staring at her with his lips parted. "Okay," he finally said after Lexie had stayed quiet. "The problem is—"

"Spark said everyone's reading my article on the bus," Lexie squeaked.

Stu sprang out of his seat. "You were right, okay? There is no problem," he yelled. "We were messing with you. You were supposed to come in here and say, 'What's the problem?' and I was going to say, 'The problem is you were nominated for a Magsy and the editor-in-chief of *Swish* magazine wants to snap you up and we don't know which news to celebrate first,' but you ruined it. So there." He flopped back into his seat, crossed his legs and his arms, and pouted.

"What?" said Lexie. She looked at Belinda to confirm the news, and Belinda was looking back at her, her lips pursed into a tiny, chic smile. "A Magsy?"

Ever since Lexie had started in the niche magazine world, she'd dreamt of winning a Magsy. She pictured herself at the white-tie banquet, wearing an evening gown—long, sparkly, emerald green, for it was always emerald green in her imagination to complement her eyes and her auburn hair—and being called to the stage to collect her award. It may not have been a solid-gold statuette, but white script on a small glass obelisk was posh enough for her.

"Nominations came out this morning," said Belinda, "so the judges' panel must have already had their eye on you. I imagine your piece in today's issue is only going to sweeten the deal."

Stu threw himself forward in his chair, reached down, and slammed a bottle of champagne on the table before retracting into his pout. On cue, Spark came through the door with flutes. "Congrats, Lex," she cheered, and then she looked around the room at angry Stu, cool Belinda, and shocked Lexie. "Wait, you gave her the news, right?"

Belinda stood up. "He did. And congratulations are in order. Here, pass me the bottle."

Feeling like she was moving in slow motion, Lexie handed it to her, and Belinda popped the cork and started pouring. Stu heaved a sigh and then dropped his pout. Belinda called out to the bull pen and invited in anyone so inclined to share in the celebration of the Magsy nomination. She whispered to Lexie, "The news about *Swish* is yours until you decide what you want to do."

"I don't understand," said Lexie. "*Swish* is, well, *Swish*. They're a weekly, their circulation is international. They're a consumer mag based in L.A. How did they even hear of me? The editor-in-chief to boot. They don't even have a New York office, do they?"

Belinda shook her head. "I know it's not exactly protocol for one editor to talk to another when poaching a reporter, but Gabby and I go back about a millennium or two, and I thought it was high time I do you a little favor."

"Gabby?" Lexie said, astonished. "As in Gabriella Alfonsi?"

With a shrug, Belinda said, "Before she was editor-in-chief over there, I may have helped her out of a scrape or two in J-school."

"And Gabby is asking for me?"

"Whoa," Belinda laughed, her hands held out to slow Lexie down a touch. "Gabriella doesn't know a whole lot of your work, to be fair. In fact, I may have been the one to call her and tell her about you. But I did send her the link to this latest story of yours, and she was impressed."

Lexie had never thought seriously about leaving Whimsy to move anywhere. The city was here when she wanted to dance to its driving beat, and now that she'd be attending the Magsy awards as a nominee, she was obviously stepping into hitherto sealed circles. Whimsy was her comfort, the robe and slippers she slid into at the end of a long day. When the shuttle from the train depot entered Whimsy Square each night, she breathed easier.

Of course, that had changed over the past week.

For the first time, Lexie wondered if it would ever change back. And if it didn't, if she and Theo didn't see their way through this bramble, what if Whimsy itself started to feel prickly to her?

She asked Belinda, "Do you know where they'd put me? What desk I'd be reporting for?"

Before Belinda could answer, Spark twisted around from behind Lexie. "What do you mean what desk?" Spark whispered.

"How did you hear that?" Lexie asked. "We were being really quiet."

Spark tapped her ear. "You work as an assistant at a magazine long enough, you pick up a few tricks about eavesdropping, m'friend." She hushed her own voice and leaned in. "Now what do you mean, where they'd put you? Who's they?"

Reluctantly, Lexie filled her in. Spark was one of the people she'd want to tell first, once she made the decision. But given that she'd only heard the news herself about three seconds ago, she was reluctant to share it with anyone. Spark would keep it quiet, though. In that, Lexie was confident.

Spark covered her mouth at the news. "Wow," she breathed through her fingers before remembering herself and putting her hand down. "That's wonderful, Lex. I mean, you know I'd hate to lose you, but this is a huge step up."

"Sure, it would be," Lexie agreed, "but I don't know anything about covering Tinseltown."

"Just 'cause you'd be in L.A. doesn't mean you'd have to cover entertainment and celebrities and stuff," said Spark. "You could work at their current events desk. They've won Ellies for some of their reporting on current events. That piece on Alzheimer's won the Ellie, and I think then it went on to win a Pulitzer." Spark gasped. "Oh, my God, you're going to win a Pulitzer."

"And you're going to win an American Fiction Award for this lovely little story you've conjured up about me," Lexie said with a laugh.

The truth was, just talking about Spark's dreamworld stirred up exhilaration in Lexie. Her goal had always been to work for a publication like that. A magazine, specifically.

Magazines were glossy and bright. They used the full spectrum of color as their stories covered the full spectrum of life. Newspapers were fine, and in fact Lexie felt her heart break a little each time she heard a publication was folding or going to a fully digital platform. But the format of papers belied their purpose: papers were black and white, while good reporting almost never was. Magazines were black, white, and every color in between. And as much as Lexie loved the features she did for *Upstate,* the investigative journalist inside her still stood poised with a tape recorder and a press pass. She wanted to one day incorporate more investigation into her journalism, but bring it to those shiny, four-color pages she so loved. She'd done it in high school. Well, she'd done as much as a teenager could. Every time there was a political scandal or shake-up in D.C., she pestered her advisor to let her travel and get the inside scoop. It never worked, especially since she pestered him weekly given all the scandals and shake-ups in politics, but she never stopped asking. She even started a magazine in college, her baby, and named it *Dimensions* to capture that feeling all those full-color pages gave her. Most of the journalism department told her it would never last, especially since the college already had an established paper. But she got it off the ground, and even handed it off to a few underclassmen just as wonderfully stubborn as she when she graduated.

The feeling stirring inside her was that same feeling she had creating *Dimensions*. What if, in a few months' time, she could turn a current-events beat at *Swish* into her next journalistic baby, one even better than her old college mag, one that catapulted her into an investigatory stratosphere she could only dream about before?

"Well?" Lexie asked Belinda, her heart starting to pound. "Do you know what desk I'd be on?"

Belinda uncharacteristically fumbled her words and broke eye contact, glancing down into her champagne. "I . . . sort of . . . know. You'd be a columnist."

Lexie and Spark exchanged an excited look. "Really?" said Lexie. "Which column?"

"Well, it wouldn't exactly be your column alone," Belinda said. "You'd work on a column. Only for a little while, I'm sure, then it would be all yours."

"Oh," said Lexie. Of course, that made a little more sense. When you started up a brand-new ladder you didn't get on at the top rung. "Well, what's the column?"

Belinda lifted her flute to her lips. Just before she took a mighty swig, she said, "'Smooches to Pooches.'"

"What?" Lexie and Spark said together.

"The column about celebrities' pets?" Spark asked, her lip curled.

"Hey," said Belinda, "didn't you ever hear it's better to be a small fish in a big pond than a big fish in a small pond?"

"No," Lexie said facetiously. "But if the fish belongs to a movie star, I'll be able to read about it in 'Smooches to Pooches.'"

"Look, Lexie," Belinda said, "you'll be out of that gig in no time, and your foot will be in the door at a fine publication. I think you're outgrowing us here, and I don't want to see you stall out when you're just at the beginning of so many possibilities. Don't hold yourself back just because for a little while the job's going to be a little less than glamorous."

"Besides," said Spark with a solemn face, "some of these pets have major dirt attached to them. Literally."

"Shut up," Lexie said, nudging her with her elbow.

"Seriously, okay," said Spark. "I'm being serious. I can see the stories: Who tracked kibble all over the floor? Who killed the field mouse in the foyer? FeeFee can't fit into her owner's purse anymore. Sources bark she's pregnant, and the glitterati of all the doggie daycares want to know, who's the daddy?"

"Don't listen to her," said Belinda. "I'll text you the number Gabby gave me for the columnist. You can set up an interview with him. But this has a clock on it, Lex. They want a call by nine a.m. Monday."

"Monday?" said Lexie. "That's the day after Christmas. This is not a decision to make the week before Christmas. This is a week for taking a breath, enjoying the season. Everyone else slows down this time of year. Besides, my brain is full of Christmasy things."

"Christmasy?" said Belinda, flinching at the made-up word.

"You know," said Lexie, "wrapping and presents and my tree. I haven't even gotten my tree."

Belinda put a gentle hand on Lexie's shoulder and gave her a sympathetic look. "I don't care. A week is more than enough time for you to figure out which road to take."

Spark muttered knowingly to Lexie, "And if you do take the 'Smooches to Pooches' road, just be careful where you step."

Lexie shoved her still-full champagne flute into Spark's empty hand. "Here, assistant. Assist me by getting me a refill."

"Uh . . ." said Spark. "Refill?"

Lexie grabbed the flute back, downed nearly the entire serving, and then shoved the glass back to her. "Yes," she said. "Refill."

When Spark walked off, Lexie said to Belinda, "I'm dealing with some personal things. I don't think my head's in the right place for making a decision about moving clear across the country, away from everything I know, my family, my home, my fian . . . boyfriend."

"All right," said Belinda, "I'll tell you what. Call the columnist. Set up the interview for January. And there, your Christmasy week's not consumed by it, and you can focus on your Christmasy and personal things." She paused, and then added, "All your dreams are coming true, Lex. Don't look so glum. In fact, don't look glum at all. People around here are already jealous of you. If you act like your success is a burden, they're just going to hate you."

The idea that she was taking this all for granted and complaining that her ship had come in but the paint job was smudged straightened Lexie up. "No, I'm grateful for all of this," she said. "I just . . ." She thought better of qualifying her gratitude, and instead switched tracks. "Thank you, Belinda. For your vote of confidence most of all. You know, burning one of what I'm sure are very few chits to call in with Gabriella."

Belinda held her flute up to Lexie. "It's only burned if you make the wrong decision. If I were you, I'd make this easy on myself. Just tell them you're on board. Enjoy the success. And enjoy your moment in the sun. What d'ya say?"

Lexie forced a smile and, since she was still sans glass, lifted an imaginary one in the air. "I say . . . I'm on board for enjoying the sun."

"Atta girl," said Belinda, and gave her a wink as she sipped.

Just as good reporting was never black and white, Lexie refused to admit that this decision only had two options: stay in Whimsy and lose out on the chance of a lifetime, or go to L.A. and give up her life here. And then there was Theo. He loved his job at the Public Library. She didn't want to ask him to give that up. After what had happened, she didn't even know where their relationship stood.

After Spark returned with another round of champagne and got to talking with Belinda and a few other reporters, Lexie managed to slip away from the celebration and sneak over to her desk. With a few clicks and a few keystrokes tapped, she brought up the travel site *Upstate* always used, and looked at the next couple days' flights out to L.A. Yes, there were other options, other colors to this story, there had to be, and Lexie was determined to find them.

Chapter
Eleven

With Christmas Eve just three days away, For the Record, like every other store in Whimsy, was packed. Margot loved it when it was like this, and not just because a happy store usually translated to a happy profit margin. She felt that Darren's dream was alive and well in these wood-paneled walls when their narrow, long nook in the Northridge Super Plaza was stuffed with music lovers. The one other time she felt this close to his spirit, at least while at work, was during opening procedures. Strange, she once realized, that the times she felt closest to him were when the store was either utterly bursting or utterly silent.

Margot had never wanted to be an entrepreneur, and until she saw Darren's spirit one early morning as she counted out cash for the register, she wasn't sure she'd be able to hold down the business at all. She liked routines, a set way of doing things. The constant uncertainty of owning a shop like this was like a skipping record. There was a groove right there for the needle to follow, but one dust mote, one hair, one bump of the player, and the needle could go all over the place and wreck everyone's hard work. The idea was maddening to Margot. She adored music, just about any genre from the 1940s through the '90s, and she knew a good amount of background info and trivia on artists and cuts. But listening to records and chatting about them was one thing; adding business into the mix created a tune entirely discordant to her.

But Darren had appeared to her in the storeroom, and he told her she'd be fine. He believed in her. Now the shop was her refuge. Whether he came to her or not in the mornings, she talked to him every day as she brought the tills to the front, straightened displays, filed new purchases of old records in their respective bins, breathed in that wonderful old wax smell of the records as she filed them, turned on the music, and lit the OPEN sign.

Today, she'd finished ringing up one decent sale of nine records and another of the Bob Dylan *Rolling Stone* collector's edition issue, and settled a debate over whether it was Neneh Cherry or Nina Simone who recorded "Woman"—it was Cherry, Margot had said, and Simone recorded "Four Women," and both happened to be in stock—when Charlotte came in. In place of a traditional shopkeeper's bell over the entrance door, Darren had installed an electronic contraption with a motion detector. Every time the door opened, a line from "Break On Through (To the Other Side)" chimed out. Usually it was a happy sound, portending new customers, new sales, "new" records that were actually old treasures from some collector's attic. Seeing Charlotte's face, though, Margot knew this was not a happy visit.

In another of her signature baggy crocheted sweaters, Charlotte bustled over to Margot at the registers. She cut in front of several people waiting in line, though to her credit, she waited to do that until Margot was finished with the sale she was in the midst of. Charlotte wasn't hiding her impatience well, but as a retail manager in her own right, she wasn't going to interrupt a sale, Margot knew.

She hustled her short, zaftig body in front of Margot's register and plumped her baggy crocheted arms on the counter, folding them with a huff. "What have you done?" she said.

Margot blinked at her. "Many, many things," she replied. "Wanna be a little more specific?"

"Gavin backed out of our Christmas party."

And here Margot had been having a pleasant day.

Obviously, this wasn't going to be a quick word. Margot grabbed one of the sales clerks from the floor to replace her on the till, and then she sauntered over to the "This Week in Music Forty Years Ago" display. Charlotte stalked close on her heels. "Maybe he doesn't like parties," said Margot as she rearranged the featured records.

"He loves parties," said Charlotte.

"Well, what makes you think it's my fault he's not going to yours? I think you're jumping to conclusions, Char."

"He said it was because of you."

"Oh."

"He said he got a vibe from you last week and he doesn't want to push you into anything if you're not ready," Charlotte said.

Margot glimpsed down at Charlotte before her deliveryman near the storeroom entrance grabbed her eye. "Good," she said, moving away, Charlotte on her heels again. "I'm not ready."

She approached the deliveryman, who let her know he'd just dropped off the several cartons of pristine albums Margot had won at an estate auction. She couldn't wait to get her hands on them. They chatted a bit as Margot signed the delivery slip, all the while Charlotte standing to Margot's side, arms a-crossed and foot a-tapping. The women followed the deliveryman into the storeroom, where he went back out the loading door. Margot made a beeline for the counter he'd left the three boxes on. She pulled a utility knife from the back pocket of her corduroys and cut into the packing tape that sealed the first box.

Charlotte cleared her throat with a loud, rough, "Ahem."

"I haven't forgotten you," said Margot, eyes like laser beams on the carton.

"For what, a friend?" said Charlotte.

This, Margot glanced up for. "What?" she said, confused.

"You said you're not ready. I'm saying, 'For what, a friend?'"

Margot snorted out a laugh. "I know what kind of friend Gavin's looking for." Once the tape was cut through, she tugged up on one of the flaps.

"What was that about jumping to conclusions?" said Charlotte.

"Look, it's only been—"

"Six years," she interrupted. "It's been six whole years, Margot."

"It has not," she said, pulling out one record. "There was that man last year—"

"You are not counting him. Dates that last for less time than your average pop song are not dates."

"Look at this," said Margot, turning the album over gently. "The Supremes' *Reflections,* still sealed."

"Earth to Margot," Charlotte snapped.

"And *Smiley Smile . . .*" She glanced at the corner of the cover and felt a little thrill. "Oh, man. This is a promotional copy. It didn't say that on the manifest. Cool."

Charlotte put a hand on her shoulder. "Can you please take a break for a few minutes so I can talk to you about this stuff?"

Under normal circumstances, Margot would talk to her cousin and friend about anything she wanted. If Charlotte had come into the store asking her to stop what she was doing and, three days before Christmas, close up shop to talk with her about the weather, Margot would do it. She'd do it for René and the kids, too. Kyle came first in her life, but the Lejeunes were a very close second. It was simply any talk about Gavin Aberline that Margot wanted to avoid.

She put the album down. "I'm sorry, hon," she said to Charlotte. "This sort of is a break for me. It's been crazy the last few days and I knew these were coming in, and I've been really looking forward to going through them."

With a shake of her head, Charlotte helped Margot rip open the other flap of the box. "Same old Margot. Tunnel vision. I swear, you get something in your head and there's no room for anything else."

Of course, the delivery was a lucky break, giving Margot just the excuse she needed to veer in an entirely different direction from where the conversation was headed. It looked like it was about to work, too, when Margot gave Charlotte a hug and thanked her for understanding. She went over to her desk and grabbed a clipboard and a copy of the auction lot manifest, which she'd had out since the day she won the thing. When she turned back, she half expected to see Charlotte walking away, but she hadn't moved.

"That's okay," said Charlotte. "You go ahead with your tunnel vision. I'll talk."

"You know," said Margot, "it's not just me. Kyle's not ready either. He nearly bit my head off when Gavin took us ice skating. Excuse me, curling." She went back to unpacking the records, checking off the manifest as she went. "Who takes people curling, anyway?"

"Um, an interesting, attractive man who's not your typical cookie-cutter guy?" said Charlotte. She shrugged. "Just a guess."

"Yeah, well, interesting or not, if my son isn't ready—"

"I'm not saying he has to open his arms and call him Daddy," said Charlotte. "But he's old enough to get past his mom being friends with a man."

"I don't want to push him. Just like I don't want to be pushed."

"Has he said he has a problem with this?"

"I'd say it was pretty obvious."

"Well," said Charlotte, "maybe it's time to sit down and have a talk with him. And do what you've always done. You don't let Kyle run the roost. You're the parent. If you want to be friends with someone, he's got to respect that."

It was true. Even when Kyle was much younger, in the first couple of years after Darren's death when he would act out or try to take advantage of his mother's guilt and vulnerability, she shut it down pretty quick. No, he couldn't skip school six months in because he was feeling sad, especially after she gave into that a few times and came home early one day to find him whooping in a very non-sad way as he hit a high score on one of his video games. No, it was not acceptable to throw the game controller at the wall after his mom caught him and use the almost laughable non-sequitur "but Dad's dead" as a defense. She was always loving, always jumping through hoops for him when she felt he really needed it, but she'd quickly gained the discerning gut of a parent in her position.

"You're forgetting one thing, Char," Margot said. "I don't want to be friends with Gavin. You know what? That's not true. If he were interested in friendship, only friendship, then maybe I'd warm to the idea. He wasn't . . . entirely terrible to talk with."

"Hardly a ringing endorsement, but I'll take it," said Charlotte. "What makes you think he needs more?"

"Oh, come on," said Margot. "You know when a man is interested. The looks, the invitations out, the cutesy 'I won't take no' overtures. It would be charming if I really were just being coy or playing hard to get. But I'm not. So it's not charming. It's uncomfortable."

"Hey," said Charlotte, "René and I have known him a long, long time. Trust me, he's not a creep. I mean, I know when some creep gets busted they talk to his family and friends and they all say, 'He always seemed like such a nice guy,' but Gavin really is. He's not an episode of some reality TV true-crime show."

"I'm not saying he's an ax murderer. I'm saying I've made my feelings clear but he just keeps pushing."

"Well," said Charlotte, her voice tweaking up.

Finally, Margot put her pen down and stopped her inventory. "Well what?"

"Have you really?" said Charlotte. "Made it clear? You did go curling with him."

Margot leaned down, opened her bottom desk drawer, and pulled out a greeting card. It had a beautiful little winter scene on the front, not entirely unlike the view of Whimsy Square from the Gallantry Bridge. It sparkled with glitter and gold lettering, addressed to "The one I love." Margot opened it, watching Charlotte for her reaction as it played, "Sometime, Christmastime, you'll walk through the door . . ." The curve inside spelled out, "Make our future a happy one."

Charlotte cleared her throat. "Well," she said, obviously hunting for some reasonable explanation, "you know, these things come back in fashion. It probably got licensed, and a company put it on their commercial, then a DJ heard that, tracked it down, and put it on the air, and it's getting its long-overdue time in the sun. Or, flipside, the royalties ran out and some marketing department snapped it up."

"And I just keep happening to run into it?" said Margot. She closed the card. "I think Darren might be trying to send me a message."

That was the first time she'd said the words aloud. She thought it'd make her feel stupid admitting that, but strangely enough, it didn't. Charlotte, however, looked startled. She knew Margot talked to Darren's spirit. Charlotte had told her that whether or not some part of him, some energy or fragment, was actually still here, she believed it was all very real for Margot, and that's what mattered. It's why Margot trusted her with this stuff about the song. But if Charlotte wasn't on

"Because he said Andy and Veronica would be there, and I thought Kyle would like it," Margot said, feeling her defenses go up.

"And is he really pushing too hard? He did say he wouldn't come to the party if it would make things awkward."

Margot tucked her soft curls behind her ears and looked back to the records, but said nothing.

Charlotte moved over between Margot and the records, held her cousin at arm's length, and waited until Margot looked up. "Honey, what's going on here? I've seen you when other men ask you out. There's no vacillation on your part. There's no hemming and hawing. Even the three-minute date was a little ridiculous. We both knew you just went out with the guy as a favor to me and there was no real future there. But this . . . this feels much different."

Charlotte bit her lip like she was mulling over exactly how to phrase her next words, or maybe whether she should phrase them at all. Then she said, "If a part of you is ready to let Gavin into your life, maybe you should explore that a little."

Suddenly, Margot's heart skipped a beat, and not in a good way. The dizzy, otherworldly feeling of a panic attack flooded her. It felt like her head was a helium balloon detached from her body and floating away, and at the same time her brain felt too tight for her skull. The first time an all-out attack like this had happened to her was a few days after she'd gotten the call from the highway patrol. "Mrs. Kobeleski? I have some very bad news . . ." She'd gotten through going to the morgue, identifying Darren, even telling Kyle. None of it had seemed real. At the funeral, though, sitting in the front pew, she'd gotten that terrible heart skip, like it actually had jumped up and gotten stuck in her windpipe. The detached feeling was so strange, she wondered if this was what it felt like to lose her mind, or have a stroke, or die. She'd turned to Charlotte, actually, who'd been sitting to her left while Kyle was to her right, and she'd whispered to her cousin to check her face. Was one side drooping? She'd heard that was a sure sign of a stroke. Charlotte had assured her she looked fine, but Margot couldn't believe it. Surely there had to be an outside sign—hooded eyes, cheeks turning purple, something—given how strangely she felt inside.

After about an hour the feeling had passed, though it came back again in waves for the next few days. Over the next year, Margot would suffer through the attacks while driving, shopping, eating out. But then they had begun to subside. Now they hit her only when certain stress triggers were touched. Like an exposed nerve, when those were hit, the ensuing attacks were intense. It didn't take a psychologist to tell her that one of those triggers was dealing with the Gordian knot that was potential romance.

Charlotte immediately saw the change in Margot and walked her away from the records to her desk chair. "A little panic there?" she said, pulling up another chair.

Margot nodded between deep breaths.

"Want me to drop this?"

At that, Margot shook her head. Yes, she [c]lotte to drop the whole matter, but more than t[] want to give in to the panic. After a minute, t[] passed, leaving behind as it always did a feeli[] discomfort, like she could live at the most rela[] have daily massages, pedicures, and facials and s[] never again feel at peace. But at least there wa[] that fight-or-flight fear.

"Char," she said, "something odd's been hap[] the past few weeks. Please, hear me out. It's goin[] little nutsy, but you're the one person I can really [] this."

"Sure," she said. "What's up?"

"I keep hearing our song," said Margot. "Min[] ren's. You know, 'A Christmas Sometime'?"

"Well," Charlotte said delicately, "it is Christn[] go to sleep without hearing carols over and over i[] from the PA system at the Orange-Clove."

"No, you don't understand. I haven't heard th[] decades. It was a B-side. One of the reasons Dar[] loved it so much was because it was so obscure. I trie[] for it online the first Christmas after he . . . and t[] digital version out there. It took me forever to even tr[] an old record of it. And all of a sudden, right when a [] new man comes into my life, it's playing everywhe[] PAs, on the radio. And that's not all."

board with this possibility, maybe Margot was way off base after all.

She started to backpedal a bit: "Maybe you're right and it's just coincidence. I mean, I would hope that if Darren's ghost had the power to create greeting cards, he'd be doing something more productive with his time, like feeding me winning lotto numbers."

But Charlotte stopped her. "I don't know how any of this works. I guess if I did, neither one of us would need winning lotto numbers. Maybe Darren can send you messages, or . . . I don't know, manipulate things somehow to get that message to you. But I feel like if he is reaching out to you, he wouldn't do it to make you feel bad. Trying to, what, guilt you into staying alone your whole life because he's not in the picture anymore? That's not Darren."

"It wasn't him in life, no way," Margot agreed. "But who knows what dying does to a guy?"

Charlotte gave her a gentle smile. "I still don't think he'd change into an entirely different person. If there's some way we go on, if the energy and essence of what we were continues somehow after death, I have to believe we retain a part of the goodness inside of us. After all, it's that same essence that made us who we are in life."

A surge of appreciation filled Margot's heart, appreciation for her cousin and that, when it really mattered, Charlotte always listened to her sincerely and with an open mind. Sure, she could be a little meddlesome, she could push Margot a bit, but it was only out of love. She wanted to see Margot happy. And for that, Margot leaned forward in her chair and threw her arms around her cousin and friend.

"Aw, sweetie," Charlotte said, patting Margot's back.

Inside Margot, emotions battled each other, every one for itself like little armor-clad warriors. Panic crossed swords with love and gratitude; sorrow wrestled with the far weaker but ever resilient hope. And then, in the midst of it all, guilt threw a grenade and lit the battlefield in a choking smoky haze.

Tears pricked Margot's eyes. She whispered into Charlotte's shoulder, "It's all my fault Darren's gone."

"No, honey, no," said Charlotte, her tone harder. "Don't start this again."

"It is." Margot backed up, blinking her eyes to dry them before the tears could fall.

"You can't keep blaming yourself. Blame the weather, blame circumstance, but blaming yourself is ridiculous and pointless. In fact, scratch what I just said. Don't blame anything. Blame is just another trap that's going to keep you stuck in the past, just like guilt and second-guessing. Stop it." She spoke in the voice she used when she had to snap her kids out of a tantrum. And, Margot supposed, she probably needed some snapping.

Charlotte stood up. "Look, talk to Kyle about how he feels about Gavin," she reiterated, "and you need to do a little soul-searching on it yourself. If you come out of all that and neither one of you wants to move on, well"—she gave an exaggerated shrug and huffed out a breath—"I'm done trying to help destiny out."

"Wait," said Margot. "What do you mean by that?"

"Gavin told René and me that he happened to meet you at the Hutch. He told us that I guess he mentioned philosophy at the rink or something? That's one of his interests too. It just seems like destiny has a plan for you two."

"You mean you really didn't send him to the Hutch looking for me and tell him all about me?"

"Margot, I love you, I want to see you happy. But do you really imagine I spend my days talking to men about you and spying on your every move so I know when to send the next candidate in?" she said with a smile. "This, right now, is the first time I've intervened on destiny's behalf, and it's not even really about that anyway. This is Gavin's first Christmas all alone, and he's in a new place. He doesn't know anyone else here, not enough to spend the holidays with them. You and Kyle have to come to the party, and obviously if I have to choose, I choose you guys in a heartbeat. But that choice means Gavin at home on Christmas Eve and Day with TV and a frozen dinner, when his whole life he's done the big fun Christmas scene. Imagine going from a roaring fire and friends all around and kids squealing with laughter and presents, to whatever's on cable and meatloaf that's still a little icy in the middle."

Margot pictured it. She hated that picture. Gavin didn't deserve that. He was a pain, but he didn't deserve to be all alone. And besides that, this obviously meant so much to Charlotte.

She stood up and hugged Charlotte again. "I promise I'll talk to Kyle," she said, pulling out of the embrace but holding her cousin's hands. "And I'll call Gavin. We're both adults. It won't be the most fun conversation ever, but I'll just come out and say a few things. Yeah. I'll put all cards on the table, so he can come to the party and still be clear where I stand."

Charlotte squeezed her hands. "Thank you. Do me one more favor before you talk to either of them though?"

"What's that?"

"Be clear with yourself where you stand."

Margot nodded thoughtfully. That wasn't such a bad idea, she supposed.

Chapter
Twelve

It had been a few years since the last time Lexie was in the back of a cab zipping down the palm-lined boulevards of Southern California. While she was less than enthusiastic about how hot the vinyl seats were despite the car's air conditioning, she had to admit she'd missed the sunshine. It streamed through her window, warming her face and highlighting her hair. Every so often she saw its reddish sparkle to the side of her sunglasses, a sparkle that normally hibernated this time of year under the Northeast's gray skies.

She'd flown in yesterday, and it had taken the whole day, thanks to connections and delays. Somehow, takeoff scheduled for 6:30 a.m. plus a six-hour flight did not equal touchdown at 12:30 p.m. When it came to air travel, mathematics and logic not only went out the window, they went out the window, got sucked into a twin engine, and were incinerated. Granted, the time change to the West Coast bought Lexie three hours, but the delay in takeoff at JFK (an hour forty-five), the layover at Dallas/Fort Worth (four hours thirty), and the maddening stop-and-go on the DFW runway (nearly two hours) put Lexie on the ground at LAX around 7:30 p.m. local Pacific time.

Lexie mentally patted herself on the back as they drove west down Beverly Boulevard. *Luckily, this ain't my first rodeo . . . or Rodeo, as the case may be,* she amended her thought as they passed two women walking their poodles and sashaying their hips in dresses that looked more expensive than Lexie's house. Having anticipated the ridiculous flight schedule, as soon as she booked her ticket for Wednesday, returning on Friday, she reserved a hotel room for the two nights she'd be in town.

Today was Thursday, and she had from eleven to twelve thirty to convince Gabriella Alfonsi that telecommuting was the most spectacular idea known to man. With a little bit of a white lie, Lexie had managed to get Gabriella's office and meeting schedule from her executive assistant. With a little bit of luck, Gabriella wouldn't decide today to arrive late, leave early, or not come in at all.

Lexie's cell phone rang, and she dug it out of her oversized purse to see Spark's name pop up on the screen. She answered silently, and waited.

"Two days," said Spark. "That's thirty-six hours and six minutes until Christmas Eve."

"Did you not hear me when I said, 'Stop calling me with countdowns'? Were you distracted by a puppy? Did you wander off to your happy-place beach resort with 1970s Donald Sutherland?"

She got an amused glance from the cabbie in the rearview for that one.

"Have you talked with Theo at all about this? Does he even know you've been offered the gig?"

"Well, I haven't officially been offered anything yet, have I?" said Lexie, adjusting her suit skirt and trying to unstick the backs of her knees from the vinyl. "Why open that can of worms until I have to?"

"Do you miss him?"

"Of course I miss him," said Lexie without hesitation. "Terribly. Don't you think I want him here by my side? I want a family, and I want it with him. Kids terrify me, but I still want them. Someday. I think. But what am I supposed to do about this opportunity I've been dreaming of since I was a little girl?"

"You've been dreaming of 'Smooches to Pooches' since you were a little girl?"

Lexie ignored her. "It's one thing to wonder what you're going to do if someday you have to choose between two things you love, but I'm here. It's happening. This is not an abstraction or a what-if about the distant future."

"You sure you're not a Gemini?"

"You know I'm a Cap. Why?"

"'Cause it'd be a lot easier to be your friend right now if I could just say, 'Well, Lex, you're a Gemini, so this sort of indecision is only natural.'"

"I don't believe in that stuff," said Lexie. "Signs dictating who you are. We all have elements of all the astrological signs. That's why it's so easy to pick up a horoscope and say, 'Oh, that's totally me.' I refuse to be stuffed into a box."

Spark was quiet, long enough that Lexie wondered if the call dropped. Then she said, "Maybe that's part of why this decision is so difficult for you. Maybe both options feel like they're someone else's definition of who you're going to become, Theo's wife or *Swish*'s cog, and neither of those definitions starts with 'Lexie.'"

It felt like Spark had just worked her magic the same way she did whenever Lexie got stricken with writer's block and Spark volunteered to bounce ideas with her. There were times she could flip an article on its head. She could turn a square draft into a cubed story with more angles than Lexie had time to explore. Just then, Lexie wondered if she gave Spark even half the credit she deserved. Oh, she sang Spark's praises, to Spark herself and to Belinda, Stu, anyone who'd listen. But for years, Lexie had spent late nights typing away, long interviews scribbling and recording, all the while telling herself that she needed to do the work, the real bulk of the work, by herself. She only accepted help from Spark, or anyone, for that matter, if she was entirely out of options and the clock was ticking. And for the life of her, Lexie had no clue why doing that was always so important to her.

However, she had no time to think more about that now, as the cab pulled up to the curb outside a marvelous steel and glass high-rise. "Spark, I'm here," said Lexie.

"Good luck, crazy girl," said Spark. "Let me know how it goes."

"You're my first call." They hung up, and Lexie turned her phone off entirely.

The Rothco, Inc. building back in New York was taller than this one, no doubt, and even if there were an eighteenth floor here and the *Swish* offices had a window to overlook the city, the L.A. skyline just wasn't the sweeping, endless urban majesty that was Manhattan. At least, not to Lexie. But sunlight must really be the best disinfectant, she thought, because the building's concrete forecourt, complete with a colossal four-jet fountain, gleamed like sand on an exclusive Malibu beach.

She carried the jacket of her suit—eggshell with a navy pinstripe—over her arm, and she was happy she'd gone with a charcoal gray shell top: the dark color positively soaked up the warm, soothing rays. If she had the time, Lexie would sit on the fountain's edge and sunbathe the rest of the day. But as much as she loved the heat, especially since her skin hadn't felt a nice eighty-degree roast since early September, she heard Spark's voice in her head, counting down to Christmas. You'd never know it was December here but for the string lights on palm fronds, a swanky glass pine tree set up behind the fountain, and the ringing of a Salvation Army bell. As Lexie walked through the forecourt, she closed her eyes briefly, listened to that bell, and got lost for just a second in a refreshing light snowfall on her favorite wooden bench by Gallantry Bridge. At the bank of doors she opened her eyes and caught her reflection in the glass, surprisingly enough, smiling back at her.

As soon as she stepped into the grand, open lobby, her heart raced with excitement. The prospect of coming to work here every day was exhilarating, just the way it had been when Lexie started at *Upstate*. After being there so many years, she'd started to see the cracks in the painted walls, the yellowing of the linoleum. Yes, she still felt the rush clutch her belly from time to time, but not nearly as often these days. Here the travertine gleamed in that tenacious sun. And the people! Lexie didn't know whether they were so stylishly dressed because *Swish* was known for its fashion-forward reputation or because there were other businesses housed here that may have been just as chic—there could be actual designers or modeling agencies here for all she knew—but she was beyond impressed, and a little intimidated. Even the main reception desk was peopled with men and women who looked fresh off a catwalk.

Ah, main reception. This was going to be Lexie's second hurtle. The first had been that white lie to Gabriella's assistant. Lexie couldn't just call and ask for an appointment. Even if

Lexie had dropped Belinda's name and Gabriella had agreed to see her at all, if her calendar looked anything like Stu's, she was booked at least a month out. And Lexie doubted Gabriella's calendar looked like Stu's. She was sure it was ten times busier. Gabriella was never going to take ten minutes on short notice to see a normal, everyday reporter who worked for her normal, everyday friend. Lexie was going to have to do a little extra, and be a little extra, to make sure she got her foot in the door.

Things might have to get a little wacky.

She'd drawn inspiration from her own recent bad luck with computers, called Gabriella's line from one of the blocked lines at the magazine—such things could come in handy for journalists of all sorts—and told her assistant she was IT. They'd had several complaints from the magazine about their calendar software, and for some reason Thursday, December 22 was blinking out. IT was in the process of accessing calendars one by one, and for Ms. Alfonsi they were showing Thursday as completely free with her in the office all day, was that the case? Lexie did feel bad for the assistant, who spent the next three minutes practically hyperventilating over Gabriella's potentially lost schedule, but then she calmed down when she saw that Thursday's meetings were all intact, and she read them off to "the IT lady named Mallory."

Main reception and then the magazine's reception were going to be trickier. Lying in person always was. But Lexie had developed the skill fairly well over the years, she thought, and she felt that since she always used her powers for good and never evil, luck would help her out when needed. Her heels clicked confidently and quick against the travertine underfoot as she stepped up to a young woman wearing a headset.

"Name?" said the receptionist, barely looking up from her screen when Lexie approached. She was pretty, with long, straight hair dark and shiny as fresh ink. At her temple, in front of the headset, she wore a flower clip, and that coupled with her hair gave her an exquisite Hawaiian aura.

"I don't have an appointment," said Lexie.

"Can't let you up without an appointment," the woman said.

"See?" said Lexie, exasperated. "That's what I told my boss. But she was all, 'Oh, Gabby's a friend, we've known each other since J-school, you won't need an appointment.'"

The young woman had moved on and was typing something. Her response was no more than an apathetic lift of the eyebrows as she kept her gaze on the screen.

"Besides," Lexie went on, "it'd be a little silly to make a whole appointment just to drop off a Christmas gift."

"So you have a delivery?" the receptionist asked, eyes still on the screen.

"Yes," said Lexie. "Exactly." She pulled from her purse a gift box wrapped in red and black plaid and tied with a red ribbon.

The woman flipped a clipboard around to Lexie, and pointed at the next blank box on the top form. "Fill this out, please, and wait for your receipt. Next interoffice mail delivery will be at noon."

Lexie saw she was going to have to turn this up a notch. She lifted her chin and said with a haughty air, "You're not suggesting I leave a gift of this value in the hands of some stranger, are you?"

Finally, the receptionist glanced up again. "And what value is that, exactly?"

With a covert peek to either side, Lexie leaned in closer and lowered her voice. "This is *the* sole surviving scarf from the collection of the notorious Aráche Mácée." Indeed, the box contained a scarf, and indeed, Lexie had picked it up from Macy's, which used to be R. H. Macy, or, with Lexie's terrible French accent, "Aráche Mácée."

Before the young woman had a chance to reply, Lexie rushed on: "I mean, you have heard of Aráche Mácée, *oui?*" She rolled her eyes at herself and flipped a wave at the woman. "Of course you have. They wouldn't let you work here if you hadn't."

Immediately, the woman said, "Well, of course I know . . ."

"Aráche Mácée," Lexie supplied with a knowing look, and the young woman parroted her as she said the name. She was starting to look annoyed and defensive which meant one important thing: Lexie held the advantage.

The woman jerked her chin at the box. "That's really the last scarf?"

"I wasn't even supposed to tell you that much," Lexie responded.

"And your boss just put it into a box?" said the receptionist. "Seems that should be laid out in its own hermetically sealed crate or something."

"Oh, no," said Lexie, horrified. "If you did that it would practically disintegrate."

This was not so much a part of the plan. Lexie's heartbeat picked up and she felt a little unsteady with the change in script. But she'd always been able to think on the fly before, and she trusted herself to do it again.

"Folding it," Lexie explained, "secures the fine silken threads. Otherwise, it would fall apart completely. Why do you think using thread from the Maldovian silkworm is so rare?"

The woman furrowed her brow. "Don't you mean Maldivian? As in the Maldives?"

Oops, cropped up somewhere in Lexie's brain, but her instincts overwrote the thought. "Please," said Lexie with the snootiest face she could muster. "Anyone can make a scarf from the Maldivian silkworm. I said Maldovian. I meant Maldovian."

Now the receptionist was looking downright mousy. It was time to grasp victory . . . which would feel a lot like grasping one of the sleek plastic visitor's tags Lexie saw people clipping to their lapels.

Lexie leaned onto the counter, which was about as far into this woman's space she could get without hopping over the thing and sitting in her lap. She clasped her hands together. With an imploring gaze so intense it refused to let go of the young woman, Lexie said, "Look, if I don't get this scarf to Gabby, or God forbid something happens to it if I leave it for delivery, my boss is going to get to talking with her, and they're going to find out pretty quick that it's missing. And then my boss might think I stole it. Then I get fired. Please don't get me fired. Not at Christmas. My little Cindy and Lou would be heartbroken if Mommy had to take back their gifts."

This gave the young woman pause. "Cindy and Lou?"

How the Grinch Stole Christmas! had played on one of the in-flight movies on the way out here. Lexie shook her head gently. "Please," she rushed on. "My fate, and my children's fates, are in your hands."

The young woman pushed her lips askew, seeming to consider her suddenly rather powerful position. "Look," she said, "next time, you make sure you have an appointment, got it?" She slapped a visitor's pass on the counter, and with her pointer finger, slid it over to Lexie.

Lexie snapped it up. "Thank you so much."

"Hang on, need you to sign in. Security's going to search your bag," she said, nodding toward the metal detectors and guards in front of a bank of elevators. "You want the seventh floor."

A flutter of guilt for talking down to the poor woman about fake silkworms made Lexie say to her, "You don't find many kind people out there, but you're one of them. You're obviously smart and an incredible gatekeeper." It wasn't her fault that Lexie had been doing this a lot longer than she had. "Keep up the good work, keep learning and believing in yourself, and you'll be a fine head of security someday."

"Well," she said, "thanks. I'm really just doing this to pay the bills until I graduate law school."

"Oh," said Lexie, making a mental note. If she did come to work here, she'd take the poor girl out to coffee a few times and teach her a thing or two about spotting a less-than-honest yarn.

As she walked to the metal detectors, Lexie shrugged into her blazer and then clipped the pass to her lapel. She breezed through security, scurried onto a closing glass elevator, and hit the button for eleven. A miniature television framed in marble told the packed car about the building, the café and credit union, the workout facilities, swimming pool, and sauna, the onsite massage therapists, and of course the Wi-Fi password. The male voiceover had to talk fast, though, to keep up with this elevator that seemed slightly more aerodynamic than those planes that can break the sound barrier.

The eleventh floor announced itself and bid a good day to whomever got off here. Lexie was one of a handful, and while the others jetted to wherever they were going, she stepped off slowly, her eyes big, taking it all in.

Whimsy was a world away. So were the *Upstate* offices, which were at the end of a painstaking, clunky eighteen-floor elevator ride that made more noises than Lexie's empty stomach when she was chasing a story. "Smooches to Pooches" was looking fine and dandy. Heck, right about now, if it meant coming here each day, Lexie would take a job sorting through those interoffice deliveries if they asked her to.

Chapter
Thirteen

Swish's offices were a glossy magazine cover in their own right. The huge bull pen, twice the size of *Up-state*'s, stretched out beyond the reception counter's curved half wall, and it wasn't technically a bull pen at all. It was divided into cubicles, each enclosed with glass walls, creating a cluster of miniature offices. Several corridors branched off from the bull pen, down which the real offices lined up. At least, that's what Lexie gleaned from where she stood. Not that she could stand in one place for very long. There were way too many people flying past her, talking on their cell phones, juggling pages, or just moving full speed ahead with serious, driven expressions. Two different sandwich carts were making the rounds, big ones chock-full of hoagies and chips and cookies and fresh-roasted coffee. On each cubicle's glass walls, black type in Helvetica font appeared on top of white paintbrush strokes, the effect coming off like a torn magazine page. This same décor was splashed on reception's half wall and down the corridors. Every so often, the slanted red line that was *Swish*'s logo underscored the "torn pages," looking like someone had gone to town with a can of spray paint.

Lexie couldn't remember the last time she'd been in a place quite so trendy.

When one of the three receptionists hung up his phone and waved Lexie over, she stepped up and asked to see Peter Jacobson. "I'm running a bit late for our appointment," she said, but the receptionist cut her off there.

"Pete's in Palm Beach covering a film festival," he said, leaning forward and swiveling back and forth in his chair. He flicked a pen madly between his fingers, and stared at her through round eyeglasses with thick black frames.

"What?" Lexie yelped. She knew exactly where Pete was, had known since "Mallory from IT" had also verified the calendars of several reporters from *Swish*'s masthead, until she landed on one who was out on assignment. "We had this meeting on the books for two months," she insisted to the young man. "I was to come in and prep Mr. Jacobson for his phone interview today."

After all this, she told herself, she would do nice deeds for receptionists everywhere to make up karma points for all the headaches she was causing today.

"Fine," said Lexie, "if *Swish* doesn't want the interview with Mr. Kubrick, I'll find a magazine that does." She spun on her heel and stalked away.

"Stanley Kubrick?" the receptionist called out. "Isn't he dead?"

Lexie spun back, her left eyebrow arched. "Well," she said, "he'll be happy to know that little lie is still working. Which is more than I can say for anyone here after I go to *Vogue* with the interview of a lifetime."

"Hang on, hang on," said the young man, jumping up from his seat and rushing out from behind the counter. "Does it have to be Pete? I can find you someone else to talk to."

"Hmm. We know Pete. One moment please." Lexie pulled out her cell phone. This next part she'd been planning to do with a good amount of distance between her and the receptionist. She was simply going to have a conversation with her powered-down phone. But with this guy breathing down her neck, she was going to need a little extra help to sell it. All she needed was the sound of another voice.

She hit Spark's number on speed dial. "So? What happened?" Spark said immediately.

"Yes, this is Alex calling for Mr. Kubrick's assistant." Normally, Lexie wasn't fond of that nickname for her full "Alexandra," but if she was outed as "Lexie" before she was ready, she was afraid Gabriella would recognize the name and refuse to see her.

"Um," said Spark, "what?"

"Yes, it's urgent."

"Did the sun do something to your head?" said Spark. "You need to wear a hat, I told you this."

"No. Would you please tell her that Peter Jacobson is not available for the interview?"

"Okay," said Spark. "Uh, am I angry at Peter on behalf of Mr. . . . did you say Kubrick? You know he's dead, right?"

"Yes, that's all correct," said Lexie.

Now Spark didn't miss a beat. "What do you mean we can't get Pete? Are you crazy? You know Mr. Kubrick wants what he wants."

Lexie held up the phone so the receptionist could hear Spark's ranting, before tucking it up to her ear again. "I know, I'm so sorry, but if you'd please just hear me out, I think we can have someone else do the interview."

Spark said, "All right, I'm calming down and not yelling at you and telling you what you want to hear . . ."

"Oh, I see," said Lexie with a hint of disappointment. "Well, I don't know if that's possible—"

"What do you mean it's not possible?" Spark bellowed.

"Okay, okay," said Lexie. "Look, I'll ask, all right?"

"You do that," Spark said.

"Two minutes," said Lexie. "Yes, if she's in the office, I'm sure Gabriella will be able to give us two minutes."

Spark snorted a laugh. "You have got to tell me what you're really up to when you get back to the hotel."

Meanwhile, as soon as the receptionist heard Gabriella's name, he waved his arms and shook his head. But Lexie turned away. "Thank goodness. Please thank Mr. Kubrick for me." She hung up and turned back to the man, who looked aghast.

"That's unheard of," he said. "A walk-in for Ms. Alfonsi?"

"Well, I can't very well call them back after all that," said Lexie. "Is she here? Can't she squeeze in two minutes for Stanley Kubrick?"

He dropped his head and recovered enough to trudge back to his phone and dial an extension. "Hi, I have a . . ." He glanced up at her, silently asking her name.

"Alex"—she paused—"Walker."

It was the first time she'd said her name with Theo's in quite some time, and a smile reflexively sprang to her lips.

"I have an Alex Walker out here to see Ms. Alfonsi. I know, but . . ." He covered his mouth and murmured things Lexie couldn't hear, but she was fairly sure she caught the name "Kubrick" in there.

He hung up. "Ms. Alfonsi's assistant will be out to greet you," he said through a simper.

Lexie thanked him, did a happy dance on the inside, and a few minutes later followed an older woman, Gabriella's assistant, down one of the corridors. It ended in a suite, with a restroom off the office's anteroom. The office itself was behind huge oak doors, anachronistic compared to the modern feel of the rest of the place.

The assistant paused outside the doors and introduced herself with a handshake. "I'm Pamela," she said.

"Alex." Lexie wasn't entirely sure why Pamela had introduced herself at all. That certainly wasn't standard protocol for an assistant who was going to spend all of three seconds with you.

"You can go right on in," said Pamela, who looked like she and Belinda could have shared the same elegant tailor.

After taking a breath, Lexie turned the ivory doorknob and stepped inside. What she hadn't expected was that Pamela would follow her in. Gabriella's back was to Lexie as held up galleys to the sunlight streaming through her outer walls, which were all glass. She had gray streaks in her ramrod-straight brown hair, and she wore wide-legged seersucker pants, a wrap blouse, and ankle boots with tiny holes cut out of the beige fabric. Pamela went to her and touched her shoulder. Without turning around, Gabriella set the galleys down on a small table, and said something to her in sign language.

Pamela relayed to Lexie, "Stanley Kubrick is dead, you know."

Oh, Lexie thought. *How did I not know she's deaf?* She supposed she really didn't know much at all about Gabriella Alfonsi herself. She just knew her magazine.

"Ms. Alfonsi," she said directly to Gabriella, or Gabriella's back, as Pamela signed, "my name is Lexie Moore. I'm the reporter—"

Gabriella's hands flew. Pamela translated, "Ah, yes, I recognize your name."

"I'd like to apologize for popping in like this, and misleading a few people to get in front of you—"

"'Popping in?'" Pamela relayed, and Gabriella spun around. She wore wire-rimmed glasses, the lenses of which had darkened in the sun. "Neighbors pop in for coffee. Family pops in for dinner. What you did was not popping in. Nor did you mislead a few people. You lied, you concocted at least one ridiculous story, and you did it knowing you'd be found out. What did you think was going to happen when you got in here and had to fess up to how you did it?"

Lexie was stuck. She had no response to that, and she felt about as stupid as she had on her first big assignment when she was still the eighteen-year-old cub in a pack of reporters all vying for attention at a press conference. She was holding out her tape recorder, hopping around the room to find an open space and having no luck. When she'd gotten back to her desk, she'd listened to her tape and heard more her own flustered movement than any questions or answers. She'd managed to cobble together a short article, but it was hardly the work she knew she was capable of.

With all the things she'd thought of to get herself in front of Gabriella, how had she not considered her endgame?

"See," Gabriella signed and Pamela said, "what you did only works when you don't have to present yourself *as* yourself at any point in the deception. But the minute you have to reveal who you are, the charade is up. Let's put it another way: how'd you get past main reception downstairs?"

Lexie hesitated.

"Come on," Gabriella signed, sitting on the edge of her desk. She gestured for Lexie to take a seat in one of her guest chairs. "Obviously you did it successfully. Tell me how."

And so, Lexie hiccupped out her story, unsure of how Gabriella was going to react. She realized as she spoke that she was less concerned the trickery itself would offend Gabriella. What really started to worry her was that Gabriella wouldn't be impressed with the lie Lexie had thought up.

But, "Not bad," Gabriella signed when Lexie had finished. "Of course, you lucked out. What if they had called up here to ask me if I knew your boss, and then I called to verify who you were? What if they had asked for ID? What if you had Pamela to contend with, who's been in the business alongside me since you were still playing in a sandbox? She'd never fall for the tactics that are going to trip up a kid."

"I don't know," Lexie admitted. "I don't know what I would've done. A lot of times I get thrown for a loop. But I'm not bad at thinking on my feet, and I've always managed to get my story."

"A lot of call for investigative stunts writing features about New York bed-and-breakfasts, is there?"

"I've worked for other publications too," said Lexie.

"You didn't get your story today," Gabriella signed. "You didn't think on your feet when you walked in here. You didn't come up with some clever, smooth line to bridge who you said you were with who you actually are. You can't be one note.

And that's what you are right now." She slid off the desk and ambled around the room, as Pamela kept a spot where she could see Gabriella's hands and Gabriella could see hers as she translated Lexie's words. "You have got to have such a wide range of tools in your belt to really call yourself an investigative journalist. And you've got a few good ones, I'll give you that. But you're still learning. You've been at *Upstate* for what, five years, I believe Belinda said."

"That's right."

"Mm. See, that's a long time to be cozy in the land of cushy articles. I wonder if you're not stunted there. You started your career digging for stories, learning new ways to break through tough ground, and then you found *Upstate:* a nice, smooth plateau that didn't call for digging of any kind."

"All due respect, Ms. Alfonsi," said Lexie, "but if we're going to talk about whether I'm stunted doing puff pieces, we should probably talk about your offer to me." Lexie held up her hands to stop Gabriella when she started signing again. "Thank you for offering it at all. I know *Swish* must have dozens of applicants a day to take any position open. But if you're implying I should be searching for a more substantial gig, I can't see how 'Smooches to Pooches' is going to be that."

"Nor can I," Gabriella signed. "Ms. Moore, when I spoke with Belinda about you, I made a suggestion based on what I knew of you at that point. Good writer, strong voice, light material. I had no idea you were interested in more than that."

"Oh, I am," Lexie said emphatically, her hands pressed to her heart. "The types of articles that come out of *Swish*'s current events desk are phenomenal. That's where I really want to be."

"Is it?" Gabriella gave her a funny little smile, like she was reassessing Lexie on the spot. "You don't like pets?"

"Pets are fine. I don't particularly get a thrill when I think of writing about them every day."

"You don't like a schedule that's fairly laidback? Not a lot of travel or long hours? Not a lot of scrutiny?"

"I like a balance," said Lexie. "I love to travel. I get a rush when I'm up against a deadline and I have work late into the night to meet it. And I like scrutiny. If I fail, how can I get better if my work isn't examined closely? How can I take pride in my successes?"

"And yet for five years you've been reporting for a mag that mostly requires local travel, doesn't do a lot of urgent stories with heart-pounding deadlines, and goes through about as much scrutiny as, well, 'Smooches to Pooches.'" Gabriella faced Lexie straight-on. "Are you happy at *Upstate?*"

"I love it," Lexie blurted out, surprising herself. The words had come from the same place as when she had to lie on her feet, but this was no lie. This was simply her instinct, overriding her thoughts.

Gabriella's eyebrows jumped in an almost amused way, and she went back to pacing around the room. "Interesting," she signed. "Yet you want more. You want, it sounds like, a spot on my current events desk."

That stupid feeling was creeping back. "I want . . . that . . . too," she said, her voice trailing off. Of course, what she wanted right now was to slink out the door for how lame the words sounded to her.

Gabriella made her way to one of her windows and stood there in silence long enough for Lexie to wonder if this was the signal that Gabriella was done with her. Pamela stayed off to the side but moved toward the windows too, to keep her boss in clear view. Just as Lexie started to stand up, desperately formulating a last-ditch effort to say what she'd gone through all of this to say, Gabriella's hands started moving, and Lexie eased back into her seat.

"When I first started in magazines," Gabriella signed, still facing the window, "I wondered if I'd made the right choice. I loved lawyer shows on TV, you see. Couldn't get enough of 'em. Especially the ones that were a little kooky, had some interesting twists and characters. I loved the idea of walking into a courtroom and pleading the case of some defendant who'd been unjustly accused, or prosecuting a really bad apple." Gabriella turned around to Lexie. "My favorite part? Those beautiful, long closing arguments that clinched the case for the good guys. So I looked into law school. I thought maybe I could work in media law, establishing things like digital rights and fair use for what was, at the time, an emerging electronic world of publication. The idea thrilled me. I loved every part of what I was doing as a reporter, don't get me wrong. But media law pulled at me just as hard."

Gabriella paused then, walked around more. Lexie just waited, ignoring her natural urge to prod and question Gabriella, ignoring the discomfort of a long silence. She'd learned to be untroubled by that discomfort and let it just wash over her. There were times a subject needed to be prodded, but more often than not, if she just waited, she got a better story than one truncated by her disruption. To Lexie, this was an extension of the journalists' old creed that the reporter should never be part of the story.

Judging by a glimpse Gabriella shot her then, Lexie wondered if it wasn't her exact intention to see Lexie's reaction to the silence. If she wasn't mistaken, Lexie thought she saw in that glimpse a flicker of approval.

"Luckily," Gabriella's words finally continued through Pamela's voice, "I happened to have a lawyer friend, and when I mentioned what it was I'd been thinking, he offered to take me under his wing for one whole day so I could see a real, live case up close. I expected witness interviews, suspect interrogations, obviously the courtroom. Real exciting stuff, right? You know what we did all day long? Sat in his office. I watched him do paperwork. He took a couple meetings I couldn't sit in on. He went into a conference room with a ton of papers. He came out with even more. We went to lunch, but that was just grabbing a couple salads from the diner down the street and we had to get right back. I'm not sure what he had to get right back to, since he just sat back down at his desk with more papers. At the end of the day, I went home." She shrugged. "That was it. And he stayed at his desk with his papers for another five hours. No witnesses. No suspects."

"And the long closing arguments?"

"Yeah," Gabriella signed, and laughed. The sound was a little nasal and a little sheepish, not dissimilar from how Lexie laughed at herself when she remembered her own youthful naïveté. "No courtroom at all. He said he hadn't seen the inside of a courtroom in ages. I asked him if being a criminal lawyer was where the intrigue and action were. He said no. In criminal law you're either defending creeps or prosecuting them. Either way it's not a fun job. You don't get beautiful closing arguments most of the time. You don't get to save someone from injustice. Mostly you're just with the darker, sadder side of humanity, day after day, until it chips away at you. And those are the lucky folks. Try to get your foot in the door as a lawyer these days. The market's saturated. I was going to rack up how much in law school debt only to find I couldn't use my degree? No thanks. I realized, I didn't want to be a lawyer. I wanted to be a lawyer on TV. And since I couldn't get that gig, I should probably stick with the thing I knew I loved: magazines.

"My point of all this," she signed, hands brushing and clapping faintly against each other, "is sometimes our dreams look a lot different from reality. I didn't want to miss out on a dream of mine, and in doing that I nearly made a costly mistake. I learned you gotta make your decisions. You can't do it all, not if you want to do any of it well. And you certainly shouldn't base those decisions on what you think the outcome may be with no practical experience. Most of all, you gotta know when it's time to jump and move on, and when to let that chance go because you'd be happier staying put."

"I don't suppose," said Lexie, "that the offer for 'Smooches to Pooches' is still on the table after what I pulled today."

"Would you want it if it were?"

"I might. Under the right circumstances."

Gabriella found her way back to the edge of the desk, and leaned on it. Pamela followed inconspicuously. "And what would those circumstances be?"

"I can't leave Whimsy," said Lexie.

Gabriella tipped her head and gave her a little smile. "Then you can't work here." She nudged herself off the desk and walked around it to collect more galley pages.

"Just like that?" Lexie said. "What about telecommuting? Consulting?"

Back down went the galleys. "What do you imagine the consulting budget for 'Smooches to Pooches' might be?" Gabriella signed. "And I don't like my reporters telecommuting. Much too cold. I like a certain feel of the traditional alongside progress. If it were up to me, we'd all still be using typewriters."

"I could spend a month here, a month back home—"

"All that for the pets beat?" Gabriella signed with a dubious smile. "Trust me, it's not worth it."

"It would be if I were working up to something else," said Lexie. "Something like the current events desk."

This gave Gabriella pause. She squinted at Lexie as though sizing her up, and then signed, "You'd be an interesting project. A good candidate. It'd be good that you're starting with some savvy. We could turn you into quite the contender." She tapped a finger against her chin in silence. Pamela said nothing. Lexie guessed this wasn't American Sign Language, but the universal gesture for, "I'm thinking."

Finally, Gabriella's hands swept around each other and Pamela spoke again: "I told Belinda you had until I believe it was next week to set up an interview, right?"

"Yes, and actually that's another thing I was hoping to negotia—"

"Consider yourself interviewed," Gabriella and Pamela interrupted. "You're hired. You can start your probationary period January second."

A strange combination of panic and elation whipped up around Lexie fast as wind gusts in a microburst. "Wait, I—"

"Stop by HR on your way out. They'll get you going on the paperwork."

Lexie jumped up out of the chair. "I can't start work January second," she blurted out. "I live three thousand miles away. I have a life. It's Christmas. I have nowhere to live here. I own a house. That's not even enough time for me to give a two-week notice." The reasons poured out of her as the panic portion of her own personal tornado took over.

"What if you were starting on the current events desk?"

Lexie sank back down into her chair. "No 'Pooches' at all?"

"No 'Pooches.'"

With her heart pounding in her throat, Lexie felt utterly untethered from reality. "I can't make this kind of decision that quickly. And even if I jumped on it, the logistics—"

"Logistics didn't stop you from getting yourself in here to see me"—Gabriella shrugged a shoulder—"sloppy as your endgame was."

"But this isn't . . . You're talking about two different . . ." Lexie asked her brain for words, but her brain suddenly became a petulant child, crossing its arms and turning its back on her. *You've been ignoring me and relying on your precious instinct all day,* it said. *Why don't you ask it to help you out of this one?*

"Tell you what," Gabriella signed. "I'll give you until your original deadline to figure this out. Let me know by Monday, the twenty-sixth. Nine a.m. I'll be at my desk. If you're not one of my blinking phone lines by nine, don't bother calling at all."

Gabriella strode over to Lexie and stuck her hand out, which Lexie took in a daze. "Congratulations," said Gabriella in her own voice. Like her laugh, it was a little nasal, but it was also soft yet authoritative. When they dropped the handshake, Gabriella went back to signing. "You got me to hire you when a week ago I didn't even know your name. Figuring out logistics about what comes next is easy. Figuring out if this is a time you jump on the chance or stay put, well, that's the hard part." She walked back behind her desk. "You can find your way out, yes?"

"Oh. Yes." She stumbled to her feet and grabbed her purse from the floor. "Thank you, Ms. Alfonsi." Then Lexie nodded to her assistant. "Pamela."

Just before Lexie left, Gabriella and Pamela added, "If you sign on, I don't want to know about moving and your house and uprooting your life. Keep it out of my office. You'll figure it all out, I'm sure."

"Right," said Lexie, and she saw herself out. She could understand where Gabriella was coming from. She struck Lexie as the type of woman who wouldn't let anything get in the way of what she wanted. She was just like Theo's superwoman, she realized, and the challenge to herself simultaneously excited her and left her feeling more confused than ever before.

Chapter
Fourteen

The last place Robin wanted to go tonight was wherever Scott would be. She'd spent the week wearing holes in the apartment floor from pacing back and forth, deliberating with Anna on whether to even go through with this. Robin would walk away from the job, except that the retainer he'd given her hadn't been fully spent yet. So far, Scott had been buying all the gifts and decorations over and above her fee, so there was still money sitting in her bank account for which she owed him about three more hours of her time.

"Just get it over with," Anna had said on Tuesday from the couch as Robin paced the living room. "Suck it up, go out Friday, get the stupid present. Then the money will officially be yours and you'll be able to enjoy Christmas Eve."

"But it would feel so good to just put a check in the mail," said Robin. "Imagine the look on his face when he opened up that envelope."

Anna glanced down at the magazine in her lap and leisurely flipped a page. "You could do that. The money hasn't been spent yet, and you've made a decent amount of moolah from your other clients, too."

Wednesday, the pacing had been in the kitchen over morning coffee. Anna camped out in her usual weekday spot next to the coffee machine, standing as close as possible to minimize lag time between cups. Robin said, "The thing is, I don't know yet how to make YOPE into a sustainable business. At the very least, I'd need to change the name."

"Why?"

"Your Own Personal Elf?" said Robin. "How does that hold up in May or August?"

"Maybe instead of trying to conform to everyone else's associations of what 'elf' means, that's your selling point. An elf for all seasons. Keebler did it."

"Maybe," Robin agreed. "The point is, even though the money technically hasn't been spent yet, it's been earmarked. It's not like this rent bump is only for this month, and unless the Hutch gets a surprise profit windfall or there's a major personnel change, this is it. This is what I have to help pay the bills. It's hard to let that go."

Both women had the day off on Thursday. As the sun set low and cast warm golden slants of light through the dining room windows, Anna sat at the table, finishing last-minute wrapping. Robin trod behind her.

Anna went about her work like a surgeon closing an incision. The current gift was one for her cousin's ten-month-old, the first baby of his generation born to the Walker family's local contingent. "One thing I never would have considered about having a baby," said Anna calmly as she folded an oddly angled corner, "is how much extra time it takes to wrap all their weird-shaped toys."

"And by the time they're old enough to even notice how nicely a weird-shaped toy is wrapped," Robin added, "they've outgrown them and you're just giving them clothes in easy square boxes anyway."

"Yep," said Anna, still hunched over her work. "It's a cruel, cruel world." She stuck the last piece of tape on and sat back. "But it's worth it."

"Yeah," said Robin. "I've been thinking I should just go through with tomorrow night."

Anna tossed herself back in her chair. "Robin, you're a weird-shaped toy."

"I know, I'm being obnoxious. I'll shut up."

"You don't have to do that." She leaned her head against the back of the chair and spoke as Robin continued pacing behind her. "Look, I'm happy to be your sounding board," said Anna. "Lord knows you've been mine enough times. But can I ask, why is this such a big deal? You've been wrestling with it like it's a major decision. It's a few hours of your life. Let it go."

"It's symbolic of so much more than that, though," Robin exclaimed, throwing her arms out the side and narrowly missing smacking her hand on Anna's chair. "King Donovan the Almighty sat there insulting me, and Scott just plain sat there. Because I'm not him or Laurence Olivier, who are apparently the only two real actors ever to grace the stage, I'm nothing. And you know what else was insulting?"

"King Donovan's assumptions?" said Anna, repeating the script she'd heard three times since Sunday's brunch.

"King Donovan's assumptions," Robin declared, clapping the side of her fist into her other hand. "It was like he was interviewing me to be his daughter-in-law or something. Scott and I are—were—just friends. Actually, we were hardly even that. He's a client. And he didn't say one word, not one word. His sister and mother defended me, but the man of the house turned into a four-year-old little boy. There was a fern in the corner with more backbone." The more she got worked up, the more frustrated she felt until she just shook her head. "You know what?"

"You're going to send the money back?"

"I am so going to send the money back." Robin thanked Anna, tousling her frizzy hair, and stomped off to her room.

She got as far as sliding into her desk chair and pulling her checkbook out of the drawer. Then she froze up. Robin had been working so hard for so long, desperate to prove to herself and the world that she could make it as an actress. To give back a piece of that, even a piece indirectly related to it, felt like failing. And she was so tired of failing. She still hadn't gotten a call, let alone a callback, from the audition she'd thought had gone so well Sunday morning. Successes had been so hard to catch that when she finally hooked one, the last thing she wanted to do was throw it back.

She felt ashamed, like she was selling out. Robin rubbed her thumb back and forth over the checkbook's plastic cover. She wanted to be the person who flipped that cover open and sent back Scott's money with a note: "You can buy my time, but you can't buy my dignity." She pushed back from the desk and went back out to the dining room.

Leaning on the doorjamb, she said to Anna, "I mean, it's not like if I keep the money, I'm party to some terrible evil, right?"

"Yep," she said, working on another study in awkward shapes.

"I'm not selling my soul?"

Anna sat back in her seat again. She said, "Everyone's got to put up with some headache or other when it comes to work, right? Just last week, I catered that Christmas party?"

"Right, the Scrooges."

"They didn't want to pay me at the end of the night, remember? They said my canapés were 'damp.' What does that even mean?"

Robin's lips sprung up into a smile despite her prevailing mood.

"Oh, the hand-holding," Anna said. "I can't tell you the hoops I jumped through for these folks. But, like most clients, when things go right, there's nothing to notice. Everything's just the way it's supposed to be. It's like a road filled with pebbles and someone's told you to pick them all up. They don't see all the work you put into picking up those pebbles. They only see if you miss one, and then that's what makes them say, 'You didn't do your job.' Then it's up to you, the consummate professional, to point out nicely that they're insane."

"Which I'm sure you did, and you got paid, and you did none of this ridiculous brooding."

Anna spread her hands. "I'm sleeping like a baby in the apartment I can afford despite damp canapés. Hon, if you wait to do business with only the people you like, unless you happen to get real lucky, you're going to have a lot of down time between paychecks."

"And the integrity issue?"

"Find a happy medium you can live with. You come in here rationalizing. Why? It's money. It's a necessity. You're not hurting anyone, so what's the problem? You got paid for a job you're doing your best at, which is saying a lot. So your client was a little fern-ish. *You* stood up for yourself. I think that's what you need to remember. You stood up for yourself. Forget Scott. He has nothing to with any of this really. You're not selling out. If you had, you would've been the fern in the corner of the room."

And with that, Robin felt better than she had since Sunday, lighter and resolved. She went to Anna, gave her a hug, and said, "But he's totally out of consideration for boyfriend material."

"Oh, absolutely. The guy's a total yutz," said Anna.

And so Robin did what Anna had told her at the outset. Friday afternoon, she sucked it up, kept on the black slacks and sweater she'd worn that day to the Hutch, left her hair down and wavy—she absolutely refused to do anything special with it for him—and was looking for Scott out her front window by six o'clock. At a few minutes after, a dark sedan pulled up to the curb, and a driver complete with a chauffeur's cap hustled around the car and up the walk.

"Anna?" Robin called out as the doorbell rang.

"Yeah?" she said, poking her freshly showered head out the bathroom door.

"He sent a car."

"He sent a car? Like a limo?"

"Not far from it. If I get in there, am I giving him the wrong idea?" Maybe, she thought, King Donovan wasn't the only one with assumptions.

"Uh, I'm gonna say look inside. If there's chilled champagne and chocolate-covered strawberries, you should probably develop a really bad cough all of a sudden and have to stay home."

The bell rang again. "I'll see you in either two minutes or three hours," said Robin. She pulled her coat on grudgingly and walked down the steps grudgingly. "Why couldn't I get an easy client?" she mumbled to herself. "I had other easy clients. Buy a gift or a wreath, boom, done. I have a car waiting for me. You know how long I've dreamed of having a car wait for me? And now I can't even enjoy it. It's tainted. It's all muddled and confused and tainted."

At the foot of the stairs, she glanced over to the first-floor door and saw Mrs. Parker standing there, watching Robin mumble to herself. Mrs. Parker shuffled out to the hallway and put a hand on Robin's cheek. "Poor dear," her voice croaked out, "the pressure of all those rejections has finally gotten to you."

After assuring Mrs. Parker she was okay, and taking a rain check on her cure-all cocoa, Robin opened the front door. To her surprise, the driver was a woman with skin the deep color of chestnuts, whose hair was piled under the cap, save a few raven black spirals framing her face. Robin immediately felt a sense of familiarity and comfort with her. "Have we met?" she asked the woman.

"I'm sure we've seen each other around town," said the woman. She held out her hand, which Robin shook. "Faye. You're Robin?"

"That's me."

"Then we're on our way," she said brightly. She led the way down the walk.

"I have to tell you," said Robin, "I'm not entirely sure I'm going to be needing your services tonight."

"Oh?" said Faye, and she turned around to face her.

"I think . . . there may have been a misunderstanding between me and the man who hired you." Robin heard herself say the words, but she was befuddled. She had no idea why she was confiding in a total stranger, familiar feeling or not. It just sort of spilled out of her the way it had with Anna.

"Misunderstanding? No," said Faye, her easy smile returning. "I don't think so." She started toward the car again.

"Okay," said Robin, taken aback. "I'm sorry to be so forward, but how would you know?"

"Mr. Donovan—that is, Scott, not his father," Faye said pointedly, "instructed me to take you to the Holly Hills Tree Farm. He said you're a business associate and this had something to do with Mr. Donovan—that is, his father, not Scott." She opened the back door for Robin.

But Robin stayed put, still bewildered. "See?" she said. "Like that. The way you said, 'Scott, not his father.' It's like you knew . . ."

Faye stood politely, waiting.

Robin pushed the thought from her mind that this woman had some kind of extrasensory knowledge of the whole situation. She probably knew the family. The car looked a lot like the one Scott had called for himself just about a week ago. Even though that driver had been a man, he and Faye were probably from the same company that had the privilege of carting around the king and his prince.

Faye leaned in. "If you don't mind my saying so, I think you'd regret it if you didn't go tonight. Have you ever been to Holly Hills when they do their special tree lighting?"

Robin shook her head. "I'm usually working. My manager's been giving me a dream schedule lately, I think because she feels guilty she can't give me more hours or . . ." There it was again, that freedom to speak her mind. But then it dawned on her just what Faye had said, and she frowned. "Wait, tree lighting? I thought this was about Donovan's gift."

"Oh, they have lovely gifts for sale there," said Faye. "The night of the tree lighting, all profits go to Whimsy schools."

The thought that Scott wanted to support kids through his father's gift softened Robin a bit. At least he had that going in his favor. "All right," she said to Faye. "Let's go."

Faye, despite the motherly lines around her lips and eyes, clapped her hands and giggled like she was one of the children. Robin found her utterly charming.

Holly Hills Tree Farm was set on snow-covered billows that hosted evergreens of all sorts, from saplings to the elders of the wood. Robin had never been here at night, so she'd never seen it all lit by a starry backdrop. "How beautiful," she uttered, stepping out of the car.

Faye had pulled up in front of the Holly Hills store; rather, she'd gotten as close as she could, given all the people milling about. It was a temperate night, and folks were huddled in groups outside, talking and laughing over hot cider. A group of carolers, which seemed to be a spur-of-the-moment chorale, sang a little ways off, where the far end of the store met the edge of the farm itself. Just beyond them stood a grand, towering conifer. According to a little placard, it was an Eastern White Pine. To Robin, it looked like a giant shrub, pillowy and soft.

Faye, standing next to her, said, "You should check it out. Get a close-up look. It's quite breathtaking."

Robin took her advice and walked up to it. When she got close enough to breathe in its fresh, spicy scent, she saw tiny unlit strings of bulbs, just waiting for their lighting.

"Pretty cool, huh?" said a man's voice behind her.

Chapter
Fifteen

Robin didn't have to turn around to know it was Scott. She did, however, turn to-and-fro looking for Faye. She didn't see her anywhere. The only thing that she noticed was a sparkly swirl of snow trickling to the ground beside her.

"Where'd Faye go?" she asked Scott.

"Who?"

"The driver? Never mind." Maybe it was asking too much that the Donovans know their drivers by their first names.

"It's great to see you again," said Scott, but Robin was hardly in the mood for pleasantries.

"You too," she threw out, and impatiently rocked back and forth, heels to toes. "So what's this gift you said you found for your dad?"

Scott ducked his head and hid a bashful smile. "I, uh, made that up."

She stopped rocking. "What?"

"Yeah," he said. "I was pretty sure if I asked you to just meet me here after my father treated you the way he did, you'd say no. And I had to apologize for him."

She shrugged. "You did that already outside your apartment."

"No, really apologize," he said. "Explain, I guess."

"Why do that here? You could've picked up the phone. Or, wild thought, you could've asked him to explain why he was disrespecting you, your home, your friend. I mean, not that we're friends," she rushed on when she heard herself say the word.

His smile vanished. "We're not?"

"Scott, you're my client. That's all." She wanted to absolve them both of the friendship notion, of any responsibility associated with it. That way, he didn't have to feel bad about what his father had said—although he should have—and she didn't have to feel bad that he'd hurt her—although she did.

"Huh," he said, his eyes downcast. "Well, then the other reason I wanted to bring you here is going to sound really stupid."

Against her better judgment, she said, "Try me."

"I heard about this, the tree lighting," he said, raising his eyes again to meet hers, "and I thought of you right away. It just seems right up your alley. I mean, especially after that mini party at your house last week. But it's everything: the party, your YOPE business and how you are the Hutch, the way you've thrown yourself into helping me decorate, the gifts for my family . . . By the way, my mom and Frankie love you."

"Well, of course they do," said Robin defensively, arms crossed. "I'm very lovable."

Scott chuckled. "Robin, you are Christmas."

Her heart fluttered at that, and she couldn't keep her arms crossed. They fell gently to her sides. "That was a lovely thing to say." Her voice had softened, and she was fairly sure the goose bumps she got were not from the December chill.

"You're joy," he said, "and you're light, and you're music, and you're cider and candy canes. I thought if anyone should be here tonight, it should be you."

When the buzzing in her ears had stopped and her eyes refocused from their daze, Robin was left with the memory of Scott's actions, or rather, inaction. His words floated away with the white plumes of their breath, but her wounds remained.

She so badly wanted to tell him how she felt, that if the roles were reversed and her father had been the one who embarrassed Scott, she would have told her father then and there how rude he was being. She wanted to tell him she was embarrassed for him as well as herself. He'd turned back into a little boy that morning. How could he let his father treat him that way, let alone his guest? She wanted to tell him it was behavior he needed to seriously consider and talk to his father about, and maybe talk to a therapist about.

But of course, she held her tongue.

These were deeply ingrained relationships and attitudes. If a person was going to change them, he needed to recognize the need to do so himself. Chances were, if Robin brought them up, Scott would dismiss them. And even if he did acknowledge them and smack himself on the forehead and say, "You are so right, what was I thinking all these years?" she couldn't be the one to change him. Because then, if their relationship ever did grow into a romance, it would fail before it ever got started. She couldn't truly fall in love with someone who didn't know himself enough to recognize when he needed to take a stand, and didn't respect himself enough to take that stand despite how hard it might be to do so.

"I think," she said, trying not to show her disappointment, "the last of your retainer would be best spent on trying to find a gift for your father."

Scott looked sideswiped. "Retainer? That's not . . . I don't care about that. Whatever's there, keep it."

Robin bridled. "Not if I didn't do the work for it."

"I think you did more than your fair share putting up with my father," he said, and laughed.

Robin didn't think it was so funny. "That's not what you were paying me for. And if you were, you owe me a lot more than what's still there for putting up with all he dealt out."

"Hey," said Scott. "I said I was sorry for that."

And here they were again, too close to what Robin really wanted to tell him. She pressed her lips together and clapped her hands once, definitively. "They have a whole artsy store in here. I think we should look around and see if anything will work for your dad."

Obviously resigned to how Robin wanted to do this, Scott followed her lead. "After you," he said, holding out a hand.

The HOLLY HILLS GENERAL STORE, as the sign over the door read, looked like it had been constructed of a few log cabins stuck together. Inside there were several rooms, each with locally made crafts and foodstuff displayed on wooden tables, shelves, and even cabinets of varying sizes. Robin put all her personal feelings to the side, and racked her brain for something besides an investment return or an autographed picture of Laurence Olivier that might make Donovan happy. Although that thought got her wondering . . .

"Hey," she said to Scott, "what about an autographed picture of Laurence Olivier? I bet you can find that online somewhere."

"He's got three."

"Of course," she mumbled to herself, going back to perusing tables. She came upon a dual-tiered table full of maple syrup, from tiny novelty bottles to gigantic cans. She said, "What about maple syrup? Your dad's plate was piled high with pancakes at brunch. Seems like his favorite breakfast food."

"Maple syrup for a gift?" said Scott. "That doesn't seem a little impersonal?"

"Well, anything can seem impersonal," Robin said. "It's not so much what you're getting a person, but why you're getting it. Like, I love those shower gels they come out with this time of year. You know, and they have those names, 'A Berry Berry Holiday,' or 'Frosted Winter Walk'? You get a gift basket of those for someone, it could seem impersonal, because gift baskets often do. But since I absolutely adore them, that gift basket is a surefire way to make my Christmas." She dropped a hand on top of one of the larger cans. "I say you get your dad a can of this, or a can and a normal-sized bottle and one of those little guys over there, along with maybe hiring a personal chef to come in one Sunday a month to make him all manner of pancakes. Blueberry pancakes, and chocolate chip, and marshmallow or walnut, whatever he likes."

Scott picked up the can. "I don't know," he said. "I don't know if he'd like that."

"I'd be surprised if he likes anything," she said quietly, only it wasn't quiet enough.

"Look," said Scott, "I know my father is difficult. But you don't know where he came from."

"Then tell me," Robin shot back. "So far, all I know about him is he's successful, he's never made a mistake, and he made me feel lousy. And, you know, the pancake thing," she added.

His eyes on the syrup in his hand, Scott said, "My dad didn't come from much. I mean, my grandparents did fine, working-class folks, decent neighborhood and all that, but it's not like he was born with the silver spoon. When he wanted to go off to New York, Broadway bound, my grandfather thought he was nuts. He could've easily grabbed a manufacturing job, a sure paycheck, but in my grandfather's mind, my dad threw that away. Dad worked so hard in New York. He couldn't go back home a failure."

Well, Robin admitted to herself, that she could understand fully.

"It wasn't easy for a while," said Scott. "As I'm sure you and all actors and creative types have experienced, the world can be pretty cold to you unless you hit it big. You're a dreamer, or unrealistic, childish. You have to work extra hard to earn money while you're chasing your goals, and you're the butt of too many jokes while you're doing it. And you have to separate yourself from the people out there who are just in it because they think, hey, right place, right time, and they'll become a star. That's what he had to contend with for a few years. He ended up putting in eight hours at some day job and then another ten between acting and studying. Years, he did that. It finally started to pay off. I remember when I was little, times were still lean, no doubt. Dad was acting at night and working as a teaching assistant while he earned his PhD in theatre. He was so happy. I've never seen him so happy as he was back then. He used to come in sometimes two, three in the morning after a show or rehearsal, and he'd kiss my forehead, right here." With his free hand, Scott touched a spot on his brow.

"Then it all changed," he continued. "He eventually became a full professor, tenured, and he didn't have time anymore for his own acting. Some professors see tenure as a way to ensure they'll always be able to teach their passion. They're dedicated to their students and that profession. And some, like my dad, see it as a box to be checked off, a finish line, permission to coast." He thought a minute. "You know, I don't even think he likes theatre anymore. What he likes is his paycheck and three parking spots on campus where he can garage his extra cars. After Grandpa died and then Grandma, he got an inheritance, made a few incredibly lucky investments, and got kind of weird."

Kind of? Robin wanted to question, but kept silent.

"He was unhappy I didn't follow in his footsteps and become a professor," said Scott. "He likes that I'm successful in my own right, but he hates how I did it. He obviously has issues with people in my life he thinks might be posers. But I think meeting you triggered more than that, especially when he saw you're not at all a poser. You reminded him of how he used to be."

Robin just let him talk. She sensed how important this was for him, could practically see the wrestling match within, between his love for his father and his disappointment.

"It's more than that, though," he said. "I bet you reminded him he *is* one of those powers. Not the kind who becomes a success and turns around, hand outstretched, to help the next struggling actor, but the kind who shuts the door behind himself after he's made it. He's a judgmental, hypocritical man who's lost his spirit." He planted his hands on his hips and shook his head. "I don't believe this. Here I was trying to plead his case to you and now I'm wondering where I was even going with this. He's my father. For the longest time, all I've wanted to hear him say is, 'Good job, son.'"

Finally, Scott set down the can of syrup. "And I think . . . I have to let that go."

Robin's head jerked up in surprise. She wasn't entirely unsympathetic to Donovan's beginnings, but the man had enjoyed an incredible amount of success, first with his passion for the stage, then in a stable teaching career, and finally with a windfall of luck. He had a beautiful, loving family. He had decided to go to bed each day miserable in spite of it all. And Scott had his own blossoming life. Robin could understand a man wanting his father's love, but when it was obvious the father wanted no part of his son's life, it was time to accept the heartache so the healing could begin.

To Robin's complete astonishment, apparently tonight was that time.

Scott put a hand to his forehead. "Can we, ah . . . Yeah, can we sit down a second?"

With a nod, Robin took his elbow. "Let's get some air," she said. "I saw a bench outside."

A light snow had begun falling, and people were starting to gather around the Eastern White Pine for the main event. The impromptu chorale had made way for the children's chorus, who sounded like they'd been rehearsing for months for their spotlight tonight. Harmonic a cappella oohs waltzed gracefully into the opening verse of "O Holy Night," as Robin and Scott ducked their heads together to talk.

Scott said, "What you did at brunch? The acting? That was fabulous. I mean, not just the acting, although if that's what you do during your auditions, you can't give up. You're good. You just need to hang in there. But I mean that you put my father in his place a little. You weren't intimidated by him at all. That was . . . inspiring."

"Well, thank you," said Robin, feeling a warm boost of confidence at the same time she wondered if that had planted the seed that was growing into a turning point for him. She admitted, "This isn't exactly how I imagined this evening would go."

"Me neither," Scott laughed, and then he went quiet. When he spoke again, though his tone was reluctant, his words were resolute. "I need to do some thinking about my father. And some talking to him. I'm going to tell him how wrong he was for how he treated you. How he treated me too. You're not the first person he's done this to. He treats lots of people this way, actually, and a couple have been my friends. And I lost those friends." He considered her. "I don't want to lose you."

"Look, Scott, this is a lot for you to digest," Robin said, touched by what he'd said, elated at his revelation, but still cautious. "He is your father. Don't go ruffling a lot of feathers if you're not sure you want to deal with the fallout—"

"He's the one who started all this," Scott said softly. "And he needs to know that." He gazed at her silently, and Robin found she couldn't tear her eyes from him. She found she didn't want to.

"The maple syrup," he said finally, "that was clever. I see why you're so successful at the Hutch. And YOPE. You have so much going for you, Robin. I feel lucky to have gotten to know you. And I wouldn't blame you in the least if you decide you don't particularly want to see me again, but if you would, maybe after the holidays . . ."

Their eyes stayed locked, and Robin felt utterly overwhelmed. She cleared her throat. "So the maple syrup is a yes, then?"

With an understanding yet slightly crestfallen smile, Scott moved back a little on the bench. "I don't know if that's quite right for him," he said. "Besides, Mom might kill me if I give him a reason to add to that waistline. Tell you what. You're off the clock tonight. I'll take you home if you want to leave, or we can stay and have some fun. If you're free tomorrow, we'll take a couple hours at the Orange-Clove and fulfill your contract. Whatever we have at the end of it, Dad's gonna have to be happy with. Or not happy, his choice."

Robin almost jumped to say, "Deal," but then she realized: "Tomorrow's Christmas Eve."

"Oh, right," said Scott. "And everyone's coming over in the morning. Look, don't worry about it then. I'll get the syrup, and we can handle the money however you're comfortable with. Hey, Frankie's birthday's coming up in a couple months. Maybe we can use what's left as a down payment for you YOPE-ing that."

Robin liked the sound of YOPE as a verb. Maybe this business had a future outside of Christmas after all. "We'll figure it out," she said. "I hope you have a Merry Christmas. Maybe wait on the talk with your dad until after the holidays?"

"We'll see how the weekend goes," said Scott. "If an opportunity presents itself"—he shrugged—"I'm not going to let it go."

"Well," said Robin, glancing at the festivities, "if you feel like sticking around for a while, I'm game. We can get some cider and look at the lights. Seems like they're getting ready to flip the switch."

Scott ducked his head and turned his eyes up to her. "I'd love to stick around for a while."

Though they sat still, she felt him pulling her into his orbit. There was that gaze again, those deep eyes. Her heart sped up as she hardly realized on any conscious level that she leaned closer to him, and he brought a gentle hand to her cheek. He glimpsed her lips, and with his thumb under her chin, he lifted it delicately and yet with the strength she was starting to see in him.

"'Scuse me," said a little voice that had popped up before them. A boy of no more than eight shoved two leaves of sheet music in the diminishing space between their lips. Robin and Scott both flinched back, startled.

The boy said, "The choir's gonna sing the 'Christmas Tree' song when they do the lights, and they want everyone to sing along."

"Thank you," Scott said, managing to sound both pleasant and annoyed at the same time.

As the boy ran off, he left Robin with a fantastic idea. "That's it," she said. "That's what you can give your father for Christmas."

Scott looked at the sheet music, confused.

"No, not the song," said Robin. "The kids. At the hospital." She hadn't thought about *A Holiday Spectacular* since she'd hung the flier at the Hutch. "An off-Broadway troupe is coming to Mercy Hospital to perform for the kids tomorrow. You said your dad doesn't even seem to like acting anymore. Well, maybe what he needs is to see some of the magic of theatre again. What better way to do that than through the eyes of a child?"

Slowly, the dimple in Scott's left cheek deepened. "I think that just might be a great idea."

"Listen, what do you guys have planned for tomorrow?"

"Nothing, really," Scott said. "We floated some ideas about watching a movie or maybe going out before dinner, but we never really landed on anything."

"Oh, this is perfect," said Robin. "Bring them here. To Whimsy. I mean, even before the show. That starts at four, but if you all come in, say, for lunch, then take in some of the Christmas sights around town, do a little shopping, maybe some ice skating, then I can meet you at the show . . . What d'ya say?"

"I say it's amazing you'd want to put up with my father again."

Right, there was that. Robin tried brushing the less-than-pleasant thought away. "Sometimes you have to take a leap of faith. Who knows? Whimsy just might have enough magic to turn your dad around."

He clapped his hands. "It's perfect. Frankie and Mom will love it." He bobbed his head, thinking it over. "And luckily you won't even have to see my father until the show anyway. I don't suppose I could hole up with you until then too, huh?"

She laughed. "I think they'd miss you."

The countdown to the lighting was about to begin, so they got up then to grab their cider. The tender beat between them had passed, but Robin thought the interruption was probably for the best. Even if Scott went through with his plans to have the mother—or father—of all talks with his dad, what would happen next? What if he and Robin did get together? Did she really want to be involved with a man whose father disapproved of her every move? Who wanted that kind of stress on top of all the stress she already had in her life?

Robin's month had begun with one goal: to cover the bump in her rent. YOPE was doing that, and it was also giving her a much-needed boost of self-esteem that she could carry into her theatre auditions. Now here she was, getting swept off her feet by a man who might invite a whole new crop of problems to Sunday dinner. Her head was swimming, especially considering that not an hour before she didn't even want to be in the same room as Scott. She remembered advice from her Girl Scouts leader long ago: if you get lost in the woods, don't move unless you're sure of the way out, because the last thing you want to do is make it harder for anyone to find you.

She and Scott were friends now, and she felt good about that. Even though a part of her wanted to wander deeper, she had to stay put until she was sure of where she was, and where they might be going.

She found herself hoping, though, that was the right decision to make, and that he didn't decide to walk on without her.

Chapter
Sixteen

The first Christmas after Darren had died, Kyle was nine, and though Margot hardly felt like decorating, she also didn't want to take her grief out on her little boy. It was then that she instituted a new tradition for their household, holding off on decorating until the twenty-third. She sold the idea to Kyle by telling him that when she was a little girl, Santa used to come on Christmas Eve and help her parents do everything: put up the tree, hang the stockings, lights, and ornaments, and of course, bring the presents. And this was true. Margot's father would go out and get one of the last trees that Old Man Harvey kept aside for his best customers. Her mother would start decorating after Margot had gone to bed, and both her parents would be up until near dawn putting the finishing touches on everything. The magic of Christmas, personified by Santa Claus, helped them do it all. Margot was sure of this even once she'd grown up. For how was it possible otherwise that two people could do it all by themselves in just one night?

Kyle loved the idea. Margot had tweaked the magic for their purposes, seeing as how there was no way she'd be able to put up a tree in one night let alone the rest of it even with Santa's help. She told Kyle that since it was just the two of them, they should share the fun, and the twenty-third would be their special day to do it. And she wouldn't be surprised if Santa's magic, and Whimsy's, blew in to them on the frosty Christmas air, even if it was a couple days early. Kyle had grown up a little since then, of course, but he still cherished the tradition. So did Margot.

When Darren was alive, they'd used all the decorations in the house, cartons' and cartons' worth. Since his death, they'd pared down quite a bit, mostly out of necessity. By the time Margot and Kyle were done with the tree and stockings and a few extras like the wreath for the front door, they were spent. They had the best of intentions. Every year they carted up all the boxes from the basement to the front hall, their staging area, gung-ho about getting through them all this time around. And every year they carted half of them right back down again, still closed up. At least it was good exercise, they'd joke, toting the heavy things up and down the stairs. Then they'd have tea, a special Christmas spice blend they had only on those three days of the twenty-third, Christmas Eve, and then the big day. In fact, it was the only tea Kyle drank all year.

This year started no different for the two. They brought up all the boxes to the front hall, layered one bushy and unwieldy tier of their faux tree on top of another until it was put together, tucked the strings of lights all around, draped their garland, and reminisced over the ornaments they hung. Kyle placed his and his mom's stockings on omnipresent cup hooks drilled into the underside of the mantle. There were three hooks, and he went into the box to get Darren's stocking as he usually did. But then, as Kyle held the fuzzy red sock with DARREN embroidered on the cuff, he paused. Margot had been watching him from the couch. When his long bangs fell forward over his eyes and he didn't bother flicking them away, she asked, "Kyle? Everything okay?"

"Huh?" He glanced up. "Oh. Yeah, it's all good."

But it didn't seem good. Margot wasn't entirely sure where the thought came from, but it struck her that this might be the perfect time to have the talk with Kyle that Charlotte had prodded her to have. "Honey," she said, "why don't you come sit here for a sec?"

Kyle went to hang the stocking, but Margot stopped him. "Hold off on that," she said. "Just come here. We need to talk a little."

He gently tossed the stocking on the side of the box before sitting next to his mom. She said, "I need you to know that I am not romantically interested in Gavin Aberline, or anyone else for that matter."

"Ew," said Kyle, dragging the word out and screwing up his face like she'd waded into a pile of muck and was tugging him along with her. "I really don't want to hear about that stuff. Not when it comes to you."

"Well, you're going to hear about it for a minute, because we need to address this," she said in her no-nonsense mom voice.

He rolled his eyes. "Yes, Mom."

"I know you have a problem with the idea of me moving on from your father—"

"What? Mom—"

"Please, Kyle, don't interrupt me." She didn't like to be interrupted by her son anyway, and she felt it was her obligation to him to keep him respectful. But more than that, just now, she simply wanted to get through what she had to say without this being prolonged any longer than necessary. "But when I am ready, if I am ready, I will make that decision for my life. I'm never going to forget your father, and I'd never bring any man, friend or otherwise, into this house if you were the least bit uneasy about it. But I need you to start asking yourself if you're uncomfortable with Gavin because there's something about him you truly don't like, or if you're uncomfortable because you don't want me having any men friends."

"Oh, my God, Mom—"

She put up a hand to quiet him. "Because if it's the latter, we're going to need to talk about that to get you past it. You can't live in the past, Kyle, and you can't expect me to, either."

Kyle buried his face in his hands. "I don't believe this," came his muffled voice. He picked up his head. "Can I speak please?"

"Go ahead."

"Mom, you're the one caught in the past," he said, erring on the side of snotty.

With the way he was looking expectantly at her, like he'd just dropped a bomb, she wasn't sure if he was waiting for her to break down in tears at this revelation or clutch at him gratefully for pointing out her neuroses. Either way, she was going to have to disappoint him.

"Of course I am," she said. "You don't think I know that? My dear, I've been on this earth a few years longer than you, and I hate to tell ya, you are not the voice of wisdom on this. So let's drop the attitude, okay? I'm working past my problems with this. What I'm asking from you is that if you're having your own problems with me moving on, please just talk to me about it. Don't shut down, don't walk away."

Kyle flopped back on the couch, looking defeated. His head dropped back and he stared at the ceiling as he said, slowly, as though the words were being extracted from him like wisdom teeth, "I *don't* have a problem with you moving on."

Margot raised a brow. "You don't?"

"No," Kyle said. "Especially not with a guy who's just a friend."

"Then why were you so upset at the rink?"

"Because you ran out of there so fast after Mr. Aberline spent all that time teaching us curling. I liked curling. I was having fun. And he seems nice. And he's already friends with Aunt Charlotte and Uncle René, so you know he's not, like, an ax murderer or something."

Margot hid her smile at the phrase she herself had used verbatim with Charlotte.

"He's obviously, you know, interested in you or whatever." This Kyle rushed over, getting the words out as fast as he could. "Even if it's just friendship, that's a good thing. That's not something to push away. Especially if it's friendship, actually." He rolled his head on the couch cushion to face his mother. "Would I be cool with you walking down the aisle tomorrow? Probably not. But it's time to let someone in, and this guy seems like a pretty good choice."

Margot fell back against the couch too, the same as Kyle had. "Well," she said, "this is a surprise." She rolled her head to face him. When the pimples on his strong jaw cleared up soon, he'd be the spitting image of Darren. She poked him in the arm. "See why talking is important, mister? I can only read your mind about, mm, three-quarters of the time. Sometimes you're a blank."

"Really?" he said. "You sure you're okay letting me in on that little parental secret?"

She patted his leg. "You're getting older. It's okay to let you in on one or two of those secrets."

"Cool. How do you do the eyes in the back of the head thing?"

"Oh, well, some things you're just going to have to learn for yourself," said Margot. "After all, they'd kick me out of the Parents Club if I revealed everything."

"Mom," Kyle said with a laugh.

"They'd make me give back my key card and my club jacket."

"Here we go."

"And I like that jacket. Very snuggly."

"Okay," said Kyle with the sort of resigned acceptance he adopted when he knew he wasn't going to stop Margot from driving home a point.

"Seriously," she said, "why didn't you just tell me how you felt?"

"I dunno. I mean, it's a touchy subject," he said. "It's Dad. I didn't want to bring it up and make you sad, or me." He picked at a spot on his jeans and mumbled, "Maybe I was feeling a little guilty. I'm never gonna forget him, Mom, but I also just want us to be happy. I want you to be happy."

She reached an arm around him and drew him into a hug. "I am happy, kiddo. I'm happy to be your mom, and to have such a great young man as my son. I'm happy for our family and friends, and for the store. I'm happy we can just take some time, sit here together, and decorate. You know what else I'm happy for?"

Kyle's mop of hair brushed against her cheek as he shook his head.

"Tea," she announced, and let him go. "We're just about done here, right?"

"Unless this is the year we dive into another box," he said.

They both leaned forward and craned their necks for a view of the four cartons in the front hall. At least they'd gotten them open this year, one with garland, another with knick-knacks, and so on, but otherwise they were untouched. In unison, Margot and Kyle said, "Nah." They stood up and had started into the kitchen when the doorbell rang.

Margot glanced out the sidelight window and saw on her porch a woman whose fuzzy purple earmuffs clamped down the sides of her spiral-curl hair. She had skin the color of chestnuts, and had to be somewhere around Margot's age, judging by the fine lines around her mouth and eyes.

"May I help you?" said Margot, opening the door in a neighborly fashion.

"My name is Faye," said the woman, "and I'm with the Whimsy Charitable Association."

"Of course, are you collecting?" The WCA was the biggest nonprofit in town. They did the most locally to help people get back on their feet during hard times, organizing job interviews, cleaning and distributing gently used business clothes, providing a pantry for food and sanitary items.

Margot started back inside to grab a few dollars from her purse, but Faye waved her hand.

"No," she said, "but thank you. We're just making the rounds to remind everyone where they can drop off donations." Faye handed Margot a list of participating businesses around Whimsy. "This time of year, coats and boots are especially appreciated."

A bell went off in Margot's head. "Coats," she exclaimed. "I've been meaning to drop off my old one. Can I give it to you so I don't keep forgetting?"

"Sure," said Faye, lighting up even more. "Thank you very much."

"Come on in out of the cold a minute," said Margot, holding the door open for her. "Want a cup of tea? We were just about to make some." Faye declined, checking her ornate wristwatch. Margot glanced up and saw Kyle just beyond the cartons, no doubt curious who was at the door. "Honey, this is Faye. This is my son, Kyle."

They waved hello to each other while Margot grabbed her old coat from the hall closet. Her hand brushed up against the music brooch on her scarf draped over the next hanger, and she got the familiar pang in her heart.

"These are my favorite types of decorations," Faye said behind her. Margot turned around to see her glancing at the knickknack box. "They bring a special meaning to Christmas, I think. Unique to each family, and it's just not the holidays without them, right?"

The pang from the brooch cut a little deeper. "That's what my husband used to say."

"For me it's snow globes," said Faye. "My whole world is a snow globe this time of year."

Kyle spoke up then, digging his hands in his pockets. "Mom? Maybe we should put a few of them out."

"Oh, you should," said Faye. "These are simply too precious to keep in a box." Then she mimed locking her mouth and throwing away the key. "Sorry. I should mind my own business."

"Not at all," said Margot. She handed Faye the coat, and they shared their thanks and goodbyes.

After Margot had closed the front door, she turned to see Kyle digging through the knickknacks box. "Mom?" he said as he pulled out a trinket. "What's this? I don't remember it."

It wasn't a knickknack, but an ornament for the tree that had gotten mixed in with the wrong box, apparently. He showed her the oversized silver bell painted with a glittery glaze, like it was encrusted with snow. Kyle flicked his wrist to ring it, but it was muted. He flipped it over, and there, taped to the clapper, was a tiny scrap of paper. "There's something written on it," he said, peeling off the tape and unfolding it. After glancing at the words, he lifted his head, and held the scrap out to his mother.

"What does it say?" she asked, taking it from him. When she read the words written in one long stream on the little strip, she felt utterly knocked out.

To my Margot: "Make our future a happy one." Merry Christmas, darling. Love, your Darren.

A date accompanied the message, a date of six years ago. "He was going to give this to me," Margot whispered. Her chest caught with emotion, and tears rushed to her eyes, though she managed to stop most of them from falling. One or two escaped, and Kyle, after giving his mom a hug, went to get tissues.

With Kyle gone from the room, the air around her turned silent and still, as though it had slowed to a stop around her. It was then that a deep voice behind Margot said softly, "That's our song."

Margot whirled around. Darren stood there, looking exactly as he had that night. He had on his long wool coat, navy blue, which made his blond hair and brown eyes all the more striking. An aura of pure light surrounded him, and when he spoke, his voice echoed as though covering a vast distance.

"'Make our future a happy one,'" Margot quoted with barely any strength to her own voice. "It's from 'A Christmas Sometime.' Oh, Darren. A happy future? You and I have no future together at all anymore."

"You've got to stop blaming yourself," he said. "None of us can move on—you, Kyle, me—until you accept the accident was my fault, not yours."

"I was the one who called you," said Margot tearfully. "I should have waited. You were already on the road. You knew how icy it was."

"I was the one who couldn't just let the phone ring," said Darren. "I took my eyes off the road. That was my mistake, not yours."

But Margot hardly heard him. "I should've let you get to dinner and then called. Or I should've gone with you."

"Maybe then we'd both be dead," said Darren, and this grabbed Margot's attention. "But you're alive, my darling. Why are you acting like you're not?"

He smiled down at the bell. "I've been trying so hard to reach you through our song. Trying to get through to you, remind you of our happiness so you can find your own. That happiness will bring you peace, and it will allow me to rest, for how can I when I know how distraught you are?" As he reached out toward the bell, Darren's light surrounded it. "I'd planned for you to find this ornament when we went to decorate the tree that year. But I see how much more it means now. Make *your* future a happy one, my darling, whatever form that takes. Open your heart to friendship and love. This man, Gavin, his companionship will make you happy, I think. Give it a chance. I know you're ready."

He moved toward her, somewhere between walking and floating, until his light surrounded them both. Her lips touched his, and with the warmth she swore she could feel from that kiss, Margot felt the burden of blame slip from her heart. She hadn't known how heavy and coarse that shroud had been until she felt it drop away.

Then, he was gone.

Margot put a trembling hand to her lips, holding the kiss there with her eyes closed. When she felt ready, she opened them.

"Mom?" said Kyle, coming into view from the kitchen. He came toward her with a box of tissues. "Tea water's on." He got a good look at her. "You okay? Did that WCA lady come back? I heard you talking to someone."

She grabbed a tissue and nodded. "Actually, I was talking to your father."

This news didn't surprise Kyle. He himself had felt Darren's presence from time to time, he'd confided in Margot, and he knew of her talks with him. "Are you okay?" he asked gently.

"Oh, sweetie," she said, pulling him into another hug. Fresh tears welled in her eyes, but this time she was smiling. "I think I am."

Chapter
Seventeen

After the spice tea had been drunk, the last decorations put up—much more this year than had been up in a long, long time—and all eyes finally dried, Margot went to her purse and pulled out Gavin's visiting card with his phone number and address on it. She'd been putting off calling him about coming to the party, just as she put off pretty much any awkward interaction as long as she could. But she'd run out of time. The party was tomorrow night, so she figured she should let the poor man know he had plans.

She went to the kitchen, tucked her hair behind her ears, picked up the "vintage," as Kyle would say, wall phone, and she dialed. But Gavin's voicemail picked up. Thinking fast, or perhaps not thinking much at all but going purely by her gut, Margot hung up before the beep. She stood there, waiting to feel relieved. That's exactly what the sound of his voicemail should have done, relieved her. A chance to avoid conversation with him and just tell him she was fine with him coming to the party? Great. She should have hung up, brushed her hands clean of it all, and if he came, he came. She'd done her part, and she couldn't care less which decision he made.

Except, she realized, she did care. And had she told anyone what she was feeling, no one would have been more surprised than she. It was the same feeling she got when an old album was playing and a new skip interrupted the song. It was lying on the beach on a sunny day when sudden rainclouds appeared. It was disappointment, pure and simple, that she couldn't talk to him.

She tried him back again, and when the same occurred, she hung up and went for the front closet. Pausing with her hand on her fur coat, the gift from Darren, she thought instead her gray coat would go best with the maroon corduroys she wore. She threw on the gray, along with her scarf with the music brooch pinned to it, and headed for the front door with Gavin's address in hand.

(Later tonight, while curled up on her bedspread and talking on the phone to Charlotte about all this, it would occur to Margot all the reasons that should have stopped her from going to his house. It was late in the day, it was rude to show up at his house unannounced, and the odds were if he wasn't picking up his phone, he wasn't home at all. But all she had was her goal clear in front of her. Charlotte's gentle laugh would come through the phone, and she'd say, "Margot's tunnel vision strikes again.")

Margot called out to Kyle that she'd be back soon, and she opened the front door, ready to bound down the porch steps. What she did instead was bound right into Gavin.

With a joint "oof" from them both, Gavin caught Margot. He wore his overcoat and his fedora, which he lifted off his head as soon as he let go of her. The sun was nearly set, but his sandy blond hair with flecks of gray caught what was left of the dwindling light. In his other hand was small gift-wrapped box.

"I'm sorry I startled you," he said. "I was about to ring the bell and there you were."

"Me too," she said. "I mean, sorry. I was on my way to see you, actually."

"Really? Well, that's a lovely thing to hear," he said.

At that, Margot dipped her head. "I just needed to tell you, you don't have to skip Charlotte and René's party. Not on my account."

He bent his knees and tilted his head so he was on a level with her lowered gaze. "I don't?" he said lightly. When she looked up again, his expression turned more earnest. "I sincerely hope that doesn't mean you and Kyle will be skipping it."

"No," she hurried to say.

His smile returned. "Oh, good."

"I just figure it's a big party," she rushed on. "Lots of people to talk to. We probably won't even get to say two words to each other."

And his smile vanished again. "I see. Margot, have I done something to offend you?" Gavin asked, tripping over his words a little.

"Not at all," she said automatically.

"Okay," said Gavin, though he hardly looked convinced. He held the gift box out to her. "I came over to wish you a Merry Christmas. You and Kyle. But this is for you. I thought you'd like it."

She took the small box, thanking him. The wrapping had little jukeboxes on it, and it reminded Margot of the novelty tree lights Robin had told her about the day she and Gavin had met. "This is really very thoughtful of you," she said.

They stood still, and Margot made no moves to ask him inside or unwrap the gift. She was quiet because she was considering him and an idea she'd just had. Gavin, obviously, took the silence to have a different meaning entirely.

He put his hat back on. "I guess I'll see you at the party then. Or not, with all the people," he said in a lackluster voice, and turned to leave.

Margot blurted out, "Would you like to go for a walk? I mean, now? Whimsy Square is just over Gallantry Bridge there, up the street. Which you probably saw when you were on your way over here."

Gavin's luster was no longer lacking. "I'd love to," he said.

They strolled along toward the bridge, quiet for a time. Then Margot said, "In case you haven't noticed, I'm not the most talkative person in the world."

He said, "My older brother introduced me to that quote from the *Tao Te Ching:* 'Those who know don't talk. Those who talk don't know.'"

Margot joined in quoting the last part. Of course she knew the old saying.

Gavin squinted, thinking about it, his hands deep in his coat pockets. "I guess you can't really take that literally in this day and age. But the kernel of truth in it still works. Although, I'm suddenly very aware how much I've been talking, and I may be getting a complex over it."

She giggled, which made him laugh, and she liked the sound.

Gavin shrugged. "I can talk enough for both of us."

It was a nice sentiment, but she couldn't help but compare him to Darren. Darren never ran from or tried to cover for Margot's shyness. He never tried drawing her out or throwing her into situations she might find overwhelming. He waited for her, because he knew that when she was ready to do or say something, she would in her own time. Large crowds or situations that called for lots of interaction with strangers often sent her into restrooms or back to the car for periods of respite. The sheer volume of people, both their noise and their numbers, would simply get to her. People naturally told Margot their problems, total strangers did at times. Darren used to tell her it was because on some level they sensed her compassion. He called her his empath. To a certain extent, she took on the emotions wrapped up in those problems, and her concerns for this person's illness or that person's divorce could follow her into a sleepless night tossing and turning, or a dazed morning drowning in coffee. This empathy, she imagined, went hand in hand with her anxiety. It seemed like her nervous system could just get overloaded and melt down. But when Darren was in her life, the anxiety and the shyness were tamped down.

Most people were uneasy being silent with another person. Darren was no different. With Margot, though, he'd learned to embrace his own discomfort, until their shared silences weren't uncomfortable at all. Gavin chattered away as they strolled, and so inwardly she turned to her group of friends, the Coping Mechanisms. Deep Breathing held her hands and said with her, "In . . . and out," while Bell Jar muted any emotions emanating from Gavin. At least, thought Margot, the evening was nice, and Gavin's emotions weren't nearly as aggressive as many other people's.

The Gallantry Bridge was lit up with festoons of multicolored lights wrapped around green garland. Just below, the kids' ice rink teemed with parents, children, and the din of whooshing skates. Twilight had risen. The ubiquitous holiday songs played over the PA, and Margot kept a wary ear out for "A Christmas Sometime." When they paused on the bridge, the aroma of hot cocoa wafted over to them from a stand on the bank of the rink. A cup sounded good, as Margot felt the tip of her nose going cold, but she wasn't sure if inviting Gavin for a walk *and* suggesting they stop for cocoa would be sending him a message she might not want to send.

Instead, she said, "I'm guessing they don't see a lot of curling on this rink."

"You're probably right about that."

"That was a fun day," she said. "Curling."

"Yeah?" said Gavin, lifting his eyebrows and looking hopeful.

"Kyle really enjoyed himself."

"Kyle. Well, that's great. I'm glad."

"Thank you for taking the time with him."

"Kyle seems like a great kid."

"He is," she said. "He constantly surprises me. You know what he asked me a little while ago? If I thought they were going to have dancing at the party tomorrow. Charlotte and René do it every year, they clear the dining room furniture out and, boom, instant dance floor. DJ and everything. But it's like it just sort of dawned on Kyle there was going to be dancing, like he's at the age where he's thinking about this stuff. My guess is . . . the next-door neighbor."

"The next-door neighbor what?" Gavin asked.

"Charlotte and René live next door to a divorcee who's raising three girls, one of whom is in Kyle's class," said Margot, "and she's adorable. She's got eyelashes longer than my hair, I swear."

Gavin laughed. "And you think Kyle's the dancing type?"

"Oh, I know it. Believe it or not, he's quite the heartbreaker already. Just like his dad."

Gavin pointed at her hand. "You should open your present."

She'd forgotten about it completely, the little jukebox-wrapped package she still held. She felt awkward he'd gotten her anything. "What about your kids?" she asked, looking at the gift but not opening it yet. "Are you seeing them at all for the holidays?"

"Sure," he said. "They'll be with their mom for Christmas, and then I'll fly out just before New Year's, spend some time with them. They're both in college, so hopefully they'll be able to fit me in between parties with their friends from high school."

Everything he said was in his usual lighthearted tone, but Margot felt a change in him regardless. She imagined how she'd feel if she hardly ever got to see Kyle. College was still a few years off, so she had time to prepare, but a home without his voice, his schoolbooks and shoes on the stairs waiting to be taken up to his room, his music, a home without those things would feel empty, especially when it was all brand new.

It would feel lonely.

She said to Gavin, "I don't know how many friends you have here in Whimsy, but if you ever feel like talking, or if you just want to, I don't know, grab lunch, you can call me. I'm a pretty good friend."

There was another change in him. When he spoke wistfully of his kids, it was as though his overwhelming spotlight had dimmed. Now the spotlight bumped right back up to full strength. "I have no doubt you're a wonderful friend. Go on, open the present."

Reluctantly, she started to tear the paper. "You really shouldn't have—" she started to say as she tore the paper.

"Don't thank me yet," he interrupted with that twinkle in his eye. "You may hate it. Course if you hate it, you'll probably still thank me, because you're a very sweet person."

Her shoulders dropped, and she froze in her unwrapping. "Please don't," she whispered, unable to stop the words.

"Um, don't what?"

She hadn't meant to talk to him about this, but she supposed she had to, especially with this gift. As she'd told Charlotte at For the Record, she'd get all her cards on the table. "It feels like," she said tentatively, "you might be interested in me. As more than friends. I'm not saying you are, I'm just saying that's how it feels. When you compliment me or"—she held up the partially unwrapped gift—"get me a present, it feels like we're on different wavelengths. You're a lovely man, but I can't be any more to you than a friend. Not right now, and not in the foreseeable future."

Gavin seemed blindsided. "Oh," he said. "All right. Well, I had my suspicions that I was making you uncomfortable. Guess I was right." He held up his hands. "I'll back off."

Hesitantly, Margot held out the gift to him. "I shouldn't accept this," she said.

"No, please," he insisted and backed away. "It's for you. Friend to friend, I promise. Except it's an engagement ring, so I hope that doesn't make things too weird."

Laughter bubbled up from Margot as the awkward fog was cleared, just like that.

"Look," said Gavin, "I'm sorry I've come on too strong. I just haven't done this in a very long time."

"Done what?" said Margot, though she was fairly sure she knew what he meant.

"Figured out how to handle a friendship with an enchanting woman."

"You did it again."

"What?"

"I'm not enchanting," she exclaimed.

"You're right," he said. "You're an utterly disenchanting woman. I don't know what I was thinking."

"Much better," she said, laughing in spite of herself.

"How 'bout I promise I'll keep working on it? The coming on too strong thing, I mean."

"It's a deal." She went to shake his hand, and then, again, remembered the gift. "You know," she said as she tore the rest of the paper, "if this *is* a ring, you better have sprung for real diamonds. I'm very picky."

"I'll keep that in mind."

From the picture on the small box, she knew instantly what it was. "The saxophone ornament," she said with child-like wonder. "Thank you." She dug into the box and pulled it out, lifting the cover on the sax's bell. Al Francis's resonant tenor crooned "I Sing You Starlight," and Margot hummed along.

Gavin said, "Sometime we're going to have to talk big bands. For a while there I was thinking I was the last person on the planet who listened to them."

"I think there are more people than we realize who value the same things we do," said Margot. "If something's not in the mainstream, we don't hear that much about it. And if we don't hear about it, we might think we're the only person who likes it, maybe we think it's a throwback or strange. Really there might be lots of people who feel the same way." She held up the saxophone. "Someone obviously thought there was enough of a market for an old big-band ballad."

Years ago, she'd had a similar conversation with Darren. He'd told her, "When you find those people who value the same little treasures you do, who share your love of wandering off the beaten path, hold on to that friendship." She could hear his voice clear as day, and she nearly shared the memory with Gavin. Then she thought better of it. Darren's presence here would only interrupt the flow of the conversation she and Gavin were starting to enjoy.

A light snow began to fall, and they started back to her house. Gavin told her he'd be taking a job consulting with the

Bonspiel Curling Club of Central New York, where he'd coached so many years before. He talked a little to her about his divorce. It was amicable enough, but there was no doubt still tension between him and his ex-wife. He'd taken a long time to heal the wounds left by the broken marriage, and he guessed that was part of the reason he stayed in Indiana so long even after the divorce. When they got back to her porch, Gavin said, "And I've been talking your ear off. How do you get people to open up to you like that?"

"Well, somebody once called me enchanting . . ." she said with a facetious shrug.

"Sounds familiar, now you mention it," he said. When she climbed the steps, he stayed put and pointed at her. "See you tomorrow night. And I promise I won't monopolize your time. You're right—we'll probably have a ton of other people to talk with." He stuck out his hand. "Friends?"

She shook it. "Friends."

Later, on the phone, Charlotte said to her, "Well, thank goodness you two are friends, at least. And you're sure you're not interested in more with him?"

"Definitely," said Margot.

"Even after, you know, the visit from Darren?"

Of course, Margot had told her about the ornament she and Kyle had found with the song lyric, and about Darren's spirit lifting six years of despair from her heart, finally. Margot chuckled at her cousin. "I had a breakthrough, yes. That doesn't mean I'm ready to start dating."

"Just asking," said Charlotte.

"Gavin and I are crystal clear about where we stand."

"Great. Because Jenna Baker, Veronica's friend's mom, has been single about a year and she's back on the dating market. I think she'd just adore Gavin, don't you? I'm going to set them up tomorrow night. That is, if you're sure you're okay with it."

"Why wouldn't I be?" said Margot, ignoring the sudden clenching in her gut.

"Excellent," said Charlotte. "See you tomorrow."

Oh, you can bet on it. "See you then," said Margot brightly. She hung up the phone.

To her empty bedroom, and to her sudden absolute need to be at the party, she said, "Now what, in the name of all that is rock and roll, is that about?"

Chapter
Eighteen

From *Upstate Magazine,* Thanksgiving Edition
(Vol. 16, No. 3):

WHIMSY (CONTINUED)

It would become clear to Margot Kobeleski
and Robin Russell that the rather enigmatic
Faye they both encountered bore a striking re-
semblance to the Spirit of Whimsy. This
dogged reporter, however, had to wait until
Christmas Eve itself, when magic shimmers
bright as freshly fallen snow, to make her most
mysterious acquaintance. . . .

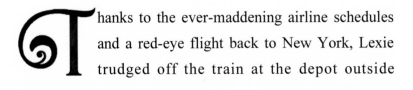

hanks to the ever-maddening airline schedules
and a red-eye flight back to New York, Lexie
trudged off the train at the depot outside

Whimsy, ready to fall over from exhaustion. It was around five thirty in the morning, she knew that, but everything else felt like a fuzzy daze. The depot was small, quaint. Lexie had always liked the feel of it, but right now what she liked most of all was that it was warm. Snow had begun to fly outside, and the temperature felt about the same as she imagined it had outside the plane at 40,000 feet.

She tugged her wheeled luggage behind her up to the attendant's window. "When's the next shuttle into Whimsy Square, please?"

"Oh, sorry," said the attendant, a motherly woman whose black spiral hair tumbled over her red depot vest. "Shuttles are down." She nodded toward the window. "Blizzard's coming."

"A blizzard?" Lexie couldn't believe it. "No one mentioned that on any weather reports."

"Came up outta nowhere," said the attendant. "It's in Whimsy, travelling southeast headed this way. They say it's either gonna dissipate in an hour or two, or pick up speed and hit the city by two p.m."

The news made Lexie feel even more out of sorts. "Do you mind if I just stay here awhile then, see if it clears up?"

With a palm out gesturing toward an empty row of seats, the attendant said, "Be my guest."

"Mind if I sleep there for about a year?" Lexie tossed out sarcastically as she walked away.

The attendant chuckled. "As long as you need, Lexie," she said.

With a start, Lexie turned back. "Did you just say my name? Have we met?" Immediately, she flipped through the files in her mind to try placing the woman, but she came up empty even though, now that she thought of it, she was sure she'd seen her before.

"I said, 'As long as you need, sweetie.'" The woman tilted her head. "Why don't you get that shut-eye?"

Lexie shook her head a little to lift the fog. She made herself as comfortable as she could stretched out over two wooden chairs, tugging her puffy coat around her as a makeshift blanket and grabbing a spare sweatshirt from her bag to use as a pillow. She powered on her phone and tried her parents, tried Spark, tried Theo, tried Anna. She wasn't sure what she was going to say if Theo actually picked up, especially since, as far she knew, he still wasn't aware of her little trip out to L.A. But she wanted some connection. Even if no one could pick her up because of the storm, even if the phone dropped the call after thirty seconds, even if a conversation with Theo devolved rapidly into an argument, she needed something.

All of a sudden she felt so alone her heart radiated a homesick emptiness so intense it made her whole chest hurt. Christmas had always meant family and home to her, and here she was spending Christmas Eve morning in a depot, contemplating moving away from all of that for good. She kept trying phone numbers, speed dial and punching in digits, even texting, silently urging the phone to connect so that she could shake the lousy feeling. The calls didn't go through; the texts all sat pending. Miserably, she silently cursed the pop-up blizzard, tucked her phone back in her purse, and dropped into slumber.

It seemed to Lexie like she'd just shut her eyes when the attendant gently shook her awake. "Miss?" she murmured. "It's just about eight o'clock."

"Morning or night?" Lexie mumbled, cracking an eyelid.

"Morning. The blizzard's lifted and the shuttle for Whimsy will be leaving in a bit."

Lexie thanked her, gathered her things, and lumbered onto the shuttle bus. For most of the twenty-minute ride she rested her eyes, as a headache, no doubt from the whirlwind travel and little sleep, pulsed behind her temples. When the shuttle let her and a few other holiday stragglers off at Whimsy Square, Lexie squinted in the sunlight that was doubly bright, both shining from above and reflected off the white snowy landscape. The sky was surprisingly clear given that just a couple hours ago a blizzard had dumped mounds of fresh powder over everything. And the square was indeed blanketed. The children's skating rink was completely buried, and as for Gallantry Bridge, only the decorative globes perched on top of its parapet stuck out above the covering.

There was a tranquil, pretty quality to the scene, but strangely enough, no one was out. The whole place was deserted. That was to be expected during the blizzard itself, but by this time, especially with the sun shining and given that it was Christmas Eve, she'd have thought kids would be out playing and parents would be shoveling walkways. There were no plows clearing the roads, no evidence of salt trucks, though something must have come through earlier because the snow in the streets only reached to the tops of Lexie's boots. Just now, though, there were no whirring engines or that awful yet reassuring sound of metal scraping asphalt. During the blizzard that had hit a few years back, people didn't even wait for the snow to stop before they went outside. For the first time in her life, Lexie felt something other than comfy and at home here. It felt downright eerie.

She walked the two blocks to her house down the middle of vacant streets, and even there she had to work to lift her boot out of six inches of snow every time she took a step. It seemed like ages had passed since she'd cruised down those balmy Southern California roads. Her light cotton suit and shell top she'd worn to the *Swish* offices were folded deep inside her rolling bag, which she lugged behind her. Not that there was any pavement available for it to successfully roll on. It bumped and skittered behind her over the snow, and after a block of tugging it, she seriously contemplated abandoning it on the side of the road.

But then, Lexie's world got a little bit brighter.

As she turned down Milliner Street and approached her house, she was amazed to see it all lit up. A big green wreath with pinecones and holly hung on the red front door, inviting her in. LED rattan orbs dangled over the white shutters, and the shrubbery out front blinked with red, blue, green, and amber string lights. In her front window, the sheer curtains gave a gauzy, dreamlike halo to the Christmas tree inside, itself alight and shimmery, complete with a star on top.

Theo, Lexie thought as a smile burst onto her face. He must have done this. She couldn't wait to throw her arms around him and kiss him to within an inch of his life. What was she thinking, telling him she needed time? They could work past whatever was holding them back, be it his monumental expectations of her, or her fears about which path to take in life.

Leaving the suitcase on the front walk, she ran—well, galumphed really—up the porch steps. She could practically feel his downy hair as her fingers ran through it, the silly way his glasses bumped her nose when they kissed, his strong arms holding her tight.

Then he opened the door. Lexie froze. "Theo?" she stuttered.

It was him, all right. But his downy hair had receded and been mowed into fuzzy stubble. His glasses were gone. He was paunchy. How in the world, Lexie asked herself, did a person get paunchy and lose his hair in a few weeks?

Despite wearing only jeans, a sweatshirt, and slippers, he stood on the threshold, pulling the front door so it was nearly closed behind him. "Where have you been?" He accused her, albeit quietly.

"L.A.," she said uncertainly. Her eyes dropped. There, on his left ring finger, was a wedding band. She put a hand to her head as her heart thumped. "What's going on here?"

"You were in L.A.," he said with a sarcastic twang. "Los Angeles."

"Yes," she insisted.

"Okay. You want to tell me how that works? Do you have a supersonic plane at your disposal? Did you beam there?"

"What?"

"My wife walks out of here seven hours ago after her bi-weekly 'Let's blame Theo for how terrible my life is' yell-athon, and now she's standing on the porch, lying to me," he said. "I think I should be the one asking, 'What?'"

Another question starting with W tumbled from her lips: "Wife?" Lexie pressed her lips together, feeling nauseous. Then, relief washed over her. "Oh," she said, understanding. "I'm still asleep. I'm at the depot, waiting to come home. This is all a dream."

"Unbelievable," said Theo. Lexie was troubled by the way he looked at her, like she'd said something vicious to him. She thought it odd for her subconscious to come up with that level of animosity between them.

The thing was, this didn't feel like a dream. Once or twice in her life, Lexie had known she was dreaming while still in the dream, and at that point she became aware of how strange the phantasmagoric world was: muted colors, jumps in time and space, the ability to run or shout hog-tied by unseen forces. The world she was in now, with Theo standing before her, the lights on the house blinking, the sun bright, and the air crisp, this was indistinguishable from the real world.

She pinched herself, and she felt it, but that proved nothing. She'd tried that in the other couple of dreams and she felt it then too. "Excuse me a second," she said to Theo. She turned away from him, took a deep breath, and screamed at the top of her lungs.

"Lexie," Theo hissed at her. He stepped out onto the snowy porch, slippers forgotten, and grabbed her arm. "What's the matter with you?"

Hardly realizing it, her hand went to the ends of her hair, which stuck out under her knit hat. She twirled them frantically and nibbled at the inside of her cheek, a nervous habit she'd kicked years ago. "I can scream," she said to him, scared. Her mind immediately pinpointed the next likely scenario. "Are you trying to teach me a lesson or something?" she asked him. "I mean, what is this? You shave your head, you lose the glasses . . . Is that a pillow in your shirt, or did you drink your weight in protein shakes to make me think you're older and I'm, what, missing out? I'm guessing it's protein shakes, because you can see it in your face, too. Pretty elaborate stunt, Theo."

Two children, a boy and girl who both looked around five years old, came running out of the house in snowsuits and boots, encircled Lexie, and sang, "Mommy, Mommy!" before hugging each of her legs.

"Holy Mother of God, whose kids are these?" Lexie yelled at Theo. "You have to bring them back to wherever you got them."

"All right, that's enough," he yelled back. His eyes flitted around the silent neighborhood as though he worried someone might come out and witness the untoward scene. Instantly he put on a smile and crouched down. "Hey, guys, Daddy has to talk to Mommy alone for a minute. Why don't you make some snow angels?"

The boy got right to it, flopping on his back and swinging his arms and legs wildly, but the girl toddled over to the suitcase and started unzipping it. Lexie grabbed it up. "That's not yours . . . little . . . person." Then Lexie gave her a stilted pat on the head, and the girl shrugged and toddled off toward her brother.

"Get in here," Theo said to her, holding the door open for her and taking the suitcase to carry it in.

When the door was closed and Theo had kicked off his snowy, wet slippers, he railed at her, "You have problems with me, you talk to me. You don't take it out on those kids."

"I don't even know who those kids are," she yelled back.

For a second, the fire in Theo's eyes seemed to blaze hotter, but then his glare cooled into concern. "You're not just trying to be funny, are you?" he said, not exactly asking but rather confirming what he was thinking. "You'd never say that about our kids. No matter what."

Lexie noticed the front hall, the stairs. Still in her slush-covered boots, she trod to the living room and took it all in. Then she went to her home office, which, apparently, had been changed back into a dining room. In fact, everything had changed. The walls were no longer different shades of light blues and greens; they were all monochrome beige. Her artwork on the walls had been replaced by framed photos. Nonplussed and her mouth agape, she crossed the living room and she peered at the pictures. There was a studio family shot of Lexie, Theo, and the two kids out front when they were a little younger. There was one of Lexie's parents, each holding a newborn, one with a pink hat, one with a blue. There was one of a very pregnant Lexie wearing a shirt that said WIN-NING! with a T stuck to the front of the word.

Lexie sank down onto the couch she didn't recognize, and her head dropped into her hands. She refused to panic, cry, throw up, or do any of the other things her body and mind seemed ready and willing to do. There was always a rational explanation for things, and she would figure it out if she could just keep her wits about her.

"I can do this," she said more to herself than Theo. "I've wriggled out of tough spots before. Of course, none of those involved delusion, alternate realities, or time travel. But it's always good to test ourselves with new challenges."

Theo sat next to her, tentatively, on the edge of the cushion. "You really don't remember our children? Our life?"

"It's more than that." She spoke slowly, trying to form her words at the same time she was trying to form her thoughts. "A few hours ago, I dozed off at the train depot after coming back from a job interview"—she took a deep breath—"a sort-of job interview at *Swish* out in L.A."

He moved to put his arm around her or maybe rub her back to console her, but he stopped, seeming to think better of it. "That interview," he said, "was six years ago."

"Something's happening, Theo," she blurted out. "I get that whatever's going on with us is not a good situation, obviously, but I don't know if I'm sick, or hit my head . . ." She sputtered a dopey laugh. "Or maybe I jumped off the Gallantry Bridge and my guardian angel is trying to show me an alternate version of my life." Her hand trembled as it found its way to her hair again. "But I don't remember any six years passing, or any of this. And you need to help me. Whoever you know me to be, apparently I'm your wife. In sickness and in health, right? As far as I know, you're still my best friend." Despite her best efforts to keep them at bay, tears glazed her eyes. "I'm scared, I need you, and I love you so much."

He reached out for her then, pulling her into a fierce embrace that she returned. He kissed the top of her head. "I love you too, Lex," he said gruffly. "I don't remember the last time you said that to me." Under her cheek she felt his chest hitch. She eased back to look in his eyes, and saw her tears reflected there.

There was something else, though, beyond the emotion. She'd seen that look in his eyes before, and after searching a moment, she found the memory. When they'd first started dating, Theo had taken her to dinner at Bucky's Pizza World across the square. Over a plastic checkered tablecloth and a fake candle, he'd told her he wanted to quit his job at the Whimsy Historical Society for an opening at the New York Public Library. They'd only been together a few weeks, but he said he didn't want to make the decision without first getting her thoughts on it.

"It's always been my dream to work at the Public Library, especially in rare manuscripts," he'd said. "It's longer hours, less pay to start, more competition and pressure, and the daily commute's harder, obviously, but I want to take the leap. What's life without adventure? I mean, not bungee jumping or exploring ancient ruins. That's cool and everything, but I think there's a whole different kind of adventure in going after your dreams."

It was that look of determination in his eyes, determination and just daring the world to get in his way, that clinched it for Lexie: she was in love with him. Here was a man who would fight for his dreams, and as he would tell her time and again as they fell deeper in love, she was one of his dreams.

His eyes held that same determination now. She knew that no matter how rocky their life together, as he knew it anyway, had been, or how it had worn him down, how defeated he'd looked when he first opened that door, he wouldn't desert her.

And she knew no matter how scared and disoriented she felt, the one thing that was crystal clear to her was how much she loved him.

Chapter
Nineteen

Strangely enough—though everything about this morning had been altogether bizarre—the plows came through as soon as Theo got off the phone with Lexie's parents. He'd explained that Lexie had a terrible migraine, and would they mind if he brought their grandchildren over to their place for a few hours? Of course, that was like asking Lexie if she wouldn't mind asking the first question in the White House press briefing room. The grandparents had planned on coming over for Christmas Eve anyway, so they'd bring the kids back home then.

When Theo had called them, Lexie sat on her hands on the edge of their bed. He paced the room in front of her, and it was all she could do not to grab the phone. Right about now she wanted her mommy like she hadn't since she was the twins' age. She was determined, though, to think as rationally about this as possible, and mute her unproductive emotions like the blaring game-day commentaries they were proving to be. Getting her parents involved, or even worse, the kids, wouldn't be helpful to anyone.

While Theo was gone, Lexie spent that twenty or so minutes going through her closet, her dresser, and the bathroom, searching anywhere she might find answers, although she barely even knew the questions. Really, what she was hoping to find was some vortex in the time line or a genie's lantern or whatever had brought her here in the first place that would be her ticket home.

She supposed the obvious explanation was still a dream, just one more real than she'd ever experienced before. "The brain is capable of so much we don't even understand," she mumbled to herself as she went through a pile of finger paintings she'd found in a kitchen drawer. She remembered an interview she'd done once with a neurological researcher who was, perhaps, a bit odd given that they'd talked while he ate his lunch of ramen noodles, which he'd at one point held up on chopsticks and offered to her as "leftover brain." (Lexie had declined and laughed, "But that gives a whole new meaning to the phrase 'brain food,'" which the researcher did not find amusing.) While his sense of humor left something to be desired, the projects he was working on were fascinating. Lexie had learned that people's perceptions make up their realities much more than they might realize. She had to wonder as she sat here, running her fingers over her children's masterpieces of construction paper and bumpy, dried paint, if maybe this wasn't a dream, per se, but a perception her brain was turning into her reality. Maybe that's why it seemed so real.

Either that, or the vortex/genie explanation.

Just before Theo got back, Lexie found her desk from what had once been her home office. It was shoved against a wall in the basement, next to the washer and dryer. Clothes covered most of it, separated piles of her clothes and Theo's, and then miniature replicas for the twins. On the far end were various detergents, dryer sheets, spot cleaners. Even the drawers had been conquered by various files, old coupons and paid bill stubs, the household junk that gets saved just in case. Nowhere was there evidence of her journalism.

Lexie didn't give Theo a chance to come back in the house. When she saw him pull into the driveway, she pulled the front door closed behind her, the lock already set, and she clomped down the snowy porch. As she opened the passenger door, Theo asked, "We going somewhere?"

"Back to the train depot," she said, buckling up. "Let's return to the scene of the crime and see if we can't find some clues."

He pulled off again, and glanced at her a few times before reporting, "Kids are okay. They don't seem to know anything's wrong, except I stuck with the migraine story, you know, just easier. Your mom's going to call you in a couple hours to check in."

"Am I not a reporter at all anymore?" Lexie blurted out.

He frowned. "Should I be telling you that? Pretty sure science fiction rule number one is you're not allowed to know your own future. Or maybe it's that you're not supposed to mess with the time line."

"This isn't science fiction, and it's not a joke," said Lexie.

"Maybe it is. How would you know?"

"What about you?" she asked. "Are you still at the NYPL?"

His jaw flexed, and he said guardedly, "It's what pays our bills, Lex."

"Don't get so defensive."

"I'm just answering your question."

"Yeah," she said, "defensively."

"Well, forgive me," he said, his voice rising, "but even though you're new to this world, I've lived in it for a long time." He kneaded the steering wheel. "This is a very old argument for us, Lex."

"Since when is asking a question cause for argument?"

"Since about six years ago." They pulled up to a red light and Theo dropped his hands in his lap. He let his head fall back against the seat, keeping his eyes forward. "You mentioned the interview at *Swish* before?"

"Yeah?"

"You didn't take the job," he said. "You said they were unrealistic, wanted you to move out there and throw your whole life into upheaval. After that you hated all things *Swish,* and pretty soon that hatred seeped into anything having to do with the industry. You publicly rebuffed the Magsy awards when you didn't win—"

"I didn't win that?" she yipped. "Those creeps."

"You started taking on all these extra assignments, but you burned yourself out. You just kept trying to prove to everyone that even though you weren't winning awards or working for *Swish,* you were still a good reporter. It's like you were out for blood the way you did it. It got worse after the wedding, worse still when we had the kids." The light changed to green and Theo started up again. "Lexie Walker doesn't have to slow down for anything. You can handle it all, and all on your own."

Well, thought Lexie, that sounded disturbingly familiar. "Guess I'm not your superwoman after all, huh?" She realized there was a bite to her tone. She couldn't help it.

Theo hit the wheel. "God, Lex, how many times . . . You know, you blame everyone, everyone but yourself. Me most of all. But I wasn't the one who told you not to take the job. I wasn't even the one who proposed."

"I proposed to you?" she said, disappointed. She'd always been traditional when it came to the idea of engagements and weddings.

"You went from not wanting to hear about marriage at all to rushing us through the whole process," he said. "And that's what it felt like, a process. An assembly line or something that you'd set to high speed."

"If you were so upset by it, why didn't you stop things?"

"I tried," he exclaimed with a bemused laugh. "You weren't having it. I tried telling you it felt like your whole life had become a checklist: get engaged, get married, have kids, get more and more acclaim at work. You didn't want to hear it. You insisted I was wrong, that you loved your life, loved the pace, 'how wonderful it is that everything's working out.' Even though all of us could see you were spinning yourself into this frenzy."

"What do you mean, 'all of us'?"

"Me, your parents, Anna, Spark, Belinda—"

"And I didn't listen to any of you?" The car fishtailed on a patch of ice, and Lexie clutched the armrest. "Wanna slow it down there a little?" she said.

"We're fine," said Theo.

Normally, Lexie wouldn't have even mentioned anything. Driving on ice and snow was practically page one in the New York State driver's handbook for beginners. Fishtailing and skidding and getting your car unstuck from a pile of slush was second nature. But this was not her Theo. This Theo was frowzled. This Theo looked like he was giving up. Just as every driver in New York knew to keep the snow brush somewhere in the car year-round, they also knew you don't drive after a blizzard when you're lost in your emotions.

"Okay," said Lexie, "so I didn't listen to you guys. But why did you go through with the wedding if you didn't think it was right?"

"And there go the accusations again," he said.

"Not an accusation," she insisted. "Not an argument. I'm asking you. God, Theo, I'm trying to get hold of what's going on." The speedometer caught her eye. "It's thirty through here, and that's on a good day."

"I know what it is."

"Then why are you speeding?"

He shot her a look and gestured to the wheel with his right hand. "You wanna drive?"

"If I weren't in the middle of a delusion."

"You got fired, Lex."

She swallowed hard. "What?"

"Belinda tried talking you down," he said. "Spark tried. Even Stu. You got so bitter. You weren't exactly the most pleasant person to be around. And your work started to suffer. I had thought . . ." He pressed his lips together and shook his head.

"You thought what, Theo?" she prodded.

He said, "I thought the wedding would calm you down. And then kids. But everything just sort of blew up."

"I got fired"—she forced herself to form the words—"before or after the wedding? And the kids?"

"After," he said. "About, oh . . ." He sighed, thinking. "Yeah, the twins were about two and a half."

She was starting to feel numb, and so she defaulted to just trying to find out as much information as she could.

"Everyone else is still at *Upstate?*" she asked. "Do I, like, do monthly cocktails with the old gang, or do they all hate me?"

His response wasn't at all what she expected. She'd thought he'd say, "No one hates you," or "Water under the bridge," but instead he told her, "*Upstate* got bought out."

"Oh," she said in a small voice. She felt sad about that, like she had when, a few years back, her elementary school was levelled as part of redistricting.

"None of the Rothco publications have been doing great, but they sold *Upstate* and it got turned into some shoppers' guide. Far as I know, you haven't seen anyone you used to work with for years."

They pulled up to a stop sign and Theo flipped the turn signal down. Lexie said, "You wanna take a right here."

"No," said Theo. "Banks will get us there faster."

"Not when there's a storm. You think it's icy here, Banks'll be your own personal skating rink."

He threw the car into park and looked at her.

"Hey," she said, "I may be missing six years, but I know this town."

"You know the one good thing about all the heartache we've been through?" he snapped. "I thought you were really starting to learn to let other people have a say once in a while. Now you're sitting here at the beginning of all that again? I can't do it, Lex. Not again."

"So, what, I'm on my own?" she said, her frustration starting to take over. "I thought that was exactly my problem."

He snorted and shifted back into drive. "One of many," he shot back, turning left.

"All right, I know this is my first day on the job," said Lexie, "but I'm guessing that I didn't tank this marriage all on my own."

"Hey, I've taken plenty of responsibility."

"I wasn't even sure I wanted to get married," she yelled. "Obviously, I made the wrong choice."

Theo slammed on the brakes, sending the car into a spin. He threw a protective arm out over her, and she clutched the center console with one hand and the overhead grab handle with the other. For five seconds and an entire lifetime, the car lost control, until it slid off into a snowbank on the side of the road, facing the wrong direction.

No other traffic came their way. No other vehicles, people, or anything else had been in the way of the car. At a complete stop, Theo and Lexie stayed frozen in their positions, his arm over her, her stuck to the console and handle, for a few seconds. The only sounds were their shallow, terrified breaths, and the wind blowing outside.

"Are you okay?" Theo managed.

"Uh-huh," said Lexie, nodding. "You?"

"Yeah. I'm sorry."

"Me too."

"No," he said, "I mean I'm sorry for hitting the brakes like that. That was stupid on this ice." He wouldn't look at her. "I would never want to hurt you."

"Well," she said, "I'm sorry for the fight. I don't want to hurt you eith—"

"Lex, stop," he said quietly. "Where we are, at least, where I am with my Lexie, six years on from where you are, that's not how it works. We don't argue and say things we regret and then it all goes away with apologies."

Her terror melted into guilt for hurting him. "I wasn't thinking," she said. "I mean about saying marrying you was the wrong choice. I was mad, and it just popped out."

"It's not the first time you've said it."

Her heart sank. "Oh."

"And you know, it'd be bad enough if you just regretted me, but I'm pretty sure you regret the kids, too."

It made her feel terrible, what he said. She couldn't picture herself that way, entering into a union, bringing little lives into the world, beautiful little babies, and then regretting all of it. All because she'd burned out? Usually when she felt over-whelmed by work or life, she took advantage of her discount at The Spa Life outside Mamaroneck, where they loved her after her feature article about them bumped profits. Could she really become this person so changed from who she recog-nized?

Theo said, "I'll, um, see if I can't push us back onto the road. You wanna come over here and hit the gas when I say?"

She considered him. Exactly what role had he played in all of this? Talk about changed. This Theo was a complete stranger. A man who married her and had children because he thought that would solve a problem? What had happened to the two of them? She was beginning to feel like they'd wandered down this road six years before, got off track, and instead of just reversing, tried continuing forward but taking this odd turn and that dirt path, until they were so far from home they couldn't even recognize their surroundings anymore.

"Lex?" he said. "Sure you're okay?"

But she couldn't ask him any of this. He'd just jump down her throat again about accusing him or throwing blame. She nodded. "Fine."

He pushed open his door. "Give me a couple minutes to clear away what I can. I'll give you the signal, and then you . . ."

She resisted the urge to roll her eyes, sitting through his instructions. She was the one who'd taught him how to shovel out of a snowbank two months after they started dating. Apparently, he'd gone from telling her she was superwoman to thinking she was clueless.

While she waited for him to dig out—luckily, he had a shovel in the trunk—she rested her head against the coolness of the side window, thinking of earlier at the house when she'd felt such a rush of love for him. Was it possible to be so in love and yet want to throttle him for the way he was acting? She wondered if she ever went back to her old life, whether they'd even have a chance at happiness.

She closed her eyes as the questions hit her, worsening her headache, like each one was a tiny little man with a sledge-hammer, pounding her brain. Suddenly, she jolted herself awake as she felt the car stop. In a split second she figured Theo had gotten them going again on his own and she had dozed off. A huge yawn swelled and she clenched her eyes, stretching. "Are we here?" she asked, but there was no an-swer. She rubbed her eyes, asking louder, "Are we . . ." Then she looked out the window. "Where are we?"

Outside the window were palm trees, blowing in the after-noon sun, in front of a sprawling house. Lexie, shocked, could barely move, but her eyes flitted around. She wore a light blue linen skirt suit. She was in the back of a taxi.

The driver turned around in his seat and said, not unpleas-antly, "You wanted 9437 Soledad Street, correctamundo? The carriage can take you elsewhere, m'lady, but the horse's me-ter's a-running."

Lexie plastered herself against the cracked leather seat. "Oh, boy," she whimpered.

Chapter
Twenty

"What's going on? What's going on?" Lexie muttered to herself like a mantra. At least this felt more like a dream—still as real as anything, the air conditioning as cool as it had been not two days before when she'd been in L.A., but she'd jumped here, suddenly, just the same as in dreams. Maybe that meant she could wake herself up after all.

The driver looked like he'd been around the block about as many times as his cab, his face as leathery and creased as the seats. He'd obviously overheard her muttering, "What's going on?" and he seemed to be no stranger to peculiar fares. Still turned around in his seat, he said amicably, "Well, miss, allow me to attempt to explain the sitchiation. You are in what we call a taxicab. A driver, that would be *moi*, gives you a ride to your destination, i.e. this lovely little domicile we have here." He gestured out the window to the house. "Then—and this is the most important part, I can't stress that enough—you pay me money for said ride."

"Pay you," Lexie said, feeling a little dizzy.

"With an eighteen percent gratuity if you feel my services have been more than adequate."

"Um," she said, her voice and words both failing her, "I don't . . ."

The driver cleared his throat and pointed to her purse. "We take cash or credit. We do not take excuses."

"Right," she said. Entirely by rote, Lexie opened a purse she didn't recognize and pulled out a wallet she didn't recognize. But inside, there was her license with her picture, issued in California with an expiration date ten years in the future. The address was 9437 Soledad Street. The name on the license was Lexie Moore, her maiden name, and she had no wedding band on. She asked, "Hey, how long are California driver's licenses good for?"

"Five years," he said with more of an edge to his tone. "My license is square, m'lady, and if you're thinking an expired license means you don't gotta pay—"

"No, that's not what I meant." Lexie did some quick math. Whatever had happened to Theo and the snowbank, it seemed she was still stuck somewhere in her future.

The driver cleared his throat. Aware that she was severely trying this poor man's patience, Lexie rushed to go through her wallet, and thankfully found plenty of cash to take care of the ride, plus tip. She shoved the bills into his waiting hand.

"Whoa," he said, his tone back to its amicable note. "This is too much, m'lady. I can't—"

"Merry Christmas," she said faintly as she got out of the car. Strings of lights and lawn decorations on most of the houses around her confirmed the season, even though her own house had none. She pushed on a pair of sunglasses she'd found in the purse. It felt like she was floating, totally removed from reality.

"Well, Merry Christmas to you too!" the driver called out. Lexie was halfway up the walk when she heard behind her, "Hey, ah, m'lady?"

She turned back. The driver had opened his door and was perched there, one foot on the pavement and his head poked up over the roof, watching her. "You need me to call someone for you? Or you want me to wait here and take you someplace else? Like, I don't know, ah, a doctor's office? Hospital or something? Excuse me for saying so, but you're looking a little what my uncle Nestor calls discombobumatated."

"Thanks," she said with a vague wave. "I'm fine." Then she turned back to the house, staring up at it and clutching her purse strap in both hands in front of her. She heard the taxi's door close and the car drive away.

Lexie just stood there, halfway up the walk, staring. She seldom did this, stood still, doing nothing, and even in her current predicament it felt nice. The sun beat down on her. The top of her head was starting to feel too warm, as was her suit jacket, under which she was starting to perspire. But the standing still, letting her eyes relax and dilate a bit, that was nice.

"Yoo-hoo," called a woman from the porch next door. "Lexie? You all right?"

The woman, in flip-flops, a bathing suit, sunglasses, and a white cover-up, bounded down her porch steps and cut across the lush lawn. She held a tall glass full of a lemony-looking drink and wore a raffia hat, whose brim measured about the same circumference as the Griffith Observatory planetarium dome. Her chestnut skin and dark, spiraled hair gleamed in the sunlight, and Lexie swore there was something familiar about her.

"I know you, don't I?" Lexie asked when the woman had reached her.

"Well, I should hope so," she said. "We've only lived next door to each other for six years. You feeling okay, hon? What're you doing home so early?"

"It's not Christmas Eve?"

The woman laughed. "Sure it is. But when's that stopped you from working 'til half past midnight?"

With the mention of time, Lexie glanced down and noticed a watch on the woman's left wrist. It was a beautiful silver piece, big and ornate with the flourishes and tiny dials characteristic of a chronograph. Yet it seemed entirely out of place for an afternoon of sunbathing.

"What's your name?" Lexie asked.

The woman lowered her glasses and gave Lexie a look of real concern. "Baby, it's me. Faye. Why don't we get you out of this sun?" She took Lexie's arm and started toward the door.

It was on the tip of her tongue: "I'd rather be alone." But Lexie stopped herself from saying it. She needed answers, she needed guidance, and if there was one thing she was starting to learn, she wasn't going to get that sitting in a room by herself.

"They're saying it's going to be a record-setting year, almost ninety tomorrow," Faye was saying. "Perfect beach weather, though. Course I don't need to tell you that."

"Why?" said Lexie, stopping again and facing her.

"Why what?"

"Why don't you need to tell me that?"

"Well, you know any news long before I do."

The wheels turned for Lexie and she felt hope rise in her chest. "You mean I'm a reporter?"

"Okay, now you're just joshing me." Faye adjusted her hold on Lexie's arm and started them walking again.

"Please," said Lexie, but she didn't stop this time. Whatever Faye wanted to do was fine, as long as she kept talking. "What kind of reporting do I do?"

"You're the senior political correspondent at *Swish*," Faye said. "My, it must have been a hard day if you need this big an ego boost."

A goofy grin spread across Lexie's face. "Well, I'm just all kinds of living the dream, huh?"

They reached the front door, and Lexie found keys in her purse, though it took her a couple tries before she matched the right one to the front door lock. The alarm was another issue, though. She and Faye took off their sunglasses and stood before the keypad in the entryway as it beeped like a time bomb. Faye stepped forward when it was evident Lexie was clueless, and she punched in six digits. "Good thing I'm the one takes care of this place when you're off hounding the suits in Washington."

"You take care of it?" said Lexie, peering around at the tall ceilings and wide rooms. "I don't hire someone?"

"You don't trust anyone," said Faye. "Took you four years to trust me, and I still say you only gave in because I made you my maid of honor for wedding number three." She thought about it. "Four? Wedding number four, that was it."

"Maid of honor," Lexie mumbled as she meandered around. She dragged her fingertips along a glass media table in the foyer. The living room was pristine, with ivory-colored furniture, throw pillows, and fixtures. The floors looked brand new. She wandered back toward the kitchen, where every stainless-steel appliance was spotless. She smelled no leftover coffee or cooking aromas hanging in the air from last night's dinner or this morning's breakfast. No pets came out to greet her, certainly no children, and there were no photographs in sight. Nothing on the refrigerator door, or hanging on walls, or nestled on the mantle. Lexie loved keeping photos of her friends and family out where she could always see them.

"Faye," she said, "do you know Theo? Ever met him?"

Faye had slowly followed Lexie as she walked through the place, her flip-flops slapping a rhythm fit for a dirge. "Theo? Can't say as I have."

"I never even mentioned him?" Lexie said in a small voice. Her fleeting joy about her job was retracted like a bogus article.

"Why don't I make you a cup of tea?" said Faye. "Nice, relaxing tea. Then you can tell me all about this Theo fellow. Did you meet him at work?"

Lexie flopped into one of the two kitchen chairs and leaned on the circular glass table. She patted the tabletop in front of the other seat, and Faye took her cue, sitting down. "You wanna hear just about the craziest story ever?" Lexie asked her. "Because apparently I don't have Theo here"—the words stabbed her heart—"but I need some help. Even if it's help from a virtual . . ." She noticed it then, and halfheartedly finished her sentence. "Stranger. Faye, are you the attendant from the train depot outside Whimsy?"

"The what from the who?" she laughed.

"You are," said Lexie.

"Darling, I'm really starting to worry," said Faye. "You know, my daughter and her whole family had the flu a few weeks back. You sure you haven't caught—"

"I'm not letting this go," said Lexie. "It's you. You're the key to all this."

Faye gave her that motherly smile. "No, Lexie. You are."

Instead of feeling angry or duped, as she might with Faye's admission, all she felt was desperation to get back home and gratitude that someone could finally, truly, help her.

"How . . . how do I get back?" Lexie fumbled, grabbing for one question out of the scurrying flock.

"Why would you want to go back?" said Faye. She held her arms out and looked around the room. "You got what you always wanted."

Lexie shook her head. "No, I always wanted to be a successful reporter, but I want Theo in my life, too."

"Well, you got what you wanted in marrying Theo, too," said Faye. "Either scenario ended exactly the same. Everyone left you alone. Just as you always want."

The realization pushed Lexie back in her chair. She just breathed and stared at her hands in her lap as the words sank in. "I always thought I could juggle it all," said Lexie, "and in trying to do that I've lost everyone I ever cared about." Then an idea occurred to her.

"I've been thinking of this all wrong. All wrong. Juggling isn't about keeping all the balls in the air at once. I mean, it isn't, is it? It's about balance. You have to let go of one while another is in your grasp."

Faye said, "And if you're lucky, you even have a partner you can throw to sometimes."

All the faces of all her friends and family rushed into Lexie's mind, and she felt a swell of love and gratitude for each and every one. "Or you might even have a whole team." She nodded with fresh determination, and rephrased her earlier question. "Okay. How do I get back so I can fix things? I have to fix things, Faye. And I think I know how to, but I have to get back."

Faye patted her hand. "You ever notice how snow at Christmas is magical, while the rest of the winter it's just snow? It blows on in sometime in December, and brings that feeling of goodwill that fills your heart at Christmastime. It makes us older folks feel like children again, and fills us all with wonder."

Lexie knew those words. "That's the story of Whimsy," she said with a touch of awe. "The blizzard that kept me at the depot. Was that the Spirit of Whimsy?"

But Faye didn't have a chance to answer, for Lexie stood up when she caught a glimpse of the unbelievable outside her window. "You've gotta be kidding me," she whispered.

With a grin as wide as a child's, Lexie ran out the front door. Record-breaking heat or not, there was no mistaking the white, fluffy stuff falling from the sky.

"This is insane," Lexie cried out in pure joy, her face turned upward. She twirled around as the snow fell furiously. She caught cold flakes on her tongue and closed her eyes, reveling in it as it melted against her skin. In no time at all, her hair dampened and clung to her cheeks. Her suit and skin were soaked.

"That holiday snow," Faye called out behind her. "No magic like it."

Lexie opened her eyes and stopped twirling.

The snow was gone.

There she was, back in the train depot.

With about a dozen or so people stopped in their tracks, staring at her.

But she didn't give them a second thought. She looked down at her clothes, and then behind her where she'd left her bag, and instantly she knew she was back in her own time. At that thought, of "time," Lexie glanced up at the wall clock over the front doors, and she saw it was approaching eight a.m. She rushed over to the two chairs she'd shoved together earlier and ran her hands over their smooth wooden arms. She breathed in deep the faint, lingering oil from over a century of trains coming and going here. This most definitely was not part of the dream, or fever, or bad fruitcake that had come with the meal on the plane, or whatever it was that had tricked her brain into that alternate reality.

Or maybe, just maybe, she thought with a tiny giggle, maybe it really had been magic. And if it had been, maybe this was still part of it. Maybe the magic was always here.

Lexie spun around toward the attendant counter. How wonderful it would be to talk to Faye about all this. But she was nowhere. Lexie's heart dropped a little, but only a little. She had a feeling Faye was never really all that far away.

The attendant who was on duty, a young man with ginger hair and a smattering of freckles across his nose, came over to her when they made eye contact. He said, "Do you need any help, miss?"

Automatically, Lexie said, "No, thanks, I'm—" Then she pressed her lips together, and with bright eyes corrected herself. "Yes. Thank you. I need help. I need help!" she cried out blissfully, tossing her arms up.

She ignored the stares and the expression on the attendant's face, which teetered between amusement and fear, and she grabbed her phone from her purse.

Lexie shook a victorious fist as soon as she heard the ringback signal, the sign that cell phones were working again. Now she just needed to connect. "Please, please, please pick up," she whispered as she shut out the rest of the world around her.

"Please," she whispered. "Please."

obin's eyes kept wandering out the apartment's front window as Anna tried pulling her attention back to their game of Christmas *Pictionary*. Really, it was Christmas "Try to doodle holiday movies to get the other to guess the title," a time-killing distraction. Robin was nervous about tonight, and Anna had turned into a five-year-old around midnight and would stay this way, bouncing off the walls, straight through today and Christmas Day.

"I'll see Theo at our mom's house tomorrow," Anna was chirruping, sitting on the floor, hugging her knees to her chest, and rocking excitedly in between doodles. "I hope he and Lexie have made up. Then we'll stop by Dad's, and then go over to our grandparents', and all the cousins will be there. I can't wait to see them all. You sure you don't want to come with me?"

"Hmm?" Robin was tucked onto the couch, her feet on the coffee table. Her gaze floated back over to Anna. "I'm sorry. What were you saying?"

"Do you want to come tomorrow?" Anna spun the sketchpad around so Robin could see it.

"Bells of St. Mary's," she guessed.

"Yup."

"My turn." She leaned over with another glimpse outside, and snapped up the pad and pencil.

"So is that a no?" said Anna with a touch of disappointment. "About coming tomorrow?"

"Christmas is quiet day for me," said Robin. "You know that. But thanks for the offer."

"You can be quiet and still come with me."

"How?" said Robin. "You have a little less than a football stadium's worth of extended family. How is that quiet?"

"We can find a room to shove you in. Hardly anyone goes into the attic crawlspace on Christmas."

Robin laughed. "Sounds like a blast." This was essentially the same conversation they had every year when Anna invited her to all her Christmases. From year to year, the Walkers changed up locations and who went to whose house in what order, but there were always a handful of very merry stops. Robin turned the pad to face her.

"Uh . . ." Anna squinted at it. *"Three Bumpy People and a Flag?* Ooh, are those Wise Men? *Three Bumpy Wise Men and a Flag?* Classic flick."

"*Miracle on 34th Street*," Robin said. "What flag? That's a street sign. Street sign and there's Santa, and what's-her-face, Natalie Wood, and the mom."

"Well, it boggles the mind how I didn't get that."

"I know." With a huff, Robin let her arms fall to her sides. Her eyes went back to the window. "What time is it?"

"Time to get a watch because I'm getting annoyed with you asking me that every twelve seconds." Anna took the sketchpad back, pencil poised.

"When Scott dropped me home last night he said he was going to call when they got into town. It's almost lunchtime. They were supposed to be in Whimsy by now."

"You do remember a snowstorm came through here last night, right?" said Anna. "Travel's not going to be great."

"But the streets are pretty clear," said Robin. "Sun's shining."

Anna shrugged. "They said there was either going to be a break in the weather or it was going to get snowy again toward the city. Maybe it's starting up where Scott is. Give him a call."

"I tried," said Robin. "Went to voicemail." Nervously, she bounced her feet against the table. "You don't think he changed his mind, do you?"

"Without calling you?"

"I don't know if I feel sad about him not coming, or relieved."

"Understandable," said Anna. She spun the pad around. "Here."

Robin looked at it. *"Elves Gone Mad?"*

"Gremlins."

"That's so not a Christmas movie."

"Of course it is."

The house phone rang. Robin leaped to her feet. "Why is he calling the house phone?" She didn't think he even had that number.

Anna leaned over and grabbed the handset from the floor next to her. "Hello?" she said, then shook her head at Robin. "Hey, Theo." She unfolded herself and took the call out of the room.

Her offer resurfaced in Robin's thoughts, and as she sank back into the couch cushions, Robin found herself considering going over to the Walkers' family Christmases after all this year. It was true, for a long time she'd enjoyed a more sedate holiday. With her family in Texas, she'd gotten used to it. Flying was not Robin's favorite pastime to begin with, not since the time in college she'd flown home and smoke starting intermittently appearing around the cabin and then disappearing. The flight attendants hadn't seemed concerned, even though no one seemed to know where it was coming from or how to stop it, but it was all Robin could do to keep her lunch down, particularly when the guy sitting next to her decided to confess all his rather toothless sins in case they plummeted to their deaths. Every few minutes, he turned wild-eyed to her, his white-knuckled hands clutching the armrests, and would say something like, "When I was fifteen I threw a shoe at the microwave because I was mad and I broke the window on it, and I told my parents it just exploded and I had no idea why."

Besides, flying from the north anytime between October and April brought with it the very real possibility of weather delays or cancellations. Even before the smoke incident, Robin had spent her fair share of hours on the runway or in the terminal, waiting for deicing or mechanical checks. She'd even spent a night here and there crunched up in an airport chair. All of that, to have a few days with family with whom she could generate about eight and a half minutes of conversation.

Robin usually liked her Christmas Days. She curled up with a good book, ate lots of cookies and ice cream, opened the presents her family sent, and then later in the day they'd call to thank her for the presents she sent to them. In the evening she'd treat herself to a double feature at home, and once or twice she'd even gotten herself dressed up nice and gone to the movies. Just now, though, the idea of kids running around and big meals and shouts of joy over getting the best gift in the world, that pulled at her a little, and then she found herself imagining all of that joy set in Scott's big living room.

What if his father did end up turning around? She imagined it all. Tonight Mr. Donovan would turn to her with tears in his eyes as the performers took their last bows, and he'd say, "I was so wrong to head down this bitter path, and I see the error of my ways. Thank you, Robin, for helping Scott, and for helping me." And then Scott would turn to her, and they would finish the kiss they'd started last night, and he'd tell her he'd wait forever for her until she figured out all she needed to about YOPE and acting and her place in the world. Then doves would appear and all the children would break out into song—

The doorbell rang, nipping Robin's daydream just as the children in her head were forming a Busby Berkeley dance number. She jumped up again and hopped around the table and a recliner toward the front window. A taxi sat at the curb, but Robin couldn't tell from here if Scott was at the door.

Anna came back out from her room. "Was that the door?"

"What if it's Scott?" Robin looked down at herself. "I'm in sweats and I have no makeup on."

Anna gasped. "Oh, my! Then he can't see you, or else the elders will have you both expelled from the village!"

"Anna, come on."

"You look fine. You look cute. Guys like mussed."

"Mussed?"

The bell rang again.

"Okay," said Anna, "I will get the door."

"But don't let him up here."

"You wanna put a bag on your head in case he needs to talk to you?"

"That's not a bad thought."

Anna put the phone down on the kitchen counter and headed toward the stairs. "By the way, the show at the hospital is off."

"Okay," said Robin. Then she got her head out of the taxi downstairs and realized what Anna had said. "Wait, what?" she called down the stairwell.

"Snow just hit New York," she called back. "The actors can't get out. Trains are shut down." She opened the front door and said, "Oh, hello."

When Robin heard a woman's voice respond, she poked her head out over the banister to eavesdrop.

"My name's Frankie. My brother Scott is friends with Robin. Is she here?"

"Frankie?" Robin called down. "Come on up."

Anna introduced herself as they climbed the stairs, and a second later Frankie rounded the landing. Her long twists stuck out from under a stylish green fedora. She talked as she kicked the snow off her boots. "Sorry to drop in on you like this, but I really wanted to talk to you and I didn't know if you'd answer a call from a number you didn't recognize."

"No problem," said Robin, gesturing for her to come inside. "Is, um, everyone else down in the cab?"

"No, they're in a different cab by now, probably, and I'd imagine they're heading to the Orange-Clove Marketplace?" she said, questioning the name. Robin nodded. "Yeah. They don't know what happened to me. I mean, they do now. I called Scott on the way and let him know I'd meet them in a little while, but I sort of ran off when we got to the depot and grabbed my own cab. I had to get at least a few minutes with you before we see you tonight. By the way, we heard on the train that we were the last one out, so I have a feeling we'll be spending the whole night in town. Any chance you think there'll be room at the Whimsy Inn?" She laughed. "Or, you know, is there a spare manger around?"

"Worst case, you're all welcome to stay here," said Robin. "It'll be a little snug, but we can manage." Anna nodded her agreement. "But what are you doing here? And how do you know where I live?"

"Oh, yeah." Frankie fished around in her peacoat pocket and pulled out Robin's YOPE card. "Scott gave it to me in case I need your expertise sometime. Which is entirely possible. Do you do weddings? I mean, not my own, not yet anyway, but I have this friend . . ." Frankie waved her hands frantically in front of her as though cleaning the slate. "Not important right now."

Frankie clutched Robin's hands, and peered into her eyes. "You really don't know me, but I'm pretty good at reading people. I'm sorry if this is ridiculously forward. Well, it is. It is ridiculously forward. But I'm afraid if I don't say it before Dad says another stupid thing, he'll ruin it all and the Donovan family will never get to see you again."

Also pretty good at reading people and situations, Anna excused herself to go to her room, giving them some privacy.

Robin smiled her thanks as she walked off, and then pulled out chairs at the kitchen counter for herself and Frankie.

"The fact is," said Frankie, "I think you and my brother click really well. It's none of my business at all, but he can't stop talking about you, and I haven't seen him light up in ages the way he did at brunch. Please don't let my father push you away. He's a lost man, a sad man. A long time ago, he took his final curtain call, left the stage, and never went back. When he did that, he sold his dreams. Sometimes I wish I could give them back to him. I keep hoping he'll come back to us, but I don't let his cynicism control my life or the people I want in it. I think Scott's starting to come around to that too. Now if this is totally out of line and neither of you is thinking about dating each other and I'm way off base here, then tell me to shut up. Obviously I misread the play and I'll be happy to back off. But I like you. At least be *my* friend," she laughed. "But whatever you do, please don't let it be a decision made because of my father."

Frankie's impassioned speech warmed Robin's heart, and she reached out and hugged her. She'd felt an immediate connection with Frankie at brunch, and now she had no doubt that they would be friends, regardless of what happened with Scott. Robin started to tell her this, and tell her about last night at the tree lighting, when she stopped short. Coming through like a freight train was an idea that halted all other traffic for the time being.

"This is going to sound crazy," said Robin, "but I have an idea, and if it works . . ." She jumped off the seat and made a beeline for Anna's door. "Hey in there, can you come out?"

Robin turned back to Frankie. "We're going to need your help—"

"What's up?" said Anna, opening the door.

Robin thumbed back at her. "Her help, Scott's help . . . pretty much everybody's help if we're going to pull this off."

Frankie jumped off her seat too and clapped her hands. "I like the sound of it. Pull what off?"

"Anna just told me they cancelled the show at the hospital," said Robin. "The weather saw to that."

"Oh, no," said Frankie. "Those kids are gonna be so disappointed."

Holding up a finger, Robin said, "Hang on, though. I think I have a way to kill two birds with one stone . . . or two partridges with one pear tree."

"I am up for anything that gets me out of the house and my mind off of how many decades it is 'til Christmas morning," said Anna.

"What're we going to do?" asked Frankie.

A slow grin formed on Robin's lips as she thought about what Mr. Donovan had mocked at brunch. "Why, we're going to stage a show in the old barn. Frankie, Anna, we need a Christmas review, and we need it now."

Chapter
Twenty-Two

ach year, Charlotte and René's Christmas Eve party was at once a source of merriment and of pain for Margot. Being around all those people triggered Margot's anxiety, despite that she knew and loved most of them. But Charlotte and René both understood her need to take a breather from the festivities, so they were used to Margot disappearing into the guest bedroom for a half hour here or there over the course of the rather long and eventful night. They set it up for her: a DVD player with new movies were set on a small table, paperbacks next to them, the bed was freshly made with a throw blanket draped over it. Charlotte even put out poinsettias and a pitcher of lemon water with a glass on the nightstand. Throughout the year, whenever she had the chance, Margot tried to do all she could for Charlotte and René and the kids in appreciation of all they did for her.

This year, of course, Margot had the added nerves of seeing Gavin and contending with whatever these feelings were for him that had popped up from nowhere over the past twenty-four hours. She was still sure she didn't want to jump into dating. By the same token, a little dark snarl of apprehension had formed in the pit of her stomach when she heard that Jenna Baker might swoop in and snag Gavin up. Even her thinking about it had changed. "Swoop in" and "snag him up"? Those weren't phrases used by a friend to discuss another friend's love life.

This was precisely the reason that Margot and Kyle stood frozen on the Lejeunes' front porch at five thirty, facing the door, in their coats, holding presents, looking like a tableau of "Mother and Son Ready to Enter Party."

"Are we going in?" Kyle asked with a sidelong glance at his mother.

"Not yet," came Margot's yip of a reply.

She hadn't told Kyle about her walk with Gavin, or her strange feelings, or the saxophone ornament. She had to process all of this herself before bringing him into the loop. He had no idea, then, why they were just standing there, which had come through loud and clear with his increasingly impatient sighs. The snow had picked up a little, and temperatures were dropping. Clouds covered the moonlight, so it seemed even darker and colder. All the windows were alight behind their frosty panes, and the big, bright Christmas tree twinkled. Friends and family and music filled the place. Laughter and boisterous merrymaking over hot toddies and pumpkin pie had only just begun.

"How 'bout now?" said Kyle.

"Nope."

He turned to Margot. "Are you punishing me?"

Margot turned to him. "In 1976, there was a band called Odd Man Rush. They were invited to a party one night and things got out of hand. The flautist . . . well, let's just say you can't just jump into a party. Otherwise, you could lose a lip. I'm just saying."

Kyle nodded. "Well, me and my lips are all about living on the edge."

Before Margot could stop him, Kyle opened the door and ducked inside. She tried grabbing the back of his coat to pull him out again, but he was too quick. Besides, Charlotte saw them right away.

"My darlings," she called out, arms wide open. Her crocheted sweater was dressed up tonight, a royal blue with reflective thread over a trumpet skirt. On his way past her, Kyle kissed her cheek and gave her his coat and the presents when she asked for them. Then he disappeared into the crowd.

Charlotte hugged Margot and said, "He looks so dapper in that suit and tie."

"Oh, I know," said Margot, handing Charlotte her coat and presents as well. "He's starting to turn into a little man. Don't get me wrong, I'm thrilled to see him growing up, but I'd still like to know who I see about slowing things down a little."

"Tell me about it," said Charlotte. She set the gifts on a table with a thank-you and kept the coats in her arms. "Veronica's in this velvet dress tonight . . . well, you'll see her. She swears she's not trying to impress a boy, but I recognize the signs." She paused and looked Margot over. "Apparently she's not the only one."

Margot held her arms out and glanced down at herself. "What? I always dress for your party."

"Not this nice."

"Thanks a lot!"

"I mean, of course you always look good," said Charlotte. Her eyes flitted around the party, and she grabbed Margot's hand. "Come on."

She pulled Margot into the bathroom off the hallway, and locked the door. "You know," said Margot, "if you're going to hide out with me and avoid the crowd, we really should sneak off to the guestroom. The hostess here does a fabulous job of tricking it out for me."

"You look amazing," Charlotte accused, pointing at her.

Margot tried grabbing her coat, which was still over Charlotte's arm. "Gimme it back."

"No."

"It's cold. I want it back."

"It's a thousand degrees in here," said Charlotte. "We didn't even have to light the fire."

"I didn't have anything else to wear."

"What about what you always wear? Besides, you know the dress code ranges from jeans to red carpet. And I know you have jeans. Margot, you look beautiful."

Margot smoothed her dress. It had long bell sleeves with a chiffon skirt that cascaded all the way to the floor. A fluttery V neckline scooped around into a stand-up collar at the nape of her neck. The color, a piercing sky blue, made her slate eyes shine and brought out the blond highlights she'd added to cover the gray in her ash brown hair. She'd worn her loose curls in a low knot, which rested against the dress's dramatic collar.

She whispered, "Kyle said I look beautiful too."

Charlotte whispered back, "Is this because of Gavin?"

"No," Margot yelped, and Charlotte flinched.

"Guess we're done whispering," she said.

"I just wanted to celebrate," said Margot. "I haven't worn this in ages. I feel a little more at peace about Darren, so I wanted to wear this." Yes, the idea of Gavin had danced through her mind when she picked this out of the back of her closet. But she could genuinely say to her cousin and friend, "I wore it for me."

"I'm so happy for you, sweetie," said Charlotte, giving her another hug. "And you're not getting your coat back until the end of the night." With that, she bustled out the door.

Margot took a breath and then followed her, but she didn't get far when she heard Gavin's bubbly voice behind her. "I had no idea Ginger Rogers was going to be at this party."

301

She turned slowly, her head shyly down. Then she lifted her gaze to meet his. His whole demeanor changed. A droll, chummy grin faded as stars lit in his eyes. "Wow," he breathed. "I mean, hi. You look amazing." A flush crept into his cheeks.

When he leaned forward to give her a friendly kiss hello on the cheek, Margot caught the faintest hint of cologne, like leather but lighter, fresher. He wore a navy blue suit that looked like it'd been made just for him. "You look . . ." said Margot, then had to swallow as her throat had apparently turned into a desert. "You look great too."

"I look even better with my fedora, but we're inside, so it's wasting away in the front closet with my coat," he said. "If the fashion gurus made the rules, a gentleman would never have to take his fedora off indoors."

"Yeah, why is that?" said Margot. "An outdoor hat, sure, but a fedora is just a classic accessory."

"Thank you," he said. "Well, I know I said I wouldn't monopolize you, but can I get you a drink? Slice of pie? Cookie?"

"I don't think a whole minute constitutes monopolizing me," said Margot. "But, you know, the clock is ticking."

"Oh, then we better hurry up on that drink." He stuck out his arm for her to take, which she did, and they headed for the kitchen.

"Cookies," said Margot. "That's new."

"I brought them."

"Aren't you a Renaissance man? Curler, music lover, philosopher, stylish, and he bakes, too."

"Ah, OC Fare did the baking, let's be clear. You don't want me anywhere near an oven. I could lose my eyebrows."

"Better than losing a lip," said Margot.

"What?"

"Nothing."

Gavin ladled a cup of punch for her at Margot's request, while she picked out two frosted sugar cookies in the shape of wreaths. She offered him one. "Wreath?"

"I'm usually more of a bell man myself, but hey, let's go crazy."

They commented on how lovely the whole spread was. Charlotte's love of baking and cooking came through as it did every year. The almond aroma of homemade *turrón* intoxicated Margot, and the *Roscón de Reyes* had already been cut, the cake's ring shape resembling more of a capital C now, but of course it still made her mouth water. Half a dozen other dishes, some sweet, a couple savory, filled the rest of the kitchen's ample island.

As she and Gavin were debating whether to try the marzipan or the mince-meat *galets* soup, René's tall figure appeared at Margot's arm. "*Mon chérie,* you are looking like the doves that fly this evening. You must save me a dance. Gavin, if I can steal you away *pour un moment,* I would like to introduce you to Jenna, the woman I was talking about to you?"

With a jerk of his head, René signaled where to look. Margot peered at Jenna. She was too tall, for starters. Her nose was too straight. And she must have had a ton of makeup on, because no one's skin outside of a baby's was that flawless. Immediately, as those thoughts passed through Margot's head, she felt like a creep. She was not one of *those* people, catty about other women. The truth was Margot didn't really know Jenna. But if Charlotte thought enough of her to try fixing her up with Gavin, she was probably a lovely person.

Gavin looked a little reluctant, but he said to Margot, "I guess I'll see you after. Maybe I can have a dance later, Ginger?"

"Sure," Margot managed.

He gave her another glance, then started walking away with René.

"Ornament!" cried Margot.

Gavin, René, and eight or nine other people in the immediate vicinity turned to her. Kyle, who had been on the other side of the room, was one of them. A moment later, most of them resumed their conversations. Gavin came back over to her. "That's not, like, my new nickname or anything, is it?"

"I just wanted to thank you again," she said. Vaguely, she was aware that Kyle was walking toward them.

"You're welcome again," said Gavin. "Quite welcome."

"That's . . . It's a lovely ornament," she said as Kyle reached them. He stood off to the side a bit. "It means so much. I have to tell you that. The music is so moving, and the lyrics are pure poetry." She put a hand to her heart. "Already, it holds a very special place."

"Mom," Kyle snapped.

She jumped a little at the startling outburst. "What?"

"I thought you were done with this. I'm sorry," Kyle said to Margot and Gavin both, "but it's just an ornament. Please just stop. You're putting so much stock in it and it's just a little trinket with a song lyric."

Immediately, Margot realized Kyle thought she was talking about the ornament Darren had left for her. She said to Gavin, "Kyle doesn't understand—"

"Yes, I do," said Kyle. "I'm not a little kid anymore, and I thought we talked about this. Please don't disregard my feelings."

She turned to face him fully, put her hands on his shoulders, and looked him straight in the eyes. "I'm not disregarding anything," she said.

"Oh, yeah, right."

"You're causing a scene, Kyle," she said calmly but firmly.

At that, his shoulders sagged. "I'm sorry," he said. "I just don't want you living in the past anymore. I thought we—"

"We did talk about it," she said. "And I'm not living in the past. I wasn't talking about the ornament your father gave me. Gavin stopped by last night and gave me a little Christmas remembrance that happened to be a musical ornament."

"Oh."

"Yeah."

"Sorry about that."

"Well, you know, next time eavesdrop a little longer before you take my head off, okay?"

Kyle thought about it. "Does it play anything good?"

She smiled and shook her head at him. "Yes. It's this little saxoph—" As she spoke, she turned back toward Gavin, but he was gone. Her eyes roamed wildly around the party, and she found him, by the front door, talking to Jenna.

"Mom?" said Kyle. "It's a saxophone?"

"Yeah. Honey, why don't you go find your cousins?"

"Look, I really am sorry," he said.

René appeared again, next to Gavin, and handed him his coat and fedora.

"I know I shouldn't have butted in like that," Kyle continued.

Gavin put on the coat and shook Jenna's hand. He started for the door, but Jenna stopped him and said something to René.

"It's just I thought you were over here ditching Gavin—I mean, Mr. Aberline . . ."

Jenna thumbed toward the front door and said something, and Gavin shrugged and nodded and said something back.

Margot grabbed Kyle's shoulders again and planted a kiss on his cheek. "Honey, it's fine. I'll be back soon, okay?"

In a flurry of chiffon, she rushed through the kitchen to the hall to the front door. "Excuse me," she said to Jenna. "Can I borrow him a minute?"

Without waiting for an answer, Margot grabbed Gavin's hand and led him outside to the front walk. "Are you nuts?" he said. "It's freezing out here."

Margot hugged herself. "Yes. Yes, it is. But I had to talk to you alone a minute. Kyle doesn't know what he's talking about. Well, he didn't know what he was talking about. Now he knows but . . ." As she babbled, Gavin put his coat around her shoulders and Margot closed it around her. "Thank you," she said.

"Look," said Gavin, "I'm happy you seem more at ease with this friendship thing, but if Kyle isn't okay with it, I'm certainly not going to push."

"No, see, that's what I—"

"And I don't think you should push him, either," he said. "Kyle's wrong, he *is* still a kid. The last thing he needs is some unwelcome father figure in his life."

"Actually, he's the one who—"

"Please, let me finish," said Gavin. "I don't want to be a distraction. I want to be your friend, maybe a pretty special friend, but if Kyle's not on board with that, then maybe some-day in the future."

Margot kissed him. She up and grabbed his lapel, pulled him close, pursed her lips, and kissed him smack on the mouth.

Passionate, it was not. Seconds later, she let him go. But it was the first real kiss she'd had in a long, long time. Her heart raced, her breath puffed in front of her in the cold, and all at once she felt exhilarated and just a little bit nauseous.

"Well," said Gavin, and he cleared his throat. "That was sooner than I hoped for."

"I'm sorry," said Margot.

"Why?" said Gavin. "It was a very nice kiss."

"No, I'm sorry I'm giving you every mixed signal in the book," she said. "The fact is, I'm not ready for a relationship. I don't even know where to start with that. Jeez, forty-eight hours ago my heart was in a completely different place. But first, you should know that Kyle wants me to move on with my life. He likes you. He was confused about the ornament, and I'll tell you about that later. But what I have to tell you right now is that I think you're a really special person. I think we'd make great friends. Or, I don't know, maybe we wouldn't. But I know I'd like to find that out. I got jealous seeing you with Jenna. I have no right to feel that or get in your way of what could be a wonderful relationship. All I know is I can't be great friends with a man who's trying to build a romance with someone else, because what happens if feelings develop between us?" She gave a curt laugh. "'If.' They already are."

Gavin took her hands. "Margot, I've been so lonely since my divorce. I thought a lot about what you said last night, about coming on too strong. I guess I was so focused on not being alone anymore that I didn't see anything but this goal line of finding a partner."

She smiled. "Sounds like you had tunnel vision," she said knowingly.

"Exactly. But I don't want that anymore. I mean, I do, but not just that. I want your friendship. Maybe that'll build into something else. Maybe it won't. But I'd rather give it the chance than settle for romance for romance's sake."

"What about Jenna?" Margot asked, wincing.

"I doubt Jenna would want to get involved with me if you and I are getting closer." He shrugged. "Maybe she'll be an acquaintance. And when she finds someone else, maybe we can all go out for dinner."

Margot smiled. "I'd like that."

A gust of snow fell softly on them, and they laughed. Margot shivered. "We should go in."

"And switch you from that punch to something warmer to drink," Gavin added. They walked up the porch steps, and he opened the door for her.

Briefly, Margot wondered where Jenna had gotten to, since she was suddenly gone. But her attention quickly switched when the DJ faded into the next song.

She and Gavin looked at each other in awe. "'I Sing You Starlight,'" he said.

"Al Francis," she said.

Gavin held out his hand to her, and she took it. "I remember you mentioned something about a dance?" he said.

"I've always found friends to be the best dance partners," she admitted. "They don't care if I step on their feet."

Gavin led her to the floor and gave her a slow spin before collecting her in his arms. Out of the corner of her eye, Margot caught a glimpse of someone leaving the DJ's table. It looked just like the woman who'd stopped by her house yesterday from the Whimsy Charitable Association.

And, Margot realized with a warm glow, she looked quite a lot like the Spirit of Whimsy herself.

Chapter
Twenty-Three

Since that morning, when Robin had announced her idea of a Christmas review to Anna and Frankie, they'd been working nonstop to make it happen. Right away, Anna had called one of the nurses she knew in the children's wing to tell her their idea, that they would like to stage a bunch of performances by local actors and singers tonight in the event room, to take the place of the off-Broadway show that had to cancel. With another couple of calls to hospital administrators, they had the go-ahead. After all, no one wanted to see these kids disappointed. The show would go on at seven o'clock tonight, a little later than the originally scheduled performance, to accommodate dinnertime and because a handful of skits and carols would be a much shorter program than a full-blown show.

Anna had also tried getting Theo on the phone to recruit his help, but his voicemail kept picking up, so she went over to his house and returned with him in tow. He looked like he hadn't slept much lately. Anna got a call on her phone from Lexie at one point, to which Theo shook his head. He left shortly thereafter, with a promise to be at the hospital early that night to help set up. It was none of her business, Robin had told herself, and nosy was a bad look, so she held back from going over to them and butting in. Besides, later she could get the gossip from Anna. Anna didn't care what Robin looked like, nosy or otherwise.

By noon, they had over a dozen off-duty employees of the Orange-Clove Marketplace in Robin and Anna's apartment. Practically everyone who worked at the marketplace had some creative talent they were pursuing, so they had a great pool of performers ready and willing to help out. The rest of the Donovan family had also come over, having altered their plans at Frankie's request. Scott and his mom had jumped right in, printing off copies of Christmas carols and holiday skits from the internet, helping to organize small groups of which performers would do what, and even calling in the group's lunch order to the local sub shop.

Mr. Donovan, for his part, had gotten involved at his wife's insistence. Rather, when Tara bopped him on the back of the head, glared down at him over the rims of her glasses, and told him to stop frowning because this was for the kids, he asked Scott grudgingly what he could do to help. Scott put him in charge of directing the skits, which really just consisted of Donovan sitting on the couch, his arms folded over his sizable belly, and bleating out a suggestion here or there. But Robin pulled Scott into the back hall at one point and said she had an even better idea for his father's talents.

"His gift was going to be taking him to the show, right?" Robin said to Scott in the stairwell after closing the kitchen door behind her. "Why don't we ask him to be a part of the show instead?"

Scott's eyes lit up, but then he said, "I don't know if he'd want to do it."

"I just sold fourteen people out there on working for no pay on their day off, which happens to be Christmas Eve," said Robin, thumbing over her shoulder. "Why? Because this is for kids who are stuck in the hospital. Who wouldn't want to bring a little joy to their day?"

He nodded slowly. "I think it'd be an awesome gift if he's smart enough to accept it. So, what, do you have another skit or something for him?"

"That's the best part," said Robin.

After she told him her idea, they started to go back inside when Scott stopped her.

"I wanted to get my father a special gift this year because I wanted his approval," he said, "and I'm getting past that need, I really am, but I still want him to have a good Christmas because he's my father. I still love him. But I have to ask, why are you doing it? If I were you, I don't think I'd care what kind of gift some old miserable coot got for Christmas."

"Well," said Robin, "maybe we can save him."

"Save him?"

"Yeah. Look, you and Frankie both know how lost he is. He may be miserable, but what if we can show him some light again? I think bringing someone back from the dark is a pretty decent use of my YOPE time, don't you?"

Scott's dimple dug into his left cheek. "You're pretty special, Robin Russell."

"C'mon," she said. "Go in there and update your dad's gift."

Scott waited for a natural break in the skit Donovan was directing before he asked to have a word with him. Donovan nodded, and Scott sat next to him on the couch.

"Dad," he started, "you said you still remember your great soliloquys. Hamlet, Amadeus, Ebenezer Scrooge. In the adaptation you did of *A Christmas Carol,* didn't Scrooge have a speech at the end, after he's changed and he's with the Cratchits?"

"Of course," he said. "It occurs just before Tiny Tim's 'God bless us, every one.' I remember it like I performed it yesterday."

"Well, I'd like to give you your Christmas gift a little early this year," said Scott, "and make you the star of this holiday review."

"What?" he grunted.

"It was Robin's idea," Scott said, gesturing to her off to the side. "She's been helping me find your gift. I think we found it. You end the show tonight. You leave these kids with an inspiring, uplifting holiday performance, one that will make this a really wonderful Christmas for them to remember. And you get center stage again, Dad, a piece of your passion back."

Tara and Frankie had stopped what they'd been doing to listen in, and Robin waited too for his reaction. She imagined this was what would crumble that rough wall he'd stacked around himself for so long. She waited for the single tear to precede a blubbering father embracing his son.

"Oh," said Donovan. His expression was still stony, but at least it had softened from one of perpetual annoyance. "No, I don't think so. But thank you."

"Reed Donovan," Tara hissed. Frankie rolled her eyes and threw her hands up before walking away.

Scott shook his head. "Sorry, Dad." He got up from the couch. Robin followed him out of the living room.

"I tried," he said to Robin. "And so did you. That was a great idea. I really thought he'd just come around. Christmas miracle, you know? But I feel like that was the last chance. I'll sit down with him and have that talk after the holidays. I'm not going to keep letting him bring us all down."

He'd reached for Robin's hand, and when they touched, she felt electricity. Here she'd been upset with Donovan, for him shooting down his son, for him sitting in her apartment and silently judging her and their whole review. But they were doing something magical for these kids. Robin was heading it up. She'd started this holiday season with an audition that had gone south because the director said she wasn't creative enough. But when she looked around the apartment, all she saw was her creativity inspiring others to be creative themselves.

And her hand in Scott's felt wonderful. She still didn't know where Donovan's disapproval left them. If the gift didn't get through to him, Robin didn't hold out much hope for how a talking-to from his son would go over. She was left with the same uncertainty she'd felt last night about what that would mean if they started dating. But that was all for later. Right now, life was good, and she was going to enjoy that for as long as she could.

She grinned at Scott, unable to contain the fireworks display of happiness going off inside her. "We get to do something really special for these kids," she'd said to Scott. "That's the Christmas miracle. Come on. We have work to do."

For the rest of the day, they rehearsed and planned and sang with all the others, until it was time to get to the hospital. Robin was vaguely aware that Tara had been pestering her husband all afternoon to change his mind, but at this point Robin didn't care what Donovan decided to do.

At ten of seven, the performers were ready to go. The hospital's event room had a small platform for a stage, an upright piano off to the side, and changing screens for the "backstage" wings. The staff had set up a few tables behind the screens, and on one were big plastic pitchers of lemon water and stacks of cups. Facing the stage were rows of folding chairs, and another, longer table at the back of the room was loaded with all kinds of snacks, from cookies to granola bars to fruit cups. Someone had even taken the time to write up cards labeling the food: in magnificent calligraphy, the cards read SUGAR-FREE or NO TREE NUTS or GLUTEN-FREE.

Robin, Scott, and Frankie were all backstage with the performers, and Tara was still muttering at Donovan in a far corner of the room, when suddenly they all heard singing coming from the hallway. They quieted down and poked their heads out from behind the screens, and they marveled at what they saw.

Anna ushered in a crowd of children, accompanied by parents, nurses, a few technicians, and even a couple doctors. The children's voices all came together in a joyous sound as they sang "Let it Snow." But they weren't just singing. Their excitement came through in laughter, and sunny squeals, and grand gesticulations. Lots did dance moves. If they were walking, they shook their hips, and if they were in a wheelchair, they shimmied their arms and bobbed their heads. A girl's fingers played against her thigh as if she were tickling the ivories, and another strummed an imaginary guitar. And that wasn't all. One little magician made coins and cards appear from behind the side panel on his wheelchair. One little Santa belted, "Ho ho ho," from behind her tie-on beard as she walked in with her IV pole.

And with that, seeing them with all their different talents, Robin had an even better idea than before.

She ducked back behind the screens and gathered all the performers over. But before she could say another word, Donovan joined them with his eyebrows and chin lifted into a magnanimous expression. Tara, looking satisfied, followed him.

Donovan said, "I have decided to agree to your request, and perform Scrooge's climactic monologue at the close of the evening's performance."

Scott and Frankie high-fived. Robin hated to disappoint them, but she wasn't going to set her idea aside just because Donovan had deigned to help them out. At the very least, she wanted to give the performers—those who had been on board the holiday review train with her from the second they chugged out of the station this morning—a chance to hear her out.

"Thank you, Mr. Donovan," Robin said, "but I just had another thought. I know you all have worked so hard today, and thank you for that, but what do you think about making the kids the real stars of the show? We'll do our skits, but let's see if any of them want to perform, doing whatever they feel like doing. Then, we can close out the show with one big singalong, which they can lead." She turned to Donovan. "We'd still love for you to do your Scrooge. Maybe right before the singalong."

She hardly finished talking when she was drowned out by a sea of "Yeah!" and "Perfect!" from her makeshift troupe, Scott, Frankie, and Tara. Donovan, however, had soured again. As the performers finished getting themselves ready, his jowls trembled as he challenged Robin.

"I suppose this feels good to you," he said. "Rejecting me the way you've been rejected so many times. Rejecting the quintessential authority figure, the epitome of all those directors who didn't cast you. Rejecting the man who happens to be concerned his son is making a poor decision about with whom he spends his time. Does it make you feel powerful? Tough to turn the tables? This was probably your plan all along."

"Dad," Scott all but bellowed, stepping forward between Donovan and Robin. "Stop it. Now."

Donovan's eyes practically shot out of his head. "How dare you speak to me with such—"

"No," said Scott, "the question isn't how dare I. It's how did I not do this long ago." He leaned closer to his father and lowered his voice. "Do you realize how close you are to losing Frankie and me? Think about that, would you please?"

Gently, Robin laid a hand on Scott's arm, and Scott backed down. She said, "Mr. Donovan, it would never occur to me to be so spiteful. I planned for none of this. We all just wanted to do something nice, for the kids and for you. No, it would never occur to me to be so spiteful, and I pity the person it *would* occur to. That's a pretty lonely point of view, a petty one, especially when I see what these kids have to go through. I wish their biggest hardship were not getting a role in some play. I don't feel powerful, I don't feel tough. I feel incredibly grateful."

She turned her back on him, and faced the troupe with a bright smile. Now she really couldn't wait to get started, with all else pushed aside. "Why don't we all go out there together? I'll make an announcement about our little change in plans, and then we'll get the show on the road. No pun intended," she said, and joined them all in laughter.

Tara pulled a stunned Donovan out to the audience, while Robin turned to Anna. "The Lejeunes literally live next door, and they're having their Christmas party. Wouldn't it be awesome if we really made this a shindig?"

"Do you seriously think they'd pack up the whole party and come over here?" said Anna.

"Not the whole party," said Robin, grabbing her purse and pulling out her phone, "but if anyone wanted to stop by in time for the singalong, we could really make this a blowout."

Anna held out her hand, and Robin popped the phone into her palm. "Can't hurt to ask," said Anna.

Just before Robin went out to address the audience, Scott snagged her elbow and asked her for a second. He led her back behind another changing screen, so they were as alone as possible in the big, open room.

"Robin—"

"Wait," she said. "I want to apologize to you because you asked me—you paid me—to make this a happy Christmas for your dad, and I couldn't do that. That said, in my defense, I had no idea he's about as merry as a lump of coal."

"*I* want to apologize to *you*," he said. "You made this an amazing Christmas for my whole family. Even Dad, and if he chooses not to realize that, that's on him. But you. You've been magnificent."

She couldn't contain her smile. "You know, I got a pretty great present out of all this."

"Yeah?" he said hopefully.

It was obvious he wanted her to say that he was the gift, and his friendship certainly ended up being just that, but she'd gotten even more out of it. "This lit a fire in me again, a fire that's been pretty much down to an ember or two lately. Any number of things may keep me from living my dream and becoming a steady working actor, but my self-doubt's not going to be one of those things. Not anymore. Especially now that I've got YOPE. Your sister mentioned hiring me for a wedding. I don't think I'm exactly wedding planner material, but a helper? An 'elf' who can take care of some of the smaller to-dos?" She shrugged. "Who knows?"

"Wow," he said. "That's so much better."

"Better than what?"

"I was hoping I was the gift," he confirmed for her.

"Well, you know," she said, "you're a part of it."

"Really?" he said. "Because you're all of it for me."

She got a flutter in her belly, and he took her hands to draw her closer into him.

"You helped me realize," he said, "that I've given my father way too much power over me. Until he and I can figure out how to bring our relationship back from the brink, he's going to need to take a timeout. I'm not compromising on what I want because he might disagree. And that includes this."

Scott kissed her gently, bringing his hands up from hers to hold her in a warm embrace. Robin melted in his arms. She could stay happy here pretty much forever, wrapped up in him and his light woodsy scent, with his soft lips pressed against hers.

As they slowly parted, Anna came rushing around the screen. "Oh," she yipped, startled. Then she smirked and raised an eyebrow. "Oh," she drawled, understanding. "Sorry, you two, but Charlotte said they're going to round up some folks to come by. And she wants to talk to you."

Robin took the phone back from Anna, glancing at a wall clock. It was just about seven, so she hoped this would be quick. "Charlotte? Merry Christmas."

"Merry Christmas, honey. Look, Anna was telling us what you're doing over there, and I just want to tell you how impressed I am by what you've managed to pull together. I mean, not even just tonight, but what you've done with this YOPE thing and how you managed to incorporate it with Hutch business. I haven't run the numbers yet, but my gut tells me YOPE helped put the 'profit' in 'profit and loss statement.'"

"Well, thank you, Charlotte," said Robin, grateful for the appreciation. "That makes me feel a little like I'm walking on air."

"Then this is gonna make you take off flying. With all the leadership you've demonstrated in just these past few weeks, René and I think it's long past due to promote you to manager of the Hutch."

"What?" Robin laughed. "That's terrific, Charlotte, but you're the manager."

"Eh, I've been thinking of taking a step back from it. Now's my chance. You can dictate your own hours as long as the shop keeps profitable and you get your work done, so maybe this'll help you out with auditions, too—and, of course, when you're cast in some hot Broadway show and you need time for rehearsals and performances. Best part, it comes with a raise, one that'll take care of that pesky rent hike."

"Oh, my," said Robin. "You weren't kidding when you said Merry Christmas." She looked toward Scott, then out to the kids, then to her impromptu troupe. "It certainly is that, isn't it?"

The spontaneous talent show was a hit. Most of the kids had some ability they wanted to share, whether it was on their own (the pianist played a Chopin prelude) or in groups (six kids knew all the verses of "Away in a Manger" and sang the song together). The grown-ups performed their skits and songs, and even helped out with harmonies or, in the case of the boy magician, playing the role of "lovely assistant." By the last skit before the big singalong, guests from Charlotte and René's party had trickled in, and the room was at capacity. Robin even recognized Charlotte's cousin, Margot, and the man she was with, the man she'd met in the novelty ornaments section at the Hutch.

A few times, Robin had spared a look at Mr. Donovan. A part of her wanted to shut him and his attitude out completely, but she meant what she said to him earlier. She felt pity for a person cold enough to believe spite had motivated her, and so, despite how rotten he'd been and how miserly he seemed about the wealth life had afforded him in so many ways, Robin still felt compassion for him.

And then the strangest thing happened.

Each time she glanced at him, she could've sworn his frown lifted ever so slightly. When the pianist played, he sat up a little. When the girl Santa recited "T'was the Night Before Christmas," or rather, what she could remember of it, his jowls seemed a little less weighed down. By the penultimate skit, he was forward in his seat, his elbows on his knees, his thumbs tapping against one another. Still, he glowered, but something was different.

Robin found out exactly what that something was when, during the skit, he stood up and caught her eye. He walked out the back of the room and waved for her to follow. Robin happened to be standing next to Scott, so he went with her alongside the room's edge, tiptoeing in their boots so their squeaky steps on the linoleum wouldn't disturb the show.

In the hallway, Donovan held up his hands. "Don't say a word," he barked. At first, Robin was ready to walk back inside. She wasn't interested if he was just going to yell at them some more. Then she noticed, he actually had tears in his eyes. He was barking not because he was angry, no, but because, unbelievably, he was moved.

"I have two healthy, happy children," he sputtered, "and I see them slipping away. How can I be the reason I'm losing you? These kids, all these kids out there, they're hurting. They're injured or they're sick. And they're in there laughing and singing. What's my excuse? What's my excuse for acting the way I have when I have . . . everything?"

He turned to Robin. "I apologize, deeply, my dear. Congratulations to you for making this production happen. And . . ." He applauded her. "That's for the performance you gave at my son's house. I owed you the proper appreciation one shows when one is impressed by an actor."

Robin had never felt so validated by others as she'd experienced tonight, and her heart fairly burst from such good fortune. With that heartfelt gratitude, she said, "Thank you,

Mr. Donovan." She kissed his cheek, and Scott threw his arms around his dad.

"Welcome back, Dad," he whispered, and Mr. Donovan clenched his eyes as the tears welled.

When they parted, Mr. Donovan cleared his throat, looking stern again. His jowls shook, and he raised a finger to Robin. "And one more thing," he barked once more.

Then he grinned. "Call me Reed."

"Will do," she said. "You know, we still have a few minutes before the end of this skit. I think we could sneak in one more monologue before the singalong, if you're interested."

Reed looked to Scott, as though asking his approval.

Scott nodded. "What do you say? Are you ready for your close-up, Mr. Scrooge?"

Chapter
Twenty-Four

Of all the Christmas Eve events in Whimsy that Lexie had participated in over the years, searching the whole town over for her boyfriend had to be the strangest and least fun of them all. And that was including the year Mo's Popcorn Palace gave out prizes for the most red and green popcorn balls constructed in an hour and the Burnell triplets ran around the store, flailing their red and green dye-covered hands and ruining any fabric they bumped into, including Lexie's favorite white sweater, which she then spent two hours trying to clean with soda water and bleach and ended up scaring the pants off some carolers when she answered the door in the surgical mask she wore to block out the bleach fumes.

Starting that morning, when Lexie had tried calling Theo from the train depot, she hadn't stopped looking for him. She actually had managed to get through to him. Looking back on it, though, she imagined she probably hadn't started the call the right way.

"I just got back from a, well, a sort-of job interview in Los Angeles, and the most amazing thing happened," Lexie had blurted out.

"Wait, you what?" said Theo. "So let me get this straight: you want to take some time and reassess our relationship, I don't hear from you for three weeks, at Christmas, and then you call me out of the blue to say you're moving to L.A.?"

"Well, hang on, I didn't tell you I'm moving—"

"What if something had happened with the flight? I didn't even know you were traveling," he said. "You know what, Lex? Good luck with the job. I'm sure you'll do great. Message received. You're done with me."

And then he hung up.

Lexie kept trying him, but he shut his phone off. She told him the whole story over the course of five voicemail messages, and kept texting, but it was clear he hadn't bothered to check them. She tried Anna, who insisted she didn't know where Theo was, even though the way she insisted told Lexie she was lying through her teeth. The women had shared one too many breakfasts-for-dinner at Bradshaw's Diner for Lexie to fall for Anna's subterfuge. But there was such a thing as family loyalty, and Lexie was well aware that as Theo's sister, Anna would err on his side in a situation like this.

Once she finally got home, had a hot shower, and guzzled down some coffee to go with the popcorn balls she picked up from Mo's for breakfast—bad memories, but darn good pop-corn balls—Lexie set out to find Theo. She'd stand outside his townhouse and yell out her whole story if that's what it took, but she needed to find him today. Gabriella wanted an answer by Monday, and tomorrow Theo and Anna would do the Walker family circuit with at least three, if not more, Christ-mases at various houses. It would be impossible to track him down. Lexie wasn't even sure where they would be and when they'd be there, since plans hadn't been firmed up yet when she and Theo went dark.

It wasn't that her entire plan was riding on whether she and Theo were still a couple or if they'd lost each other, but if he expressed any interest at all in trying to work back to their happiness, she had her answer for Gabriella. And she wanted that so badly. Lexie's heart had been aching since she woke up from whatever had happened to her this morning—dream, delusion, Whimsy's magic. If Theo washed his hands of her, it would break her heart. Then again, if Theo wanted her back but refused to accept some of the responsibility of how far off course they'd traveled, she might have to wash her hands of him . . . which would also break her heart.

At that point, she wasn't sure what she'd do. A change might be best. She wasn't ready to say goodbye to Whimsy, Spark, Belinda, and Stu, but maybe some time on the West Coast would help her heal. Not forever, but for a while. She could throw dust covers over the furniture here, lock up the house and ask her parents to look in on it from time to time, rent a place in L.A. Maybe she could even swing a deal with *Upstate* similar to what she'd been trying to get with *Swish,* and freelance from afar. Either way, she was going to have to make up her mind fast. If she didn't at least have a chance to talk this over with Theo to see where he stood, she could end up regretting it for a long time. Maybe even for the rest of her life.

Theo, obnoxiously, was not at his house. Lexie tried the doorbell, and when that didn't work, she tried her key. If Theo wanted her locked out, he could have set the chain, but she opened the door no problem, and a quick survey of the place told her he wasn't around. To the empty, dark living room, she cried out, "Don't you know I'm trying to find you because I'm madly in love with you, you big blockhead?"

Lexie had spun through Whimsy. She had started with Anna's place early that afternoon, which was hopping with some kind of show they were putting on that night at the hospital—Lexie was only half-listening and Anna was distracted by a gazillion other things, so she didn't get the full story—but Theo wasn't there. She drove the winding, undulating road that led out to Holly Hills, got stuck behind snowplows on Frog Hollow Lane and then again on Carriage House Drive, did three laps around the Orange-Clove promenade, stopped at both the Whimsy Ice Rink and the kids' rink at Gallantry Bridge, and knocked on more doors than she could count of friends, neighbors, and acquaintances. Aside from lots of offers to come in for wine or eggnog, she came up empty-handed.

It was about quarter of eight that night when Lexie, exhausted and sprawled out in an armchair in her living room, leapt up with an idea. Anna had said they were doing their show at the hospital. The hospital, as it turned out, was just about the only place Lexie hadn't looked for Theo, maybe because that was one place that, under normal circumstances, she most certainly did not want him to be. But what if he was just there to help out with the show?

She jumped in the car and drove the six blocks over to Mercy. A few questions at the front desk brought her to the children's wing event room, and by eight o'clock she'd stopped cold at the room's open double doors. There was Theo, finally, standing on the other side of the stage, in Lexie's sights.

With a dazed smile she watched him. Given that the last time she'd seen him, or dreamt him, he was weighed down by six years of unhappiness, it filled her heart to have her Theo back. His glasses, his downy brown hair, his athletic build under what happened to be one of her favorite sweaters, a forest green he liked to wrap around her because, as he said, it brought out her eyes. It always smelled of him, that spicy-lavender mix. Her heart ached again, thumping loudly as though calling out for its mate.

Like he could sense her staring, Theo glanced over then, and their eyes met. She gave him an apologetic look, but he apparently had no interest in apologies. He turned just enough to keep her out of view. On stage, a man Lexie had never met was performing a monologue from some adaptation of *A Christmas Carol,* and it seemed the children were rapt. They sat forward, eyes wide, some mouths agape at this actor's booming majesty. The journalist in Lexie, who never really went off duty, wanted to know his story. Instinctively, she nearly pulled her notepad from her purse to jot down first impressions. But the job was going to have to wait a little while.

She kept Theo in her gaze, and crouched down to creep past the audience at the back of the room. It was standing room only in here, and she managed to step on a few toes. She tried moving only when the actor got loud enough to cover her bumping into a folding chair or even just her walking, which was surprisingly noisy in boots and a coat.

Theo glanced back over to her a couple times and kept turning his back toward her, depending on where she was. Finally, she made it to the other side of the room, Theo's side. Ebenezer Scrooge was wrapping up. He'd seen the light, the true meaning of Christmas. He'd gotten the Cratchits their prize turkey and was on the cusp of living happily ever after. Lexie zigzagged around the upright piano just behind Theo, but she didn't see the bench.

On stage, Scrooge proclaimed, "And let there be—"

"Oof," popped from Lexie's mouth as her shin caught the piano bench. Its feet screaked against the linoleum floor. In slow motion, she saw the bench toppling over, and she lunged to try catching it. But it crashed down on its side, and Lexie crashed down with it. Theo, standing right there, dove for Lexie when she started to drop, but he was a little too late and lost his balance. He did, however, manage to break her fall. Within a second or two, Theo had Lexie in his arms, both draped in a most inelegant and rather painful position across the rolled piano bench.

Several people around them helped them up, Lexie and Theo both assuring them they weren't hurt too badly. They muttered apologies to everyone, especially to Scrooge, who had paused but not broken character. As they tried to melt into a wall, Scrooge finally finished his line with a resounding, "Peace on earth!"

The room erupted in applause and good-natured laughter, and Scrooge took his bows. When it was obvious another performer was coming over to play the piano, and Robin Russell came on stage to announce a big finale singalong, Lexie and Theo hightailed it out of the room.

"Are you sure you're okay?" Theo asked her, following her as she hustled down the hall and peeked into windows.

Lexie found what she was looking for—an empty room where they could talk privately for a few minutes—and she pulled him inside. "Thank you for catching me," she said. "I'm fine, thanks. Are you?"

"If you're talking about the fall, I'm okay," he said.

"But you're not okay otherwise?"

"What do you think, Lexie? No, I'm not okay. What's going on with us?"

"Before I say anything else, first I need to know . . ." She stopped her question.

"What?"

"That's not right," she whispered to herself. "First, I need you to know. I love you, Theo. I am so crazy in love with you. Any apprehension I had about marrying you was my own stuff I had to work through. But I had what I guess you can call an epiphany, and I'll tell you more about it later because you're probably going to need some kind of alcoholic beverage to help you understand it. I know I could use one."

"Lex—"

"Wait, please. My whole life is about asking questions and getting information out of people, and for once I need to be the one to spill it. Because if I don't, I could lose you. I don't know, maybe I've already"—she took in a sharp, panicked breath—"lost you. The thing is, Theo, I've figured it out. And by that I mean I've figured me out. At least when it comes to our relationship, my insistence that I can plow ahead with full career ambition *and* be a wife and mother, my daily refusal of help from Spark or Belinda. I've had this need to do it all so I don't miss out on anything, and it's got me strung too tight and spread too thin. I don't trust people the way I should, the people I should, because for the longest time I was afraid that if I asked anyone for help and they got it wrong, what if it caused my whole house of cards to tumble and *that* made me miss out? I've placed my entire life on the back of 'If you want it done right, do it yourself.' The problem is I'm pretty sure that back's gonna break, and then who do I turn to when it does?"

Theo's gaze shot to the floor. He was quiet for a while, and Lexie did nothing to interrupt his thoughts. Finally, he said, "I, uh, suppose it didn't help, me calling you super-woman all the time."

"Well . . ."

"You always seem to have it together, Lex," he said, eyes still down. "That's why it hurt whenever it felt like I got brushed to the side for your job. And I know how that sounds. I promise I don't mean it like some caveman thing where I need my woman to put me first all the time. It just seemed like if you could juggle anything, how come I was the one who'd get dropped when your job always came first?" He laughed shortly and shook his head. "I'm hearing myself say this stuff and I feel like an idiot."

Finally, he looked up at her. "I'm sorry for the way that night at Rendezvous went down. I know how it must have looked to you, me having dinner on our special night with an-other woman. I was hurt, and I wasn't very understanding."

"If I could've known how to fix the article without going in—" Lexie said with beseeching eyes.

"I know," he said. "Wish you would've told me about L.A., though."

She shrugged. "It seemed like it would just make you upset, and if I didn't have to lay that on you, on us, if I went out there and it was a bust, I didn't want to make you mad for no reason. But I am sorry."

"No, you were probably right." They laughed gently. Theo took her hands. "Ah, Lex," he said, "these past few weeks have been awful without you. I'm so crazy in love with you too."

She threw her arms around him and kissed him with all the passion in her heart. The entire world disappeared, anything outside of this kiss. All there was existed between them, her hands in his hair, his glasses bumping her nose so tenderly, his lips pressed fervently against hers as they shared one breath. She didn't lose herself in his strong, loving arms; she found a whole other piece of herself there. This was how their very first kiss had felt to Lexie, as though she'd never felt true love before and never would with any other man.

When they slowly parted, they stayed locked in each other's arms, their foreheads touching one another. A while later, Lexie looked up into Theo's eyes. "Promise me something."

"Anything," he whispered, and brushed her forehead with his lips.

"Let's stop the guessing," she said. "Enough with acting based on what the other 'seems like' they might be feeling. Honesty and open communication only from now on. How else is any kind of future between us going to work?"

"So you want that future with me after all, huh?" he teased.

"We're not guaranteed tomorrow," said Lexie. "But if there is one, I know for sure I want to spend it with you."

He kissed her again. "You know," he murmured, "if you want this L.A. gig, we'll figure it out."

"Really?" she said, shocked.

"Hey, I've been at the NYPL a long time. Maybe it's time for another adventure."

Lexie grinned at the glint in his eye, the one she first fell in love with. "You'd come with me?"

"Anywhere, Lex. Anywhere."

"Thank you," she said, burying her head in his chest. Then she resurfaced. "But that's a decision for later."

She pulled him out of the room. A passing nurse gave them an admonishing look, cleared her throat pointedly, and to Theo, wiped a finger across her lips. Lexie got the message, pulled out a tissue, and told him it'd probably be best to wipe her lipstick off before going back inside the event room to the kiddies.

Even with her head delightfully in the clouds, Lexie's inner journalist still picked up on a rather interesting conversation going on as they walked back inside the event room. The performance was done, and folks young and old were talking and eating in small groups. Anna, Robin, and a rather formally dressed woman Lexie didn't know were huddled together, and it was their conversation that roped Lexie in.

Anna hugged her, apologized for hiding Theo, which Lexie waved off, and introduced her to the last woman in the group, Margot. "Robin was just saying," Anna explained, "that this Christmas seemed even more magical than usual."

Margot nodded emphatically. "I think the Spirit of Whimsy might have been working overtime. You wouldn't believe my story."

"I know," said Robin. "I started out the season trying to make rent. Not only did I find some extra income, I found myself again." She shrugged coyly, a blush rising in her cheeks. "And a pretty special man . . ."

The ladies cooed. Lexie said, "I had my own brush with Whimsy. Hey, would you two want to sit down and talk with me about it sometime soon? This might make a great article."

They agreed, nodding, and Margot added, "Only in Whimsy, right?"

More to herself than anyone, Lexie said, "Right. Only in Whimsy." And those words rang in her ears true as a bell on Christmas morning.

She excused herself and took her cell phone out of her purse. She hit a button for the speed dial.

"Hey, Spark? Merry Christmas. Listen, I have an idea for a story. When we're back after the holiday, I want to get started on it right away. And I will most certainly, most definitely need your help."

Epilogue

One Year Later

From *Upstate Magazine,* Thanksgiving Edition (Vol. 16, No. 3):

WHIMSY (CONTINUED)

It was this reporter's delight last year to publish *Upstate*'s first profile on a Christmas in Whimsy, even with the rather roller-coaster journey we had losing the article, rewriting the article, and finally getting that article to layout and into your hands, Dear Reader. But we had to come back to Whimsy this year. After hearing how the Spirit of Whimsy touched Margot and Robin, and the experiences of yours truly, we at *Upstate* felt compelled to share the magic of this special town with you once again. We hope you've enjoyed a "Christmas

Back in Whimsy." Maybe, just maybe, you'll take the train and enjoy a day trip to the Orange-Clove or the tree lighting at Holly Hills. If you do, be on the lookout: for when holiday snow shimmers in starlight, the Spirit of Whimsy may be visiting tonight.

The entire party had gathered in Lexie's living room, which last May had become Mr. and Mrs. Theo Walker's living room, and Belinda clinked a fork against her wine goblet. "Attention," she said, her voice smooth as her chin-length hair and signature skirt suit. "May I have everyone's attention?"

Lexie, in a sweater dress, sat in her favorite armchair, with Theo perched next to her, holding her hand. Christmas Eve was tomorrow night, and most of the people here would be seeing each other again then, at Charlotte and René's annual party. Tonight, though, was about the people in Lexie's life who'd made the last year in particular so special. This party was her thank-you to them. With the fireplace roaring and the glorious scent of pine from their grand Christmas tree, surrounded by her family and friends, Lexie felt an abundance of goodwill, more than she ever had before.

When Belinda had an attentive room, she said, "First off, I'd like to thank Lexie for agreeing to keep 'Christmas Back in Whimsy' in her pocket until the Thanksgiving edition to keep it topical. I know how hard it is for a reporter to hold any story, especially for nearly a year, but it seems to have been worth it. Sales for that edition broke our record, and Lexie has been nominated for another Magsy award."

The whole party cheered. The Magsy loss earlier this year had been a little disappointing, but Lexie had found she really didn't care. Just being nominated, she'd said in a red-carpet interview, actually was a big enough honor. Besides, the winner, with a three-part piece on new funding for local artists, deserved it. Lexie was happy. She'd gotten to dress up in a gorgeous sequined gown—emerald green, just as in her daydreams—appear with the love of her life looking handsome as ever in a tux, and rub shoulders with the elite of the artsy New York press. She'd had the most delicious lobster tails and chardonnay, and come home to her warm, cozy house. Not to mention, she had lobbied Stu for Spark's promotion, and she and Lexie were now, more often than not, a writing team. Her life was too full for the loss of an award to get her down.

"Thank you all, thank you," said Lexie from her chair. "I had no problem holding the story. While you do need to live in the moment, it's true, there's something to be said for patience . . . especially when it affects circulation and profit margins."

Everyone laughed, and then Belinda continued, "I do have one piece of news I'd like to announce—"

"Nope, now . . . Nope," Stu interrupted, just joining the party. His explosion of curls poked out from the front hall, and he rounded the corner into the living room. He had a corduroy blazer on, which Lexie knew meant his husband wasn't far behind. Otherwise, Stu might just have shown up in a T-shirt stained with taquitos from Señor Jalapeño's food truck. "This is my announcement," he said. With quite the show of it, he cleared his throat and squared his shoulders. "On Christmas Day, the *Sentinel,* New York's preeminent lifestyle magazine, will be reprinting 'Christmas Back in Whimsy.'"

Lexie gasped and sat up straight. "Are you serious?" She found Spark's huge eyes and dropped jaw staring at her from the couch.

"That's awesome," Spark cried, flipping her purple bangs out of her eyes. She got up and rushed over to Lexie, giving her a hug.

"That's acclaim," said Lexie.

"That's a pay bump," Spark murmured to her, and Lexie laughed.

"As many of you know," said Stu, "and against my better judgment because about a million things could go wrong with this, Lexie will be starting a lighter schedule and working from home as of January first."

"What can I say?" she defended herself to her friends from the magazine giving her good-natured boos. "I have an amazing writing partner to help me"—she gestured to Spark—"and now that I'm starting to show, I'm realizing chasing stories doesn't seem as fun as chasing a little one around. Though I'm sure that will all change when he or she starts teething."

She looked up at Theo, and he grinned at her. They'd found out just that morning that it was twins, and no one else knew yet. In the doctor's office, upon hearing the news, Lexie had a flash of panic, for she'd had twins in her vision of that terrible future with Theo. But almost immediately she felt at peace. Her life had changed. She'd made sure of that. Having twins didn't condemn her to that awful future. They brightened the new future she and Theo were building for themselves and their family. And that was just it: they were building it together. The fear she used to have about whether she was fit to raise children had faded, now that she knew she didn't have to do it all alone.

Last year, when Lexie had called Gabriella and declined the offer at *Swish,* she'd left things cordial, appealing to her sense of the traditional. With Pamela translating on Gabriella's end, Lexie told her that Theo had proposed to her on Christmas Day in the living room they'd share, in the town where her heart had grown up and still belonged. She told her about Robin and Margot, and even a little of her own vision that she believed Whimsy was responsible for. How could she leave this town where magic was real? Not just the magic of the Spirit of Whimsy, but the magic of Whimsy itself, such a special community, where friends and neighbors helped and loved each other, where old traditions were relished and new ones welcomed. Maybe if her vision had been the only enchanting and mysterious event of the season, Lexie wouldn't have felt the same. That's why she was so grateful to have heard Robin's and Margot's stories. They helped her remember just how charming Whimsy was, and helped her see that the wonder here thrived. Lexie still had a hand in the fast-paced magazine world of Manhattan, and she and Theo were looking forward to the new adventures in their life together, but her life just wouldn't be as full and joyful if Whimsy weren't a part of it.

Belinda stole the spotlight back from Stu, and wrapped up the toast with, "Here's to our hostess."

Lexie sipped her cider, and as she set her flute down on an end table, she caught a glimpse of someone out on the sidewalk, watching their house. "Is that . . ." She stood up, and started for the front door.

She passed by Robin and Scott, who were talking with Scott's parents and sister about the upcoming nuptials. Robin's engagement ring could light all of Whimsy, Lexie and Anna had agreed earlier. Reed Donovan had lost a lot of weight thanks to his recent stint off-off-Broadway, and because, as he insisted to anyone who asked, he had to look as good as his business partners: his wife and his future daughter-in-law. Reed and Tara had taken a huge portion of their personal wealth and invested it into Your Own Personal Elves, which was now a nonprofit that identified struggling communities, and helped residents rebuild. As Robin had told Lexie earlier, YOPE was fun, but directing the community last year to bring some joy to kids who really needed it had left an indelible impression on Robin's heart. Aside from the new

YOPE, she'd ended up getting the role she'd auditioned for the day she met Scott's family, and from that, two other small but precious parts had come her way this past year. Between YOPE, still managing the Holiday Hutch, and acting, Robin's plate was nearly full. Still, though, she and Scott found time to play with an idea they'd had. Someday, he wanted to build a destination train, a resort on wheels, that included a murder mystery weekend for Robin to act in or direct. "But that," Frankie had said, "will have to come after the gorgeous wedding and my little niece or nephew who I am not going to stop asking for."

On her way to the front door, Lexie also passed Charlotte, René, Margot, Gavin, and the kids—although Gavin's kids, who'd made the trip to Whimsy this year, weren't kids anymore. Neither was Kyle, Lexie noticed. She'd first met him when interviewing Margot for the article, and he'd sprouted into a handsome young man this past year. Margot had introduced Gavin to Lexie as "my good friend." That, they most certainly seemed to be. They finished each other's sentences, fairly glowed in each other's presence, and in what seemed to be an inside joke, kept getting each other cookies shaped like wreaths and bells from the tray Gavin had brought. While they weren't dressed as formally as they were when Lexie had met them last Christmas Eve, they both looked amazing, especially Margot in a new dress and fresh blond highlights. As Lexie passed them, she heard Margot say something that gave her pause.

"Gavin and I are serial nostalgics," Margot said. "Seriously, this is a thing. We long for the past. But then we realized, one day *this* moment is going to be in the past, and we're going to long for it too. So why not enjoy it to the fullest while we're living in it, rather than spending this time longing for a past that is gone no matter what?"

Lexie rubbed Margot's back and nodded, encouraging the notion. Then, through the sidelight window, she caught another glimpse of the figure out front, walking away. She rushed out the door and stood on the wintry porch, but by the time she got there, the figure was gone. It had been a woman, Lexie was sure. A woman with curly raven black hair and skin the color of chestnuts, wearing a watch whose silver glinted in the moonlight. Now, in her place, only a swirl of crystal snow remained. By the time Lexie blinked, it had blended in with the light flakes falling from the sky.

Lexie took it all in. Festive lights blinked around her neighborhood, in her town. Firewood-scented smoke rose from various chimneys, including her own. Lexie hugged herself and whispered, "Merry Christmas, Whimsy."

Theo came out with her coat and swaddled her in it. They shared a loving, long kiss and then went back inside, hand in hand.

THE END

My heartfelt appreciation to Diane Taber-Markiewicz and Daniel J. Markiewicz Jr.; Jeanne and Bud Fadale; Mary Ann Sawyer-Wade and Jack Wade; Julie Sisson, Cassandra Moffitt, Terra Osterling, and Marcia Sisson; the Fadale and Markiewicz families; Lara and Jeff Adams; Sharon Cassano-Lochman; and Christina Ramirez. Thank you all so much for your support and help in bringing a little Whimsy into the world.

Find out more about Clarissa J. Markiewicz at

www.clarissajeanne.com.